UNDER THE
GREEN HILL

Laura L. Sullivan

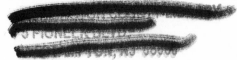

Henry Holt and Company
New York

Henry Holt and Company, LLC
Publishers since 1866
175 Fifth Avenue
New York, New York 10010
www.HenryHoltKids.com

Library of Congress Cataloging-in-Publication Data
Sullivan, Laura L.
Under the green hill / Laura L. Sullivan.—1st ed.
p.   cm.
Summary: While staying with distant relatives in England, Americans Rowan,
Meg, Silly, and James Morgan, with their neighbors Dickie Rhys and Finn
Fachan, learn that one of them must fight to the death in the Midsummer War
required by the local fairies.
ISBN 978-0-8050-8984-4
[1. Supernatural—Fiction.   2. Fairies—Fiction.   3. Brothers and
sisters—Fiction.   4. Superstition—Fiction.   5. England—Fiction.]
I. Title.
PZ7.S9527Und 2010   [Fic]—dc22   2009050772

First Edition—2010
Book designed by Elizabeth Tardiff
Printed in September 2010 in the United States of America by
R. R. Donnelley & Sons Company, Harrisonburg, Virginia

1   3   5   7   9   10   8   6   4   2

For my mother
Barbara Ann Sullivan
A Great Patron of the Arts

UNDER THE
GREEN HILL

Prologue

IN A DANK, MOSSY HOLLOW beneath the shade of ancient oaks sat two stones, man-sized boulders that must have been tumbled in the last ice age to lie unmoved for centuries. One of the stones yawned, showing craggy fangs of knapped flint in shale gums. He uncurled himself and stood, becoming a man, or what looked like a man, stocky and weatherworn. He spat, scratched his armpit, and kicked the other stone.

"What? Oh, is it time already?" the other stone (who was still a stone) said sleepily.

"Not yet," replied the man, who was now not so much a man as a slimy man-shaped thing. "But the time draws near. Can you feel it?"

The stone shifted against the earth, testing its currents. "Yes . . . yes! It is coming! *They* are coming!" The stone quivered now. "Ah! I have never known the like. Can you feel the power in them?"

"Aye," replied the first, who shed his slime and stood resplendent in jeweled feathers, catching the dappled light beneath the tree canopy. "I have seen the first wren hatch from the first egg. I have drunk the waters and tasted the salt before they joined to become the oceans. I was born in the earth when the earth was born . . . and never have I felt power like this." He changed again, the feathers becoming green skin as he shrank and sprouted butterfly wings. He flitted to land on the stone.

"You are no older than I," the stone said testily. "And I want my sleep. We have some time yet before the battle will join. Why, they are not even in England yet. They wait in a newer place. But they will be here soon. Patience. And stop that infernal shape-shifting, if you please. I am going back to sleep. Wake me when the time is ripe, when the little fruits are ready to be plucked."

The winged fairy changed one last time, becoming a boy of about fourteen with an insolent, grubby face and turned-up nose. He gave the stone another kick and skipped away, laughing, into the woods.

Across the Ocean—East

"OH DEAR," SAID PHYLLIDA ASH as she read the telegram. Even in these days of telephones and e-mail, the only messages that reach the Rookery are hand-delivered by a sly-faced young man who pads down quiet paths from the nearby town of Gladysmere. "They want to come here, 'Sander. On the first of May. Oh, this will never do at all!"

She ran her free hand distractedly through short, thick curls that in some lights were almost lavender. Though she had, even at her great age, a brusque force to her movements, there was something about the way her fingers lingered at the ends of her curls that hinted she'd once been a coquette. Lysander stifled a grunt as he pushed himself up with a stout, gnarled cane and crossed the garden kitchen to put an arm around his wife of sixty years.

"Why now?" she moaned, leaning into him. "Of all the years, of all the times, why does she pick the most dangerous to send her children here?"

Lysander Ash took up the telegram and scanned lines written in the age-old truncated style. *Dear Aunt Uncle Ash, stop.* "Aunt and uncle, hogwash! Great-aunt and -uncle, maybe. . . ."

"One more 'great,' I think."

"Be that as it may." He read aloud: "*Urgent favor needed, stop. Fever rampant in States, stop. Can you take children for summer, interrogative. Awfully grateful, stop. Arriving May One, stop. Rowan, Meg, Priscilla, James, stop.* Do they think we don't even know their names?"

"Well, we've never seen them. We've never seen any of them, not since Chlorinda left."

"Your sister wasn't able to take on her responsibilities," Lysander began hotly.

"Now, don't open old wounds," his wife said, with a reproach so gentle it was obvious she'd been repeating it for many years. When people have lived together for six decades, and played as children in the years before that, many of their conversations go by rote, and often entire arguments can take place with a brief glance.

"Four generations living across the ocean, and those children so far removed from what's in their blood. And now they want to traipse across the ocean just in time to get themselves captured or glamoured or torn to shreds!"

"It's not as bad as all that," she said, wondering, as she frequently did, whether he became deliberately contrary just to force her into an opposing tack. She'd been dead against the children's coming the moment she read the telegram, but now, in the face of Lysander's opposition—it was her family, after all—she was almost reconciled to their arrival. "We can take precautions. . . . They'll be all right if we keep them on the grounds. The house and gardens will be enough for them, and there's nothing that can hurt them there. It will be safer than staying where there's fever. A lot of children are leaving the States, I've heard, or going off to the mountains. I'm ashamed I didn't think to invite them here. Why, our house could hold a hundred children, with no danger to anyone! What harm could four come to?"

"Four children here, at Midsummer, on a seventh year? Even the villagers hide their children at the teind times."

"They'll be fine," she assured him, squeezing his hand. "Bran will look after them. Oh!" She gave a little gasp. "Someone has to tell Bran." She looked worried, perhaps even a bit frightened.

Lysander turned away from her abruptly to poke the low fire that burned winter and summer. "Well, it's not going to be me." After all, he had to put his foot down somewhere.

Across the Ocean—West

IF YOU LOOKED at the four Morgan children from above—say, hidden in the branches of an apple tree, as Finn Fachan was at that moment—you might think that their heads looked like nothing more than a bag of mixed nuts. There was Rowan, the eldest, whose sleek, burnished hair gleamed chestnut in the late-April sun. Beside him and next in age (though, being a girl, she frequently seemed somewhat older) was Meg, tall and often far less certain than she appeared, with dark, coarse hair exactly the color of a Brazil nut. Silly, whose real name, Priscilla, hadn't been used in nine years, had a cropped, boyish cut that made her head the same shape and light, rich shade as a hazelnut. And little James, who at just four was treated more as a favorite pet than as a brother, had very pale almond-colored curls. They all had skin fair as nutmeats, and freckles that came and went with the seasons. Their parents, Tom and Glynnis Morgan, were professors at Arcadia University in the hilly wilds of western New York.

"But I don't want to go to England," Silly said morosely as she tore the purple petals from a crocus. "I want to stay *here*!"

"That's just because you have a *boyfriend*," Rowan replied, giving taunting emphasis to that offensive word as he snatched the flower from his sister's hand. "He *loves* me, he *loves* me not . . . ," he began, plucking off the last two petals, and was rewarded with a kick to the shin.

"Jasper's not my boyfriend," Silly insisted, giving a little shudder at the thought. "But he beat me in the cross-campus race, and I'll be hanged if I'm not here to take back the title this summer." Silly had gone through an intense pirate phase several years ago, and despite her family's best efforts, some of the phrases still stuck. An occasional "Avast!" or "Belay that!" would crop up in her conversation, and she'd been known to call her brother a scurvy dog. But at least her piratical interjections were better than the things she'd learned one weekend when a biker convention motored through town. Her mother never quite recovered from being called Silly's old lady.

Meg made a face. "I don't think a race is much of a thing to worry about, when there's a chance you could get sick and . . ." She censored herself just in time, glancing from Silly to the apparently oblivious James.

"Get sick and what?" Silly demanded.

"Nothing, dear," Meg said, putting on what the others called her Mother tone. This time, Rowan forbore teasing her about it—he quite agreed with her intentions. The two eldest Morgans had been reading the papers, and though they didn't wholly understand things about virulence and infection and questionable vaccines, they gathered enough to know that some people were dying from a fever that was spreading insidiously across the country. Most people, they read, only got very sick and weak, and eventually recovered.

But she'd overheard her parents talking late one night, when she was supposed to be asleep, and for the first time in her life she'd heard real fear in their voices. "The vaccine is probably safe," her father had said soothingly. "'Probably' isn't good enough for my babies," her mother countered. "And children are the most vulnerable to the fever. Betsy's sister's little boy died of it in Vermont, and there have been cases all through New York City. It's only a matter of time before it gets to Arcadia. We have to send the children away." Father had asked, "But where?" And it seemed to Meg that her mother had taken a particularly long time before she said, "To my relatives in England. My great-aunt. There's no fever in England yet, and, besides, the Rookery's so far from anywhere that the fever probably couldn't find it. It's the safest place for them." Meg thought the grimness in her mother's voice came from the idea of parting with her children.

Meg didn't tell the others what she heard, though the children had a pact always to share the fruits of any eavesdropping they accomplished. The prospect of going to England was thrilling in itself, and her first impulse was to bound back upstairs and whisper the news. But with each step her feet grew heavier, until, finally, at the top of the stairs, she turned and sat, looking back at the dim light downstairs where her parents still sat talking, now unheard.

They weren't just going on holiday—they were fleeing. People were dying...children were dying. She'd never met Betsy, or Betsy's sister, or Betsy's sister's baby, but somehow the thought that it had perished, and that her parents worried that she, too, could suffer that fate, made her feel vaguely queasy inside. The idea of telling Silly or little James about it made her feel even worse. Though Meg could at times be very sensible and adult, and put on her maternal voice, at the moment she felt horribly young and ineffectual. Mother would know how to tell the others, she decided. It occurred to her how hard it must be, at times, to be a parent.

The Morgans didn't tell their children about their summer plans for a week, and in that time Meg burned to tell her siblings, and itched to confess what she'd overheard, to glean some comfort from talking about it. If she could only hear her mother tell her she didn't have to worry, she would feel better. It didn't mean that she *wouldn't* worry. She was a member of that tribe of people who always worry, at least a little bit, even when there's really nothing to worry about. But she was still of an age to be vastly comforted by a mother's reassurance.

When the news broke, Meg was surprised to find that her parents glossed over their fears of fever. It would be a nice treat for the children to meet their great-great-aunt and -uncle, and to visit England. It really was a lovely place, with ancient woods and fields of clover and thyme, and mossy banks of brooks. . . .

"Then why haven't you ever been there, Mom?" Rowan had asked. "If it's so nice, I mean."

"I just never had the time," she said, rather too breezily. "But you should know your family. They've been so kind, always sending presents."

Meg watched her mother narrowly as she rambled on. Her biggest fear had been reduced to one barely noticed sentence: "Now's a good time to go, what with the fever here." She made it seem really no more than a vacation. Meg was almost hurt—exactly why, she could not say—that her parents refused to make clear to them the real reason they were being sent away. She knew that she herself had not felt able to talk about the grim possibilities, but she'd trusted her mother to be able to present it all in a cool, rational, calming way. This was, Meg thought a little too dramatically, probably the biggest, most significant thing that ever happened to them, and no one was giving them the true reason for it. She wondered, a little resentfully, what other things in her life her parents hadn't seen fit to tell her.

Between learning their fate and this day under the apple tree, Meg talked it over with Rowan innumerable times. In his good moods he told her not to worry, which somehow didn't sound as reassuring coming from him. And in his sour moods he told her to dry up and not be such a baby. But Rowan was cheerful by nature and only snapped back at her when she'd pestered him for the thousandth time. He didn't seem too concerned, and was excited by the prospect of a trip across the Atlantic to a foreign country. To go to England, virtually on his own (he didn't think much of the controlling influences of a pair of octogenarians), was practically like being an explorer, discovering new realms. But he agreed with Meg that it wouldn't be a good idea to tell the younger two the real reason they were going.

Rowan and Meg were great readers, and each had rather romanticized notions about England. Rowan had read one or two books by Dickens and quite a few stories by P. G. Wodehouse, and to him, England was London, though he wasn't sure if it consisted of seedy Victorian streets or the Edwardian sophistication and shine of lunch at the Ritz. Meg, of a more rural disposition, knew the greenwood of Thomas Hardy and the Brontës' moors, and thought it all sublime. (Have I mentioned that their mother taught English literature at Arcadia? The children took to her specialty more than they did that of their father, which was physics.)

"Mother's right," she told Silly, shifting the topic away from disease and fear of death to something more pleasant. "It will be beautiful there. She said they have a great old house with a hundred rooms, all full of odd things, and gardens all around. It's in the middle of the woods."

"Big deal," Silly said, scuffing her shoes and yawning elaborately. "I've got all the woods I want right here."

"Well, we're going, whether you like it or not," Meg said with an air of finality. "And stop destroying those flowers." She snatched a cluster of purple, white, and yellow crocuses out of Silly's hands and absently set to making a chain of them. There weren't enough for a good necklace, so she contented herself with making a crown for James's golden head. Accustomed to being made much of by his sisters, and sometimes even an indulgent brother, he submitted to this indignity with great aplomb, and continued to dig up swaths of turf at their feet.

"But I just don't see why we're going," Silly whined, defiantly picking more flowers but making them into a bracelet for James instead of shredding them. "And why do we have to leave so soon? May first, Dad said. School isn't even over till June. We'll miss all our exams. Why can't we go in July, after the cross-campus race?"

" 'Cause your parents are coddling cowards, that's why!" a voice said from nowhere, and before they could search for its source, a long, lithe body dropped pantherlike among them. The Morgans reacted in ways typical of their natures: Rowan gave a start, but almost instantly looked as though people dropped out of the sky on him every day. Silly jumped back in a half-crouch and looked as though she was ready to fight anything from a boy to a bear. Little James, unperturbed, moved his toy tractor several inches to the west to get out of the apparition's shade. And Meg, much to her embarrassment and personal disgust, gave a shriek and found that her hand had sped to her mouth.

Now, Meg was no coward. Truth be told, she was probably the bravest of them all, for she had purpose and determination, whereas Silly had bluster and Rowan a rapidly maturing composure. But she was very easily startled, a fact that her siblings took full advantage of. She wasn't afraid of roaches or spiders, for example, but if one of them happened to scuttle or fly unexpectedly toward her face, she was apt to scream before she knew what she was doing. Rubber snakes and even dish towels that came out of nowhere frequently had the same effect, and though she would quickly regain her equanimity, it caused her acute embarrassment that she appeared to be afraid. It was such a very *girlish* thing to do, and among the Morgan children that was considered the worst of sins.

It was especially galling to Meg that she should be at anything other than her best in front of Finn Fachan. Finn was about the same age as Rowan, but slightly taller and built on longer, leaner lines. He had silky black hair, and a face that tended to look its best when he was saying something unpleasant. Meg thought he was very handsome, which, for many good reasons, she had never confessed to anyone.

Finn strode slowly among them with his hands behind his back, just the same way his father walked when he was teaching political science. ("It's not a science at all," their own father had been heard to say. "Physics. Now, that's a science.")

"You take that back!" Silly was seething. "Make him take that back!" She looked to Rowan. Though she was perfectly willing to settle the matter herself, she had a fine sense of the chain of command and felt that it was Rowan's duty, as the eldest, to be first to thrash anyone who called their parents cowards. She didn't understand exactly why Finn thought this, but she knew that, nine times out of ten when she met Finn, she wanted to hit him.

Finn ignored her—at nine, she was beneath his notice—and winked at Meg before breaking into an elaborate pantomime apparently meant to represent someone falling suddenly ill and dying.

"Stop it!" Meg cried. "Just . . . just stop it!" She placed herself between Finn and Silly, close to tears to think that her little sister would learn how frightened their parents were for them, how real the danger was. Fortunately, Silly had decided that sulking was the better part of valor, and turned to stalk away, annoyed that Finn was getting away with whatever he was doing.

Finn picked himself up from the grass, brushing off his pants and laughing unpleasantly. "Running off like rabbits!" he said, much amused. "*My* father would never do such a thing. You won't catch us flying scared from some fever." Still laughing, he walked off, gathering a few of last fall's horse chestnuts to throw at the chipmunks.

"Isn't he the vilest thing you've ever seen?" Rowan asked Meg before Finn was out of earshot.

"Mmmm," she said, scooping up the garlanded James to follow Silly back home.

That evening, as the Morgans were finishing off a late dinner of rosemary chicken and sugar snap peas, Tom Morgan was summoned from his chair by the phone's imperious ring. They saw their father scowl as he said, "I don't think that would be possible," to whoever had interrupted the meal. Then he left to continue the call in the other room, while everyone, even their mother, stopped talking to try to listen. It wasn't very difficult—this was one of the few times in memory when their father raised his voice.

"They don't get along very well. Don't you know that?" he said, and then, "No, it's not nonsense. Children know their own minds just as well as adults. Well, my children do. Anyway, it's not up to me. They're not my relatives. Of course I can't tell her what to do. Are you a caveman? Well, you can talk to her, but I just don't see how it will be possible. They wouldn't like strangers staying with them. Hold on."

His head popped back through the door, and he beckoned his wife by gesturing with his chin. With raised eyebrows and an amused look, she slipped past him, murmuring, "You caveman!" as she went. Whatever she said on the phone remains a mystery.

When Glynnis Morgan was happy, her voice would ring through the neighborhood. But the more annoyed she was, the softer her voice would become, and when she reached a whisper she was very dangerous indeed. Back in the dining room, their father added another splash of Scotch to his drink and hunched in his chair, and the children knew better than to ask him any questions.

"Tom," she called a moment later, "come in here a minute."

On the pretext of clearing the table, Rowan, Meg, and Silly migrated to the part of the room nearest the door and heard their mother's tense whisper: "What can I do? His boy's in the same position as ours. He doesn't have anywhere else to send him."

"Well, he should have stayed on speaking terms with his relatives. I've heard even his parents won't talk to him. Anyway, with that TV commentary slot, he makes twice what we do. He can send his kid to boarding school. Or military school. Silly says she can't stand him, and Rowan isn't too keen on him, either."

"But he's a child, Tom. What if it was your boy? Wouldn't you want him to be safe?"

"It's up to you. They're your relatives. But I don't think they want to run a hostel for American children."

"They have a huge house, and probably dozens of servants. They won't even notice one more boy. His father will set up an account there to take care of any expenses. I'll wire them and let them know."

"Our kids won't like it."

"Well, I don't have any choice. I can't say no."

"I can."

"You're not a mother."

By now, of course, the Morgan children had more than an inkling of what was coming, and they exchanged distraught glances.

Their parents returned, and their mother took a breath to compose herself. "I have some news for you, duckies. Your friend Finn Fachan will be going with you to England."

"Well, there's one consolation," Rowan said to Meg as they were brushing their teeth. "At least we know Finn's dad's a coddling coward, too."

Flying to the Rookery

THE AIRLINE CLERK who would escort the children to the gate told the Morgans boarding would commence in ten minutes. Then she discreetly melted into the background to let them say their good-byes before the children passed through security. Glynnis Morgan gathered her children around her and looked at them so sternly the other passengers must have thought she was angry with them. But she wasn't—she was only very, very worried at the idea of letting them travel on their own.

"Someone will be meeting you at Heathrow. I'm not sure if it will be your great-great-uncle or great-great-aunt, or if they're sending someone. If you don't see them right away, *wait* for them. For goodness' sake, don't go wandering around Heathrow trying to find them. Just sit down and wait until someone comes for you."

"What if they never come?" asked Silly. "Do we stay there and starve and petrify?"

"Yes, baby, you stay there until you fossilize. Now, do you promise me you'll be good, and careful, so your poor mother doesn't have to worry herself sick?"

The children promised, of course, wondering how their mother could have such a low opinion of their common sense.

"They just started boarding first-class passengers and travelers with special needs," the clerk whispered, and stepped away again.

"What are special needs?" Silly asked.

"Oh, someone with a disability, or maybe with a baby," their father said.

"Since you're traveling alone, you could probably board now," their mother said. "But I want to keep you with me as long as possible." She managed to hug all four of them at once, to their acute embarrassment. That embarrassment was trebled when, from down the terminal, there came a sort of tumult, and the crowd parted to reveal none other than Finn Fachan, accompanied by his parents, his Colombian nanny, and a little round hunched figure that seemed caught in their wake and looked as though it didn't belong there.

Finn's eyes skimmed over the Morgans, and he stopped a little way from them. He shook his father's hand, nodded to his mother, and sidestepped the arms of his nanny, who seemed to have more affection for him than his parents did. But as he headed for the plane, Silly shouted after him, "Can't get on yet! They're only boarding first class and special needs!" She was hoping to see him turn away awkwardly, but it was Silly who felt her cheeks burn when he flashed her a malicious grin and said, "I *am* in first class." She shook with rage as he swept by without a backward glance to them or his parents and disappeared down the gang-plank.

"Don't let him get to you," Rowan said in an undertone. "He's probably lying—he's boarding under the special-needs category. They have to seat the idiots first so they don't get in the normal people's way." But he thought of his own economy-class ticket, where he would be seated squished between Silly, who fidgeted, and James, who occasionally drooled or, worse yet, vomited, on long plane rides. He hadn't ever envied passengers in first class, because it always seemed an unimaginable luxury—he would no more think to envy people who lived in palaces. But here was a boy, no better (and, he thought, far worse) than he, who would be wallowing in whatever decadent delicacies and private bathrooms first class might offer.

Now his parents were talking with Finn's large, loud, boorish father and pale, distant mother. The round little person with them turned out to be a boy a bit younger than Meg, a bit older than Silly, whom the Morgan children knew vaguely. He was one of the faculty children, but they'd only seen him at Arcadia staff gatherings. His name, if Rowan remembered it correctly, was Dickie Rhys, and his father taught philosophy. His mother had died when he was a baby. What in the world was he doing here? He certainly wasn't a friend of Finn's come to give him a tearful sendoff. Dickie was carrying a bag too heavy for him, and he dropped it with a thud, then winced as it landed on his toe.

"Bit of a surprise for you, Tom," Mr. Fachan said, pointedly leaving Glynnis Morgan out of the conversation. "Ran into Rhys t'other day and told him where I was sending my boy. Said why don't he send his along for the ride. Owed Rhys a favor for a while, got out of it pretty cheap, don't you think? Couldn't hurt to have another along. You said they have a big house. Rhys's boy's a round one, but not too tall. Won't take up much room, and that grandmother or whatever of yours can put 'im on a diet. Works out well all around." His voice, accustomed to filling a vast lecture hall, echoed through the terminal. Several people stopped to stare.

Tom Morgan looked as if he might explode, but his wife, seeing how miserable Dickie was, gritted her teeth and said, in the low voice she reserved for her darkest moods, "Of course Professor Rhys's son is welcome." And in a very motherly way she drew Dickie into her own fold, away from the Fachans. But to herself, she wondered what kind of impression this caravan of children would make on her relatives. Years—generations—of the most sporadic contact, and then this. *We'll be disowned*, she thought. Then she corrected herself. That had already happened decades ago, when her grandmother Chlorinda Ash left England under circumstances that were never spoken of, though occasionally alluded to.

Many embraces and a few secret tears later, they were through security and all aboard. When the *Fasten Seatbelt* sign was turned off, the Morgans had a visitor.

Sauntering down the aisle from first class, carrying a glass of something that to Rowan looked suspiciously like champagne (though it was actually ginger ale), came Finn. He lounged against the seat in front of them, and looked down at the Morgans.

"Enjoying your seats in steerage?" he asked, oblivious of the resentful looks the other economy-class passengers were giving him. "I'd bring you my leftover filet mignon in a doggy bag, but the waitress said it would only stir up rebellion. What are they feeding you back here?" He looked with some distaste at the limp salad and questionable chicken sitting on Meg's tray. "Hmm, yes. Well, as my father says, you get what you pay for. So what can I expect from this place we're headed? Father says it's in the middle of nowhere."

"Mother says it's very pretty there," Meg began, not quite looking at Finn.

Finn looked disgusted at the very idea. "I mean, what's fun? There's a town, right? Is there a movie theater? An arcade?"

"I don't think so, Finn," Rowan said, more inclined to sound pleasant in the middle of a crowded plane than he might otherwise.

"Well, Father set up a bank account for me there, so money won't be an obstacle. And I've brought my collection of video games and DVDs, so even if there's nothing to do the summer won't be a total loss. Did you know there're only a few channels on British TV? Maybe if you're good little boys and girls I'll let you play some of my video games. If only so I can see how lousy you are at them."

As you might imagine, it gave Rowan real pleasure to reveal the following fact: "Sorry, Finn. They don't have electricity at the Rookery. It's an authentic old manor, and they haven't allowed improvements. Hope your collection wasn't too heavy."

Finn's jaw gaped slightly, and for a moment he was at a loss for words. At last, sounding a bit less cocky than before, he said, "Doesn't matter if they're heavy. I can pay a porter to carry them." He managed to maintain his composure better than the Morgan children would have liked, but they could tell he was thinking of the grim prospect of being cooped up in a place without electronic diversions all summer.

"I'm going back where I belong," Finn said loftily, and returned to his seat.

Many tush-numbing hours later, the plane touched ground and taxied up to the terminal. It was midmorning local time, and the children, wrinkled and bone-weary from their confinement, filed out. There was a peculiar light in their eyes that came from not sleeping, and knowing that they wouldn't sleep for another twelve hours at least. They felt almost as though they were dreaming, sleepwalking through a crowd of strangers, looking for the one who had come to collect them.

Dickie fumbled in his bag and retrieved a small contraption, which he held to his mouth and quickly inhaled.

"What's that?" Silly asked.

"It's for my asthma," Dickie replied in a small voice. "I don't feel an attack coming on, but since it's new air here, I figured I better be careful."

Silly, who didn't know much about asthma but was intrigued by the word "attack," began to press him for details on his condition as they went through customs and looked around for whoever was supposed to meet them. Some of the passengers marched straight on, as though their future was perfectly mapped out before them; some lingered at the gate, greeted by smiling and squealing loved ones. But no one showed any interest in the children.

Finn, straddling a chair off to one side, was ostentatiously thumbing through his new checkbook. "If no one comes in ten minutes," he said, "I'm getting a hotel. Someplace modern enough to have electricity."

Just then Meg saw a figure striding, almost charging, down the nearly empty corridor. He was tall and dark and seemed to be moving in shadow even under the fluorescent light of the airport. At first glance, Meg thought he must be rather old, fifty or more, for though she could not yet see his features there hung about him a dourness she associated with age, and though he moved quickly his shoulders seemed somewhat hunched, as if he might be hiding an old pain. He wore high boots that looked as if they belonged outdoors, and the low heels clicked as he walked straight toward them.

"I'm late," he said in a gruff, gravelly voice, not apologizing but almost as if he was challenging them to object. "But not very. You're the children?" He looked them up and down with no sign of approval, and Meg saw that he was much younger than she had first thought, perhaps not even thirty. His hair was wild, looking as if it had been chopped with a knife, and his eyes were a peculiar light brown that Meg would almost have called orange, if she'd thought it was possible for anyone to have orange eyes. They looked like a fox's eyes, but the rest of him made her think of a dark, shaggy wolf.

"I'm t' take you to the Rookery," he said. He didn't seem very friendly.

"Is it a long drive?" Rowan inquired politely, as the man of the family. But their chauffeur looked around at the children, seeming to take a long time counting. At last he said, "There's more'n four of you. Supposed to be four."

"Well, yes, you see . . . ," began Rowan, but Finn stepped forward, holding out his hand to the man as if they were both wearing suits and standing in a bank lobby.

"I'm Finn Fachan. Pleased to meet you," he said, more nicely than the others had ever heard him speak. "Dickie Rhys and I have come along for the summer. Don't worry, it's all been arranged." His hand still stuck out before him, ungrasped, as the man looked disapprovingly down at him. At last the man turned away, and said only, "Come along," without looking back to see if they were following.

"The *nerve* of him!" Finn said to Rowan as they set out. "Who does he think he is? He's just a gardener or someone, or a filthy gamekeeper, or whatever they have around here. Bet I can get him sacked when I tell your relatives."

Somehow, Rowan didn't think so.

They trudged behind the man to collect their bags. Dickie and the Morgans rented little trolleys with pound coins they'd exchanged before coming, and Finn, true to his word, found an elderly man in airport livery to load his bags and push them along. But Finn balked when they came to the vehicle, an ancient-looking, open-backed contraption they couldn't readily identify. It was somewhere between a pickup truck and a piece of farm equipment.

"Little 'uns up front, big 'uns in the back."

"I'm not riding back there!" Finn said, but for all the good it did he might as well have been talking to the truck itself. The man opened the front passenger door (on the left) for Silly, who dragged James up after her, and then started the car, looking impatient to be off. Meg, Rowan, and Dickie heaved their bags into the back and then settled themselves as best they could on the scraps of hay and old burlap sacks that lay strewn in the bed. Finn mumbled something about getting a taxi, but he wasn't quite brave enough to follow through with his threat (though Rowan had his fingers crossed), and finally directed the porter to throw his bags in as he scrambled up into the truck. The moment Finn was in, the man pressed the gas. As far as Meg could tell, he hadn't even turned around to make sure everyone was aboard.

Meg never expected it to be a pleasant ride, but she found that once they got into the countryside she didn't mind the violence of the wind on her face or the growing heat of the late-spring sun. The land was hilly and green, divided into oddly shaped fields and pastures by rows of hedges or low rough stone walls that looked as if they had been in place for eons. White balls of sheep dotted the hillsides, and she saw that some of them, when they turned toward her, had black faces. She wished she'd been inside with Silly and James, though, if only so she'd have a chance to talk to the man. He might seem stern and taciturn, but Meg figured he could hardly refuse to answer her questions if he was trapped in a truck with her.

Inside, Silly was meeting with little success. It took her a while to get over the fact that they were driving on the wrong (that is, the left) side of the road. Twice she almost grabbed the man's arm to pull him over to the other side, but she controlled herself. It made her dizzy to see the cars zooming past them on the wrong side. Eventually, she got used to it, though she would still sometimes flinch if she'd been looking down for a while, then, suddenly, looked up to find herself in the unaccustomed place.

She tried to strike up a conversation right away. "What's your name?" she asked. It seemed a fair question. He replied with something that sounded like a grunt.

"What?"

"Bran."

"Oh." She expected to be asked hers, but then she realized he must already know. She tried a different tactic. "Is it going to be a long drive? I love long drives. Especially out in the country. What's the speed limit here? Do you go by kilometers? What's the name of that town over there?" She said it all in a rush. It seemed that, with so many questions to choose from, he'd find it easy to answer at least one of them.

"Don't talk while I drive. It distracts me."

Silly was talkative and persistent, and not one to be bullied. All the same, she found herself cowed by the dark, rough man driving them, and didn't dare talk to him for the rest of the three hours it took to reach the Rookery. She did, however, occasionally talk to James, and glanced defiantly slantwise at the man to see if he'd object. He never did, and the first time she almost thought she caught the faintest trace of a smile; it looked as if such a thing rarely touched his mouth.

In the end, Silly decided that the man might have a real reason for not wanting to be distracted. He drove much more slowly than any of the other cars were going, and though he was careful he seemed . . . well, too careful. Perhaps he had only driven a few times in his life, or knew all the rules of driving without ever having had to put them into practice. He seemed to think for a very long while every time he shifted gears.

The landscape was gradually changing. The smoggy, crowded streets around London were left far behind. The first two hours of driving were on a broad highway, but as they progressed, the towns were spaced farther and farther apart, and the small pockets of woodland that interrupted the fields grew bigger. They took an exit down a narrow lane that could barely be called paved, so dusty and rutted had it become. It was closely bordered by a hedge twice as high as the truck, and wound so sharply that Meg, looking forward through the dingy glass that separated them from the inside of the vehicle, held her breath in terror that they might run into some sheep or an old man idling by the roadside. She was certain there would not be room for two cars to pass each other. But they seemed to be the only travelers on the road, and followed it for quite some time, feeling trapped behind a maze's tall walls.

The way opened up at last to country far more wild than any they had passed before. The trees at the shoulder looked impossibly ancient, with trunks so wide that all of the children together, linking arms, couldn't have reached around the circumference (even if they let Finn help). The road dipped down steep hills, and here and there jagged rocks jutted from the earth, too random to be monuments, too odd to have sprung up by their own means. In the distance they could see a line of dark trees, behind which must be a black wilderness. A little town was nestled in a hollow on one side of the road, the houses made of stone and thatch—Gladysmere, Meg figured. They were driven along a dirt road that skirted the edge of the forest, and over an arched wooden bridge that groaned under their weight as it carried them over a stream. And there, bursting on them as they passed through a copse of cedars, rose the Rookery.

Welcome

OUTSIDE OF MOVIES, Meg had never seen a place like the Rookery. Calling it a house wouldn't do justice to its size. It was somewhat less imposing than a castle—it had never been built for pitched battles or sieges, and had no moats or high fortifications. It was a wealthy gentleman's country house, from the days when hereditary titles made the man, when a king (or a queen) might give a courtier riches unimaginable for complimenting his wig or serving him a good meal. Phyllida's ancestors had held the land for nearly two thousand years. Then, in the 1640s, a Gladysmere squire gave the disguised and hunted teenage Charles Stuart his own horse from under him. When that harried youngster became King Charles II, he remembered the kindness, and Phyllida's ancestors earned fortune enough to build the Rookery and ensure that they would never shirk their hereditary duties for want of money. But Phyllida Ash would have done what she had to even if she must do it from a mud hut. Her duties were in her blood, and her ties to that particular piece of England so strong that no force, not the National Trust or the queen herself, could shift her.

The Rookery was untouched by any wars or revolutions—it was so isolated that when strife came to England no one ever thought to attack it. Time itself had done little to the Rookery. The centuries had taken the sharpness from the corners, and moss filled the shady cracks so that where the façade had once been a light-gray rectangle, it was now almost a dark-gray oval, softened in its harsher angles. The Rookery was built in the shape of a massive U, with the arms extending at the back of the manor to create a partly enclosed courtyard.

There was a little lawn in the front, in the semicircle formed by a wide curved driveway that approached the vaulted front doors, but the landscape was dominated by trees standing so thickly it could almost be said the Rookery nested in the middle of a forest. But Meg had seen the forest proper, and by comparison, this was only parkland. Though oaks predominated, there were also alders and ashes and lindens and towering evergreens. Here and there, in an open spot, were single fruit trees—apples, pears, and cherries—all just past bloom, leaving a lingering sweetness where their petals dried on the ground.

The Rookery stood five stories and had a great many windows. Meg tried to count them to figure up the number of rooms, and was so staggered by the quantity that she lost count. She'd assumed that whoever said the Rookery had a hundred rooms must have been exaggerating, but now she believed it. Why, how could two old people live alone in a house so grand? Even if they had frequent guests (and Meg had the idea that they didn't), most of the rooms must have stood empty for years. She was intrigued at the thought of what treasures might be hidden inside rooms no one ever entered . . . and yet somewhat uneasy when she pictured all the places where people (or even ghosts, though if you asked her she'd say she didn't believe in them) could hide.

Overhead, a cloud of great shining black birds rose above the roof, winging in a circle to examine the newcomers before settling with hoarse caws on the trees and chimneys.

The children didn't have much of a chance to contemplate the house itself, for as soon as the truck stopped before the broad stone staircase an old woman in a flowered dress emerged from a normal-sized door hidden in the carved wood and brass of the great arched doors, which stood perhaps fifteen feet high. Phyllida Ash walked—one might almost say "skipped"—down the steps and hurried to meet them as they tumbled out of the truck.

"Welcome! Welcome!" she cried cheerfully. "I'm so happy to meet my relatives at last!" The children didn't make a very impressive group. They were wrinkled and tussled and had been sitting so long they could hardly stand. Their eyes were heavy, and James was covered in grape juice from an unfortunate incident on the plane. Finn looked surly, and his black hair was standing on end from the wind. Dickie looked as if he might burst into tears at any moment, though it might have just been his allergies.

Phyllida figured out a bit more quickly than Bran that four boys and two girls don't add up to four children, but though she was surprised, she was used to taking far more unusual things in stride.

"Come inside, dears, you must be exhausted. Let me get you settled and fed and watered, and then I can learn all your names. I never can remember anything I hear when I'm standing up. I think comfort is the key to a good memory." She ushered the children toward the door, rather like a mother hen herding her chicks. She didn't try to hug or kiss them, which, though the children didn't particularly notice this at the time, raised her in their subconscious estimation. (Perhaps it was only because she hadn't sorted out which four properly belonged to her.) But she did take James's hand after he stumbled on the first step, and when the others weren't looking, she patted Dickie's back reassuringly.

"We'll go into the garden kitchen. It's by far my favorite room. There's another kitchen way off somewhere—I'm not quite sure where—that's used by the servants, for themselves or if we're having a banquet. But this one looks out over the herbs, with the rest of the garden behind it, and from late March until . . . well, until the end of October, it's open for the breeze and the pennyroyal smells to come in."

They passed first through a great hall with shining wooden floors and walls, and silver sconces holding low, dull flames. There was no furniture save for a few chairs upholstered in burgundy pressed against the far walls, leading Meg to believe that the rest of the rooms might be similarly empty (which made the prospect of their exploration far less enticing). She later learned that the reception hall was an exception—most of the other rooms were cluttered with old wardrobes and trunks and great dusty canopied beds, with antiquities and dubious treasures and tapestries of scenes too faded to be seen.

"We don't live in most of the house," Phyllida said as they continued through a hallway. On one side they glimpsed an enormous room dominated by a wooden dining table, its unlit candelabra like ghastly dead spiders with their legs in the air. "The ten or so rooms we use often are near the center here, and they look out on the garden. The bedrooms are on the second floor. I had four of them made up. I didn't know if any of you wanted to share. But I can have two more dusted and aired by tomorrow, if you can make do tonight. Here we are."

She directed them into a bright, breezy room that hardly seemed to be inside a house at all—and certainly not inside a stately mansion. It was decorated like a country cottage, and a none-too-modern cottage at that, with heavy brass or cast-iron implements hanging on walls covered in a floral paper that would have been garish if it wasn't faded by the sun that streamed in from an open door and two wide French windows. There was a twiggy broomstick in one corner, and an old-fashioned refrigerator that baffled Meg until she saw that it was cooled by a large block of ice. A fire smoldered in the hearth, hardly alive at all as it glowed red in the charred blocks of wood, though every now and then a tiny salamander of flame would crawl out to lick a fresh branch.

In the garden kitchen, the outside and the inside seemed almost the same thing. The sun, creeping to midday, lit the flowering herbs to brilliant hues of green and pink and white. Cut flowers and potted plants covered nearly every surface except the large white table where Phyllida placed a jug of milk and a dish of butter before turning to cut thick slices of new bread. "This will tide your stomachs over until I can whip up something more substantial." Dried bunches of leaves and flower heads hung from the rafters, and tendrils of some fragrant vine growing near the windows had snaked inside. It was as much a potter's shed, apothecary's workshop, and summerhouse as a kitchen. Meg had never seen anything quite so pretty and homey. Dickie began sneezing.

"Health to you!" said a voice from the doorway, and the children looked to find an elderly man leaning on a heavy gnarled cane that was almost a club. Lysander Ash had one of those peculiar faces that seem unwilling to divulge their true meaning. It was often hard to tell if he was looking cross or amused, and the heavy white mustache entirely covering his upper lip didn't help.

"Dears, this is my husband, your great-great-uncle, Lysander Ash." Meg wondered if she thought they were all related to her.

"Couldn't be there to meet you. Had a deal of work for today." As when Bran said he was late, there didn't seem to be anything of an apology in Lysander's words.

"It's May Day, you know," Phyllida said to the children. "That's an important day in these parts."

It was on the tip of Meg's tongue to ask why, but then Lysander said, "Have you told them the rules yet?"

"Of course not! Can't you see they've just arrived and they're hungry and dead tired? Wouldn't do any good to tell them anything now. That can all wait. Nothing could happen before sundown anyway."

The children exchanged glances at the idea of rules. They weren't very used to them, aside from the obvious ones about looking both ways before crossing the street and not accepting rides from strangers. Perhaps the Ashes were not as easygoing as they seemed. But Phyllida, for one, didn't appear to have any strictness about her. "Eat up, dears!" She laid out honey and jam. "We'll have an early supper tonight, but this will do for now. Please, tell me your names whenever you're not busy chewing."

"I'm Finn Fachan," Finn said, wiping milk from his mouth with the back of his hand.

"Oh," Lysander said dryly. "*Not* a Morgan, then?"

"No," he said with what looked like a grateful smile. "Tom Morgan said he'd tell you. I hope I'm not a surprise. I'm a friend of the Morgans."

At this, Silly spattered breadcrumbs into her hand as she stifled an explosive laugh.

"*Glynnis* Morgan didn't tell us ... but no doubt the message is on its way," Lysander said. "News travels very slowly here. At least news from the outside does. But rest assured that any ... friends of my relatives are welcome here. We certainly have the room for them."

"Yes, that's what my father, Professor Fachan, said. He sent you a check to cover any expenses. I'm sure it will be enough."

Lysander's look shifted more noticeably to the cross side, but Phyllida said quickly, "Oh, that's very thoughtful, but there's no need. I'll send it back as soon as it comes. And are you a Morgan?" she asked, looking at Dickie.

"No," he said, sniffing loudly. "I'm Dickie Rhys."

"*He's* a friend of ours," Silly spouted, rather too loudly.

"Good to have you with us, Master Rhys," Lysander said,

pulling a large white handkerchief from his pocket and handing it to Dickie. "Catching a cold there?"

"No, sir. I have allergies." He blew his nose softly, as though to do the job properly with so many people around might be rude.

"Oh, you poor dear!" Phyllida said. "And I suppose the garden is making them worse. I'll give you a bedroom facing the front of the house. There shouldn't be too much pollen blowing there. Will you be all right here for now?" Dickie, red-nosed and puffy-eyed, nodded and tried to disappear back into his chair.

"My deductive powers tell me that the rest of you must be Morgans," Lysander said. And he proceeded to name them all, in order from eldest to youngest. "Well, that's it, then. The formalities are over. I'll go back to work, if you please. I'll return before dinner to go over the rules." He cast a look that might have been ominous, though James, who, it seemed, could see right through him to his better nature, giggled and threw a crust of bread at him. It stuck in his hair, and he frowned very severely, which only made James laugh harder. Meg pulled his hands down and, since she didn't know what else to do, dipped her napkin in her milk and scrubbed at the impossible grape-juice stains, turning them a sickly mauve.

"Don't bother with those, dear," Phyllida said to Meg, deftly snatching her napkin from her. "I'll give them to Lemman to wash. She has the patience for it."

"Who's Lemon?" Silly asked.

"She takes care of the dairy. You'll meet her later. But don't be offended if she doesn't talk to you. She never talks."

"Oh, she's dumb, then?" Finn said.

"'Mute' is a nicer word for it, dear, but, no, she's not mute. She just chooses not to speak. Are you all finished eating?" They had bolted their food, and there was nothing left but crumbs on their plates and sticky white rings in their glasses from cream that hadn't been wholly separated from the milk. "I'll show you your rooms and the main part of the house. I daresay you'll want to explore the rest of it on your own. Better save that for tomorrow, though. You're apt to become lost, and all of the household will be gone tonight. No one will think to find you until morning, and who knows what might be creeping in some of those old rooms. I haven't been in half of 'em since I was a girl your age." She nodded to Meg, who was fascinated and a bit unnerved by the idea that Phyllida Ash had ever been her age (or, worse, that she, Meg, would ever be in her eighties).

"But first you can meet the rest of the household." Phyllida Ash pulled a little lever on the wall, and in some distant room a bell tinkled. She led the children back to the main entrance hall, where they found a dozen men and women lined up along the wall. There was a spindly older man dressed in black who could be no other than a butler (though his duties these days were few), and a younger fellow, similarly dressed though with a less staid demeanor, who was his under-butler in training. Several cheerful-looking, pretty girls in ruffled white aprons served in the kitchen or as parlor maids, performing their light duties where they were required. There was a roughly dressed pensioner whose sole job was cleaning muddy shoes or snow-covered boots before they could foul the house. A man in his twenties leaned casually against the wall, looking as if he thought himself too good to be there—or almost anywhere else, for that matter. He sometimes ran errands into town, or repaired things with lazy taps of a little hammer, but mostly he hung around the kitchen, chatting up the girls, until the cook shooed him away. The cook was there, too, a stout, pleasant, matronly woman who had evidently been baking bread and just washed her hands—they were clean up to mid-forearm, beyond which they were plastered in flour and gummy gobbets of dough.

Phyllida Ash introduced the children, then went down the line. Each bowed or dropped a curtsy, except the young man who liked the kitchen girls, who only scowled deeply with his eyebrows, no doubt wishing they'd get a move on so he could go back to his proper business of flirting.

"These are the servants, then?" Finn said, looking them up and down as though he had just purchased them at a slave market and was unsure whether he'd gotten a good buy. Meg, a proper middle-class American who really did almost equate servants with slavery, was horrified. They might be servants, she thought, but did he have to rub it in their faces?

Phyllida made a little noise of acknowledgment, and Meg saw some of the servants give Finn odd looks. He sure could get on the wrong side of people in a hurry, she thought. Still, he had never said anything horrible to her (though that was probably more from negligence than anything else), and his eyes were a dark sort of blue that sometimes made her seem to lose her powers of speech.

The cook began to talk to the Morgans and Dickie about what they'd like for supper, and the aproned girls sallied off in a flurry of titters, followed by their admirer.

"Is that Bran one of your servants?" Finn asked, in the same overloud voice his father used. There was a quick hush—the cook broke off abruptly in her description of the Rookery's applesauce, the retreating girls slowed their pace and stopped giggling, and both the older butler and his butler-in-training stiffened and looked twice as formal as before.

"He was very rude to us on the way here," Finn continued, thinking he could get the man in trouble. "Put us in danger by making us sit in the back without seatbelts, and his driving is atrocious. He shouldn't be allowed on the road. I just thought you should know, so you could do something about him."

Phyllida looked at Finn with the first trace of annoyance she'd shown yet, though it quickly passed, leaving her face, if not her thoughts, serene.

"Is he one of your servants?" Finn pressed.

"No," Phyllida said slowly. "He's a sort of relative."

Finn seemed vaguely surprised. "A close one?"

"You might say that," Phyllida Ash said archly. "He's my father."

A Lot of Silly Rules

"LOONY, THAT ONE," Finn said while they unpacked. He'd walked into the room Meg and Silly were to share that night, until the other rooms got made up. "Thought she was a bit crazy, but that settles it. Her father! Simply raving!"

"I think she was just kidding," Meg said, tossing aside a pair of Rowan's socks that had gotten mixed in with her own. "He's evidently a close friend of the family, and she was irritated that you were criticizing him. You should be more polite."

"Oh yes, Mother!" he said, dropping down onto the foot of her bed. "I'll be so very good and not make the poor servants cry! And I won't even fear for my life when I have to drive with a big oaf, or live with a crazy old lady. Her father indeed!"

"Drop it, Finn," Rowan said as he sauntered in. "No one wants you here. Remember that. But since they're stuck with you, you ought to make yourself more agreeable to the Ashes. They were kind enough to let you come. But nobody wants you here."

Whatever Finn felt about this speech he kept well hidden. He smirked, as if to imply that Rowan was obviously mistaken—who wouldn't be delighted at his presence?—and began to juggle with two pairs of Meg's socks and one set of unmentionables. "What do you think this May Day business is all about?" he asked casually.

Meg, who thought Rowan was being far too hard on Finn and watched his face narrowly for any signs of hurt, said, "All I know about May Day is there's supposed to be a Maypole. And don't say that about Finn," she added. "Of course we want him here. We'll all get along just fine." But Rowan still scowled, and Silly grinned, obviously backing him up.

"The loony old bat—or should that be batty old loon?—said everyone would be gone tonight. They must be having a big party somewhere. Did you notice we weren't invited?"

"I don't care," Silly said, yawning. "Probably some dull bunch of farmers. I'll be happy to get to sleep."

"Well," said Finn, "while the babies are asleep, we have to decide what to do with our night of freedom. Whole house to ourselves, no servants—I think that's the perfect time to explore."

"But Auntie Ash said not to," Meg said.

"Do you really think you could get lost in this house? Come on, there's only two reasons she wouldn't want us exploring. Either she just doesn't want us to have any fun . . . or there are things she doesn't want us to find. I bet there's treasure hidden in this place, or corpses in the cupboards, or a crazy old uncle locked away in the attic. Are you babies telling me you're not going to take advantage of tonight?"

"I'm pretty tired, too," Meg began. But Rowan, though he despised Finn as much as a good-natured boy can despise anyone, liked the idea of exploration and any rule-breaking that didn't seem too serious. And he'd be hanged (to steal one of Silly's old piraticisms) if he'd let Finn go off and have all the fun.

"We'll wait and see what time they all leave," Rowan said decisively. "And when James is in bed, those who want to can explore the house."

Finn gave him a look of utmost scorn. "Think you're in charge, do you? I'd watch that, if I were you." Rowan rose abruptly, squaring his shoulders. The boys had been on the verge of fighting several times before, but nothing had ever come of it. Once again, it failed to come to blows. Finn merely looked at him like a particularly haughty cat and gave a little laugh. Another boy might have punched Finn for that laugh alone, but Rowan was too honorable to hit someone who was obviously not ready to fight. He was the sort who would sit down with his opponent to discuss the rules before the fisticuffs began; Finn was the kind who would wait till his enemy's guard was down and get in the first, and probably only, blow. He was taller and a little older than Rowan, but not as strong, and he wouldn't fight unless he was sure from the outset that he would win. So he sat coolly, thinking of nasty things he could do to Rowan if he wanted to.

"Let's go down to supper," Meg said quickly, getting up and shoving Rowan toward the hall. "It should be ready soon."

They were in fact met at the door by one of the girls in frilly white aprons, come to fetch them. "Is it true everyone's going to be away tonight?" Rowan asked.

"Oh, laws, yes!" the girl replied. "Everyone in the village who can walk will be on the Red Hill tonight—and most of those who can't walk will find someone to carry them."

"It's a big party, then?"

"More than a party, I'd say. But aren't you going? I'd have thought any relations of the Ashes . . . but then, it is your first day here."

"Where's the Red Hill?" Finn asked, sidling up to her.

"'Round the other side of Gladysmere, just beyond the Commons."

"Why's it called the Red Hill?" Silly asked.

"Because it's not the Green Hill," the girl replied. She added, almost as an afterthought, "And because of the fires." With this mysterious comment, she preceded them down the stairs and directed them to the grand banquet hall.

"Hello, dears! Have you had a little rest?" Phyllida Ash, looking rather small, waved at them from the far end of the table. "Lysander and I usually take our meals in the garden kitchen, but I noticed it was a bit cramped with all of us in there at once. I'll have another room made ready with a smaller table, but I think for tonight we can sit at the proper groaning board . . . or at one end of it, at any rate." She rang a handbell, and hidden doors swung open, admitting three liveried men carrying plates and a girl with long matches to light the four candelabra. "We usually eat somewhat later, but with your journey, and all the goings-on tonight, I thought it better to eat now. Here's Lysander, never late to a meal."

Lysander asked if they were all healthy and happy, then took his place at the head of the table, with his wife on his left and

Rowan on the right. Conversation was strained and hesitant through the soup and fish courses, but by the time they dug into a bloody roast they were all feeling easy with one another. Phyllida made each of the children feel clever and interesting by asking all of them about things they knew. Lysander's wry and often sardonic humor at first made the children feel younger than they were. But as they became used to him, they realized that he was actually treating them as if they were much *older* than they were, and it is nice to be treated like an adult, without having to take on an adult's responsibilities.

"He scared me at first," Silly told Meg later that night. "But now he makes me think of Santa Claus. He pretends to be very concerned about whether we're naughty or nice, but inside, he's just thinking, *Ho! Ho! Ho!* I like him."

It wasn't long before Finn asked the question everyone else had been thinking. "Will we be allowed to go to the party tonight? Some of us aren't very tired, and we'd like to go."

The Ashes hesitated before answering. "No, I don't think you'd better," Phyllida said at last. "It's not really a party. More of a . . . a ritual. An old custom in these parts. May Day, or Beltane, they call it here. It's not really for children. The folk drink too much cider, and there are bonfires everywhere. No, I'm sorry. You won't be able to go. But the procession will pass this way near sunset, on the way to the Red Hill. You'll be able to watch that. It's as good as the Beltane night, without getting your toes stepped on by drunken revelers."

Finn and Rowan both thought the same thing at the same time, and they exchanged quick glances across the table: They'd have the whole summer to explore the Rookery, but there would only be one night of—what did she call it?—Beltane? Surely, with everyone gone, they could sneak out and just have a look, see what it was all about. On his own Rowan probably wouldn't have gone through with it. He wasn't a goody-goody (or at least he generally wasn't), but he was anxious to make a good impression on the people he would have to live with for four months, and didn't want to begin by disobeying them—and getting caught. But Finn would undoubtedly try to sneak out, and Rowan couldn't bear the thought of what he'd have to listen to the next morning if he didn't go, too.

After supper, they repaired to what Lysander called the smoking room. Neither of the Ashes smoked, but it turned out that the fireplace did, and filled the room with a heady, fruity smell of burning apple wood. There was a billiard table at one end, and several deep armchairs of burgundy leather with brass trim. The children felt very important as they were served coffee (with very little coffee and a great deal of milk) and tiny, ornate glasses of blackberry cordial.

"Not very good for you, I'm sure, but after all it is a festive night, for several reasons," Phyllida said. "The cordial will help you sleep tonight, but the coffee will keep you awake while we turn to serious things for a moment." She pulled a folded piece of paper from her pocket.

"You'll have a great deal of freedom here," she told them. "I wouldn't have it any other way—I don't like to see children or animals confined or too constrained. But you must understand that there are certain ... dangers here. And this place isn't quite like the places you're used to. There are customs here so old that they are almost laws, and it would be very unwise to break them. I've compiled a list of rules for you to remember. Some of them will seem arbitrary to you, some foolish, but you must do as I say. And don't ask me why some of these rules exist. I won't have a good answer for you. But be assured that they *do* exist for a reason."

She looked very serious, but for some reason the children had already, in their own minds, almost dismissed the warnings that were to come. She herself said they would sound arbitrary. And what dangers could possibly exist here? They'd had full run of Arcadia, from the Arboretum to the Arts Quad, and had managed to stay alive so far.

Phyllida shook out the piece of paper and rested a pair of spectacles low on her nose. "You may have free run of the house and the garden, and you may go into the village, Gladysmere, whenever you like, as long as you tell one of us, or Bran, where you're going. But the forest—you passed it on the way here—is absolutely off limits!"

"Why?" Rowan asked, immediately ignoring her request for no questions. "Are there dangerous animals?"

"No, there haven't been wolves or boar in England for hundreds of years. Trust me, it is very dangerous nonetheless. Now listen, and no more interruptions."

Rowan fell silent, feeling chastised. When he looked up at Finn across from him and saw a challenge in the boy's smile, he knew they'd be going into the woods, too.

"There's a spring at the foot of the garden, and a little stream that runs south. You may play there until it cuts past the bridge.

Beyond the bridge, you must not enter the water. There are several deep pools along its course. Don't even get close to those."

"We're all good swimmers," Silly began, but stopped at Phyllida's stern look.

"You must always be in by sunset. Inside the house, or in the gardens." That put a double nix on their plans for that evening. "You must never try to ride the wild ponies, no matter how friendly they may seem. We have two or three good, steady horses in the stables, if any of you would like to ride."

"I'm allergic to horses," Dickie volunteered.

"What aren't you allergic to?" Finn asked in an undertone, rolling his eyes. He had no sympathy for anyone weak or incapable in any way.

"Now, these next may be hard for you to remember all the time, but they are, if anything, more important than the others. You must never, under any circumstances whatsoever, eat any food that does not come from this house, or a member of the household. Don't eat anything you find, no matter how tempting it looks. And don't accept food from anyone, not even if a farmer's wife offers you a slice of cake. Be polite in your refusal, but always refuse. If you feel you've given offense, just say it's what we told you to do, and anyone from these parts will understand. And never offer food to anyone. If they ask you for it, you can give freely, but never make the offer. If there's anyone needs food, they know they can always come here. Sometimes the tinkers pass through—they're like Gypsies—but they know to stop at the Rookery if they need anything. Can you remember that?"

They all nodded, but, despite Phyllida's earnest looks, they thought this was only a rather severe variation on the standard rules about accepting candy from strangers.

"You mustn't give your name to anyone you meet outside the village. And yet you must not refuse to give some answer. If you pass a stranger in the fields, and he asks who you are, you can say you are children of the Rookery. Or say, 'Oh, I'm just myself.' I know it must all sound a little silly to you, but they're simple rules, really, and shouldn't hamper you in the least. If you follow them, I think you'll have a marvelous summer. Now, let me see...." She bent her head to consult the list again. "Sunset, stream, forest, food, ponies, names ... have I forgotten anything?"

"Dunna kill the emmets," said a low voice from behind them. The children turned to find that Bran had crept in.

"What was that?" Finn asked impatiently, doing nothing to disguise his instinctive dislike of the fox-eyed man.

"The emmets, lad," Lysander said. Bran seemed to sink again into the shadows. "The ants. Or the spiders, for that matter, though that's another story."

Finn had an immediate impulse to find a magnifying glass and a column of ants.

"Ah yes, I'd forgotten. The ants. That's very important indeed."

"We don't kill insects," Silly said. She had in fact pounded several people for that very crime, and all the Morgans thought badly of people who killed bugs.

"As well you shouldn't," Lysander said. "The smallest among us often have the greatest strength. And though they lie lowly, if they're crossed they can be quite fierce indeed."

"But why ants in particular?" Meg asked.

Lysander was silent for a time, much as Phyllida had been when Finn asked her about Bran's relation to her. Then he said, "Because ants are really fairies who have grown very old."

Finn gave an explosive laugh, but Lysander ignored him and continued quite seriously. "Fairies never really die, you see. They can all change shape, some more fluidly than others, but every time they change back to their real form, they become a fraction smaller than before. Oh, not much, just a tiny, minuscule bit. But over hundreds of years it adds up. Eventually, all fairies become ants, and then they get smaller and smaller—I don't know what happens to them in the end. But, then, I don't know what will happen to me in the end, either. Who does?"

Finn had, through great effort, managed to put on a serious face, but the corners of his lips were twitching. "Oh, are there fairies around here?" he asked, clenching his fists to keep from laughing.

"Of course there are, boy!" Lysander said proudly. "There are more fairies here than any other place in England!"

The Brownie

"MORE CRAZIES IS MORE LIKE IT!" Finn said when they'd been herded to the front steps to await the Beltane procession. "If my father only knew what kind of place he sent me to. Fairies!" He shifted his voice to a falsetto. "Oh, I think I see one flitting in the pansies! Look at the little wings!"

"Fairies aren't like that," Dickie said timidly from behind Rowan's shoulder. "I've read about them. They're not little and dainty. They can be dangerous."

"Has Mr. Sniffles read his fairy tales? Then you can keep me safe from the big, bad fairies. What a place! I get stuck with not only you pack of wimps, but a pair of insane old fools who believe in fairies." All the same, Finn looked as if he was having a good time. He was only bored when there was no one to insult and nothing to criticize. The Rookery was providing him with plenty of fodder for amusement.

"I don't think they really believe in fairies," Meg said,

somewhat uncertainly. "She said there are a lot of traditions here. Probably centuries ago people believed in fairies, and they still stick to the old habits, even if they don't believe them anymore. So the people in the village would get upset if they saw us killing ants. It's like black cats and spilling salt. She just wanted to help us avoid trouble."

"You know," Finn mused, looking down the road, where they could just hear the faint tinkle of bells, "it probably would never have occurred to me to kill ants. I'm glad she told me. Why, I reckon I probably stepped on a dozen fairy geezers on the way out here."

Meg pulled James into her lap to keep him from falling down the stone stairs, and began to talk to Dickie. The sounds of merriment were growing louder, jolly high-pitched jingles like bells tied to a horse's equipage, and resonating peals like portable church bells. The road curved sharply just before the Rookery, and they couldn't see what was coming at them from their perch at the top of the steps. Now they could hear laughter and singing, and a strange reedy piping—an elusive melody they couldn't quite catch. There were clomps of horses' feet, and sounds like dancing on the hard-packed dirt road. Cartwheels creaked, and from the festive tumult rose a girl's joyous laugh and a sudden chant of masculine voices.

The party sounded as if it was right on top of them, yet they could still see nothing. For one wild moment Meg thought that the troupe must be invisible—surely, with all that gay sound seeming so close, the cavalcade must be right in front of them, a ghost parade, joyous and unseen. She shivered at the thought.

But then, from around the corner, came a boy who looked about her own age, dressed in green and brown, dancing and leaping with wild abandon. He saw them, and stopped almost mid-leap with a look of great surprise, then ran back around the corner toward the advancing parade.

"What was that about?" He looked as though he was afraid of being seen . . . or perhaps only unwilling to be seen by them.

Phyllida and Lysander came out behind them just as the first riders (as if on command) rounded the bend on piebald horses with flowers braided in their manes and tails. Earlier in the day, the Ashes had worn clothes that, though somewhat rustic, didn't seem all that different from something one of their professor parents might wear. But now Phyllida wore a flowing skirt of vivid spring green and yellow, and a gauzy top covered with a light jacket that was formed of a loosely woven multitude of crocheted flowers. A garland of ivy and foxglove perched atop her silver curls, and she carried a sort of jester's bauble festooned with flowers and tiny beaten silver bells. Lysander wore a close-fitting green jacket and pale doeskin breeches, and his hair was covered with a pointed red cap. His staff had trailing pink and green ribbons wrapped around it.

"Good day to you, revelers!" Lysander called out. There were now more than a hundred people lined up before the house, and though the procession had ceased its forward momentum, the participants seemed unable to keep still. Some merely shuffled their feet and jangled their bells, but others twirled like dervishes, on their own or grasping a partner's hands.

"Good evening to you, caretakers! Have you put your fires out?"

"The hearth is cold and the house is dark," Phyllida said. It sounded as if they were reciting lines from a script.

"Then join us, and make free!" And with that the rider in the lead let out a whoop and the horses marched, the people danced, and the wagons rolled on, as the Ashes walked down the stairs and took up a place at the end of the line. The children could see other members of the household coming from around the sides of the Rookery, similarly dressed in bright finery, to join the advancing line.

"Be good, little ones," Phyllida called out. "And mind what I said."

"Can you believe they're leaving us all alone?" Finn asked, wonderingly. "I'm used to a little more of a challenge. . . ."

But Rowan wasn't listening to him. Finn followed his gaze and found the object of his interest. Borne on a litter that was a veritable bower of flowers was a girl, sixteen or seventeen, with flowing blond hair and very white skin. At this distance she was the most beautiful girl Rowan had ever seen. Young men were clustered around her, and when one seemed to please her she would turn smilingly to the lucky swain and present him with a flower from her verdant carriage. There was a magical aura about her; everyone who looked at her seemed to worship her.

"Not bad," Finn said laconically, raising an eyebrow at the retreating figure.

Meg, noticing what they were looking at, said, rather huffily, "She's not so pretty." And she was right—if they'd seen her more closely (or with a more critical, feminine eye), they'd have found that her features were somewhat rough, she squinted, and each fingernail was broken off short. She was a dairymaid and some-time hog-tender, pretty enough, no doubt, though certainly no more exceptional than any other cheerful, hardworking farm girl. But under the glow of so many admiring eyes, she became spectacular. Each worshipful gaze served (more than any charm she herself possessed) to heighten her beauty, so that the more people looked at her expecting to see beauty, the more beautiful she became. It was the children's first encounter with that thing called a glamour, and even then, Meg saw through it more readily than the rest.

"I wonder who she is," Silly said.

"She's the May Queen," someone said, and from around the hedges came that boy who had led the procession and disappeared so quickly at the sight of them. He was thin and brown and lithe, with a tip-tilted nose and eyes that darted about much too quickly, until they settled unnervingly, unblinkingly, on you for a too-long stare. He'd evidently had time to overcome whatever surprise he might have felt at seeing strangers at the Rookery.

"I'm Gul Ghillie," he said, "and you're Phyllida and Lysander's relations. Or some of you are. Doomed to stay in all night while the rest sport on the Red Hill?"

"Not if I can help it!" Finn said.

"That's what I thought," Gul said with an impish grin. "Well, meet me at the bridge crossing and I'll escort you there meself." He looked at the two older boys. "Which one of ye's of the family?"

"I'm Rowan," he said. "The Ashes are my relations. These are my brother and sisters." He nodded to his own.

"Pleased to know you," Gul said, eyeing him shrewdly. "Yer

likely enough." He turned abruptly away. "Just after sunset, at the bridge," he said, and scampered off.

"That was odd," Rowan said. "Wonder who he is?"

"I liked him," Silly said. "He'll show us all the fun around here."

Meg said nothing. She was apt to be suspicious of people who seemed too friendly right away—they often had their own reasons for it. But she told herself that a little village like Gladysmere must not see many strangers, and he was probably just anxious to be the first to meet the newcomers. He seemed nice enough, and she supposed it was better to be welcomed than shunned. But why had he fled at the first sight of them?

"Which of you are in?" Finn asked, with a look that clearly implied he'd think very poorly of whoever skipped this adventure.

Rowan and Silly said "I am!" simultaneously, and Dickie, who looked as though he'd really rather not, raised his hand as if he were still in school and said, "Me, too!" between two loud sniffs.

"What about you?" Rowan asked Meg.

"Well . . . someone has to stay behind with James. Even if he's asleep, he can't stay by himself, especially in a strange house."

"Sounds like an excuse to me," Finn said, making Meg bristle. She was keen for adventure, too, though she was the kind of person who would always think to bring water and wear sturdy shoes *before* the adventure, whereas the other Morgans generally set out first and thought about necessities and comforts later. She was often criticized for her forethought, and Silly had been known to call her a wet blanket . . . but they were always thankful for the drinks, or the sunscreen, or the flashlights she remembered to bring. She didn't want to be left behind on this excursion—and, even more than that, she didn't want the others, particularly Finn, to think she was afraid to go out at night. But there really was James to think of. . . .

"I wanna go t' the party!" James said shrilly. Meg looked at him in amazement. She had almost forgotten that he could talk. He was usually so self-absorbed, they all took it for granted he wasn't paying attention to whatever they were saying. He had been the baby for so long, they forgot he was now nearly sentient, and might have opinions of his own.

"But you can't go, baby love," Meg cooed. "You have to go to the sleepy-sheeps very soon."

But he had been dozing on and off for the past twenty-four hours, and at the moment felt wide awake. He wanted to go wherever the others were going. " 'Fyoo leave me, I'll follow you," he said with unusual craftiness.

"Not if I tie you to the bed!" Silly growled.

"All right, he can go," Rowan said, and Meg looked at him resentfully. After all, Mother had put her in charge of James. Sometimes she thought Rowan was just *too much* the older brother. It went to his head.

James looked as though he'd accomplished a great victory, but Meg resolved then and there that she'd get him (and all of them) home in bed as early as possible.

"Well," she said, patting the once-again silent James, "I'm going to get us jackets. It's bound to be chilly after the sun goes down."

"That's the ticket, Meggie!" Rowan said with approval.

She sulked as she left them all and trudged up the steps.

Somehow, the adventure didn't seem as exciting as it once had. There was still an hour or more until their rendezvous, and she determined to stay away from the others all that time. That would show them! she thought, though she wasn't quite sure how. In case Rowan decided to follow her, perhaps to apologize, she went not to her room but to the garden kitchen. It was funny that, even while she was harboring a grudge against all of them, she was thinking that she really should make a few sandwiches to take along, in case any of them got hungry.

She eased open the kitchen door, and there, seated on a low stool, was the oddest man she'd ever seen, working a great butter churn. At least, she had to say it was a man, because it certainly wasn't an animal. But she'd never seen any creature quite like this. It was short and barrel-chested, with thin legs and arms, sallow skin, huge watery eyes, and lank hair that hung greasily in its face. It was dressed in a ragged sort of loincloth that barely covered the vital parts. Most peculiar of all, it wore no shoes, and its bare, leathery feet were blunt and perfectly square at the ends—it had no toes!

It wasn't because she was brave that she didn't scream. It never occurred to her to be afraid of the bedraggled laborer, who was too gaunt and pathetic to seem any sort of danger. In fact, her first thought was that it was some poor deformed soul doomed to work unseen, forbidden (just as they were) to go out to enjoy the festivities. Once, when she was a very small girl, she cried and pointed at a man who had no legs, and her mother had been quite sharp with her. Since then, she was very careful to display no outward surprise at anyone's appearance, even the tattooed, pierced, green-haired youths that sprouted among the college students at home.

But she couldn't help staring at him for a very long time, until she realized she was being rude, blinked, smiled, and started to introduce herself. For a second her eyes seemed to be losing their focus . . . and then the little man was gone. The stool was still there, and the butter churn stood before it. But the thin, tattered creature had disappeared. No, she hastily corrected herself, not disappeared—ran away, because you stared so rudely.

"Come back!" she called. "I'm sorry! Come back!" She ran to the still-open door to the fragrant herb garden, and collided with Bran.

"Oh!" He'd frightened her more than the little butter-churner. "I thought everyone was gone!"

"And ye'd get into mischief," he replied gruffly, frowning down at her.

"No, I wasn't . . ." She broke off guiltily, thinking about what they had planned for that night. "I was just . . . hungry."

He looked down at her suspiciously. "Ye just ate."

Meg stared at her feet.

"Well, get a plateful and be off with ye." He blocked the door, a monolith with folded arms, and Meg crept back to the kitchen and made herself a hasty snack of ham and pickles under his watchful orange eyes. "And mind ye stay in the house tonight. Ye could do with an early bed."

She started to go, grateful to be out of his baleful stare, but she couldn't resist asking him about the little man she'd seen.

"Who is it that churns the butter?" she asked.

"Ah, sometimes Lemman in the dairy, sometimes the lady does it her own self. Why d'ye ask?"

"I mean the little man with the long hair, and no . . . proper clothes." She'd been about to say "no toes," but though she'd seen it with her own eyes, it seemed too far-fetched.

To her astonishment, Bran's entire aspect changed. He bared his teeth in what could only be a smile (though it made him look even more wolfish) and clapped a hand on her shoulder. "So 'e let ye see 'im, did 'e?"

"Who was it? I only saw him for a moment, then he . . . ran away."

"Let ye see him from one blink to t'other. Still, it's something." He seemed to be talking to himself now.

"Yes, but who was he?"

"Him? Oh, he's the brownie of the house. Helps with things now and again, when no one's around. Keeps the servants in line if they get lazy."

"Is he ill? He was so thin. Don't you feed him enough?"

"Shush!" he said, looking vaguely alarmed. "We don't feed him anything!"

"But . . ."

He pulled her out of the kitchen into the dark hall, and for a moment she was frightened. He lowered his voice to a harsh whisper and bent close to her ear. "Ye don't *feed* a brownie, lass! If a brownie thinks you're *feeding* him, he'll pack up and find another establishment. Ye just leave things out for a brownie— new milk or oatcakes or a raw egg now and again—and he helps himself. But he'd be insulted if you fed him."

"But why?"

"Just a brownie's way. They all have their ways, some odder'n others."

"*Who* does?"

"The Good Folk, lass! The fairies! Haven't you been paying attention? That's what all those rules are about!"

"But I thought that was just to keep us safe."

"It is! It is! You don't know fairy ways. There's dangers here ye couldn't imagine! I told her not to let you come, but she said you were of the blood, that it was your right. And I suppose it is, if the brownie let you see him. I'm surprised, though. They're secretive, gotta get to know ye, t'trust ye. But ye *are* of Phyllida's line. Guess they knows that well as I do."

Meg had backed a step away from him, and was looking at him as if he was crazy. But some part of her—maybe it was, as he said, her blood—believed him. And, after all, she had seen the brownie with her own eyes, and the more she thought about it, the less likely it seemed that the strange little creature was human.

"But why doesn't he have any toes?"

Bran shrugged. "Just the form he takes. He can change into anything, like they all do. They say, when he first moved here— oh, hundreds of years ago—he stubbed his toe on the front stairs. 'Too much trouble to take away the steps,' he shouted. 'I'll take away me toes instead!' But I don't know if that's true."

Meg was silent a while. "Then it's real, what Uncle Ash said—there are fairies here?"

"Aye, and you're lucky to have seen one. But yer not to go looking for them. It'll only stir up trouble, and could be dangerous.

And I'd not tell the others what ye saw. They won't believe you. It's safer that way. Fairies usually don't bother the ignorant.

"I'm off," he said. "Mind ye, remember the rules, and keep an eye on the others. Ye know how serious the rules are now." He looked stern again. "And don't set foot outside this house tonight. This is one of the troublesome times. Not as bad as Midsummer, but the Good Folk do get about on a festival night."

When he reached the door, Meg had a sudden panic and ran after him. "Is the . . . the brownie still in the house?"

"Aye, but he'll be no bother to ye. He's safe. Well, safer than most. G'night!" And he pulled a loden hat (rather like something Robin Hood might wear) down over his head and set out into the gloaming.

Of course, her first impulse was to rush to tell her brothers and sister. But she knew there was something in what Bran had said—they hadn't seen the brownie, and they would think she was either seeing things or just making it up. Would she believe Silly, or Rowan, if they told her they'd seen a creature that wasn't supposed to exist? She herself still half felt that Bran and the Ashes were playing an elaborate joke on them all, or perhaps inventing tales of mysterious, potentially dangerous creatures to keep the children in line. Most of the time, she'd consider herself too sophisticated to fall for something like that. But, then, as she had to keep reminding herself, she'd seen the brownie, and it disappeared the moment she blinked.

Now there was that evening's escapade to consider. Loath as she was to open herself up to mockery, it occurred to her that it might be positively unwise to go out on this particular night. If there were more things like the brownie traipsing about the countryside, she, for one, didn't really want to be out. Making up her mind all at once, she dashed back to the front steps, where the rest were still assembled, speculating on what they'd find that night.

"Rowan, I need to talk to you," she said, beckoning him away from the others. She could tell he was in a bad mood, and Finn's smirk made the cause clear. No doubt he'd been needling Rowan, who seemed almost ready to snap.

"What is it?" he asked with a twitchy impatience as they moved just out of earshot. Before she could begin, he said, "Finn wanted us to go now, before it gets dark. Said I'm afraid to get caught. Well, I *don't* want to get caught, and it's a good thing we waited, 'cause I just saw that Bran leaving. Maybe everyone isn't gone yet."

"No," Meg said, "he was the last one. The last *person* in the house," she amended. "Rowan, I have to tell you something. We shouldn't go out tonight." And with great hesitation, and in a very small voice, she proceeded to tell him what she'd seen, and what Bran told her.

She looked to Rowan expecting to find some sympathy, some understanding—even if he didn't believe her, if she made it clear she didn't think they should go out, she hoped to find some measure of support from him. But no—he was looking strangely like Finn, mocking and almost unpleasant.

"Don't tell me you've started to believe that hogwash!" he said, loudly enough for the others to hear. They all turned to stare. "If you're afraid to go out, just say so."

"I'm not afraid . . . not very." She heard Finn laugh.

"I'm not!" she almost screamed, feeling tears of rage spring to her eyes. "But we don't know what could happen. There could be anything out tonight!"

The only one who looked worried was Dickie. The others openly scoffed.

In the end, she agreed to go, partly to look after James, who still swore he'd escape on his own if he wasn't allowed to go, and partly, though she was afraid, from curiosity to see if there really was anything to what Bran said. She was too old to believe in monsters, and didn't think there was anything actually malevolent out there. If they went to the Red Hill, they'd be near all the villagers, and what could happen to them in a crowd, even if it was nighttime? But she was sorely disappointed in Rowan.

Beltane Fires

DUSK CAME MORE SWIFTLY than they'd expected; once the sun sank behind the trees, it was very nearly black at the Rookery.

"We should have set out sooner," Meg said. But the others (even James) only looked at her scornfully. She had become the official old lady of the party.

They moved with some stealth until even the highest windows of the Rookery were hidden behind the trees. The others looked over their shoulders for any servant who might betray them; Meg searched each window for the gaunt yellow face of the brownie. When they rounded the bend on the road to Gladysmere, they began to walk more freely . . . all except Meg, who searched each tree and hedgerow for the things she feared (but didn't really believe) might be there. But aside from the low drone of crickets bidding one another good evening, the night was still, and Silly's strident laughter was the only startling sound.

Gul Ghillie sat on the arch of the bridge, swinging his feet and tossing flat oval stones into the trickle below. When he spied them he waved, and called out with a lilting halloo that sent little shivers along Meg's bare arms (she had forgotten the jackets after all). He greeted them with a smile, but there was still an appraising air about him as he looked the assemblage over.

"Ah, so ye *all* decided to come," he said, spitting off the side of the bridge. "No matter—there's room enough in the woods for the lot of you."

"Woods?" Meg asked as they gathered around him. "I thought we were going to the Red Hill."

"Aye, the Red Hill. That's where the fires are." And, for reasons Meg couldn't fathom, he winked at her.

Gul Ghillie set off with an almost skipping walk, as though the world was too jolly for a more conventional pace. While the children hastened to keep up with him, he began an engaging monologue about the history of Gladysmere.

"There was this sword, y'see? Forged from a hunk of iron that fell out of the sky. Sword out o' legend, wielded by a king who meant to unite all the folk in these parts. This was, oh, thousands of years ago, even before Phyllida Ash's ancestors became the Guardians. But this king was met with strife. His dearest friend betrayed him, and he was slain by his son. In the end, the sword was thrown into the lake down the way."

"That's not the history of Gladysmere!" Rowan said. "That's the story of King Arthur!"

"Dunno any Arthur," Gul Ghillie said amicably. "This feller's name was Aelred or some such. That's the story they tell around here. Who's this Arthur fellow?" And he and Rowan walked abreast, comparing their versions of the legend as they had heard it.

The town, crouching in heavy shadow, was as still as a grave-yard. Not a single soul roamed the cobbled central street, and no light shone in any of the windows. The loneliness, the emptiness were almost worse to Meg than if there'd been murderers or ghouls haunting the lanes. She preferred a danger she could see to this disturbing feeling that something might jump out at her at any moment. She told herself not to be silly, that they were all perfectly safe in this, surely the quietest part of England. Still, as the silent houses looked down at her with their lifeless windows, she wished she were safe at home in bed.

"Is everyone at the May Day party?" Meg called up to Gul Ghillie, who was walking some distance ahead.

"Aye, not a one would miss it. Wouldn't care to be left in a house with nary a fire. Babes at the breast go, and grandmothers so ancient no one knows from one minute to the next if they're quick or dead."

"And they told us it wasn't for children!" Silly said.

"Well, you're still strangers, see," Gul explained. "Even though you're the Lady's kin, they'd want a proper introduction, in good bright daylight, before they'd let you go to the Beltane fires. Townsfolk, I mean. They're used to one another, used to things being a certain way."

"Shouldn't we stay away, then, if they don't want us there?" Meg had visions of their being hauled home in disgrace. That would be almost as bad as facing unknown fairies.

Gul stopped. They were on the edge of the town, just before

the grassy field known as the Commons, where on other days wooly sheep would graze, and girls herding geese would meet to exchange gossip. But on that night it was as dead as Gladysmere—even the livestock were elsewhere.

"You're afraid," Gul said to Meg in a low voice. If Finn had said it, he would have been trying to hurt her; if Rowan had said it, he'd be trying to embarrass her into a better show of bravery. But this strange brown boy with the keen, darting eyes that seemed to see so much more than anyone else, spoke the dreadful words with a flat kind of sympathy that surprised her.

"I'm not!" she insisted, tensing her lips to be absolutely sure they didn't tremble.

"Well, if you are, you know a sight more than the others!" he said. Rowan laughed and started boldly across the starlit Commons, but Gul held her gaze a moment longer. "There's naught to fear tonight," he whispered to her. "This night's a merry time for all who love the land—man and Good Folk alike." For a moment he seemed very old, very wise, and there was something in his aspect that reminded her of Bran. Then he was a boy again, running after Rowan to take the lead himself as they trooped across the deserted field and passed through a little grove of old, nearly barren apple trees.

The land began to rise, almost imperceptibly at first, so that their legs felt the strain of the grade before their brains had sorted things out. It grew more rugged, too, with rocks and roots reaching up to knock their toes and grab their ankles. They could hear life ahead of them, singing and laughter and a low crackling sound like armies of mice marching through dry leaves, which

Meg didn't recognize until she saw the first glow of the bonfires through the trees. Gul made them stop near a thicket of brambles that had flowered but not yet fruited, then moved the spiny curtain of leaves aside to reveal a broad, gently sloping hill swarming with people. At the crest burned three fires, and their flickering crimson licked light to the farthest reaches of the clearing. All around the hill, the woods were dark and dense.

Finn started toward the hill, but Gul pulled him back. "Are ye daft? Didn't I say you're not welcome there? You've come to see what it's all about, not take a part. Do you think they won't know you don't belong if they see you?"

Indeed, though the strolling or dancing forms moved occasionally into deeper shadow, the top of the hill was well lit. Even at this distance, Meg could make out Phyllida Ash near the center of the group, her hair shining like moonlight. And there was the cook, throwing her stout body about in a lively jig as around her men clinked their glasses and sloshed amber liquid onto the ground. An assortment of woodwinds played a melody that sounded like wind moving swiftly through rocky crevices, and a verse reached them:

> *"My staff has murdered giants,*
> *My bag a long knife carries*
> *To cut mince pies from children's thighs*
> *With which I'll feast the fairies. . . ."*

Yet all seemed merry and gay, with no fear of what Bran had intimated lurking anywhere around them. It was a grand sight to watch, almost as good as being a participant. Had she been in the thick of things, Meg might have felt uneasy, wondering if she dared to dance, worrying that people thought her out of her element. But watching it from the foot of the slope, hearing the music and seeing so many throngs of happy people, filled her with a vicarious sort of pleasure. It was like giving someone a particularly lovely gift, she thought, one you'd like to have yourself. It was almost better to see them enjoying it than it would be to enjoy it yourself.

Hidden in the brush, the children tried to make sense of the assorted peregrinations on the Red Hill. At first they thought it was like one of their parents' cocktail parties, where people milled at will in their own pursuits of pleasure, here and there, as they fancied. The more they watched, though, the more it seemed that there was an order to it all, that everyone was gradually moving to some preordained place, for some purpose that would be unfolded. The younger people were nearest the fires, along with the fair girl still perched in her blossomy bower. They adjusted themselves in a way that made Meg think of a prelude to a square dance, and seemed to Rowan like the starting positions of some obscure sport. As it happened, it was both.

"They're about to start the Love Chase," Gul Ghillie said. "Oi, Finn, flatten yourself a bit!" Finn had started to crawl forward, and was craning his neck to get a better look at the May Queen, who was descending from her litter to stand very close to the fire.

"What's that?" Meg asked. But even Gul Ghillie seemed to have become spellbound, and he didn't answer, only looked intently up the Red Hill.

At first it really did resemble a stately dance, or perhaps a pantomime. If the participants spoke, their words were too hushed to reach the interlopers. The May Queen was surrounded by a bevy of girls her own age, who seemed to be adjusting her clothes and setting new flowers in her hair. Then they parted, and the girl stood alone for a moment in the shifting orange of the three fires. She looked much smaller than she had in her regal and flowery throne, held high above her admirers, and Meg wondered if she felt frightened.

Two women came from the crowds of older people that were assembled farther down on the slope. One—who might have been the girl's mother, for she, too, was fair and had the same rough, cheerful prettiness—reached her first, and took her in her arms in a swift, fierce embrace before turning abruptly and almost running away, without looking back. The second woman was Phyllida Ash, and over her bright garments she had draped a dark veil that covered her from her head to the hem of her skirt.

She seemed more shadow than flesh, so dark was she among the bright young folk who swayed as firelight played on their bare limbs. They all seemed to draw away from her, except for the May Queen, who stood very still when Phyllida touched her forehead and then placed a switch of wood and a hunting horn into her hands. This was fashioned from the curved black horn of a bull, charged over with red scrolling, and suspended from a strap of leather. The May Queen placed it to her lips, as Meg and the others strained forward to get a better view.

Meg wasn't at all sure what was happening—everything seemed so strange and solemn, as though the smallest actions held meanings as deep as the earth's very foundations. She was no longer frightened, but she felt as if something profound was happening right before her, and she didn't quite have the wit to understand it.

The May Queen blew the horn . . . and all that emerged was a shrill squeak that tapered off into a rude noise. Much to Meg's relief, the May Queen laughed, high and floating, and Phyllida's veil fell back to reveal her own mirth. The spell seemed to dissolve, and they were no longer players in an esoteric mystery, but only revelers gathered in celebration.

"So it has begun!" Phyllida Ash cried out across the hill, and the May Queen, plainly smiling even at a distance, looped the horn across her shoulders and set off at a run down the hill. When she was nearly at the base, a score of the young men (and a few not so young) set off after her.

"Is this the Love Chase?" Meg asked.

"Aye, hush!" Gul hissed, pressing himself lower against the earth.

The boys in pursuit clearly didn't push themselves to their full speed. The May Queen ran lightly but not too quickly across the dewing grass, and the boys loped some distance behind while she completed a circuit of Red Hill. Their path brought them within a few feet of where the children hid, but the brambles were thick, and the participants so intent on their task that the children were in no danger.

When she was making a second lap, the boys closed in upon the May Queen, but to Meg's astonishment the girl turned as she ran and struck out at the nearest of them with the switch Phyllida Ash had given her. The branch was light and supple, capable of inflicting no real damage, but she seemed to be lashing at them with all of her strength, and when runners passed by again, Meg saw that most of the boys were bleeding from slashes along their cheeks and throats. Only two were unscathed, a strapping, handsome fellow not yet twenty, whom the May Queen seemed deliberately to spare, and a man with an auburn beard, older than the rest, his sleeves rolled up on sinewy arms, who appeared to avoid her blows by skill rather than her favor.

These two took the lead, and the chase became more earnest. The May Queen's feet moved more fleetly, and the two men jostled with each other to take the lead. The May Queen veered a bit to come nearer the younger one, but the red-bearded man's foot snaked out, sending his competitor into a headlong sprawl. The older man leaped over his opponent and made a grab for the May Queen. She gave a little scream, though she seemed no more than startled, and stumbled over her long skirts. But before she fell, the victor scooped her up with a triumphant yell, like a red deer's call, and bore her to the crest of the Red Hill.

Cheers rose from the crowd, and all—save perhaps the boy who had come so close—looked well pleased at the outcome. The May Queen (who by now looked quite disheveled—hardly any flowers were left in her hair) panted at her champion's side, and was allowed to rest a moment before he led her to one of the fires.

"They're not going to . . . No! She'll catch on fire!" Meg dug her fingers into the earth as the couple, holding hands, took three running steps and jumped through the fire. More cheers rang out, clapping and ululating cries, and—lo!—there they were, leaping through the second fire, laughing and apparently unhurt. The flames had died down a bit, burning only knee-high, but they still looked viciously hot to Meg, who watched in awe as the couple crossed the third fire.

Then the rest of the company followed suit. Most jumped with a partner, holding hands and taking it at a run, and not a few balked at the last moment and, to the jeers of the others, had to try again. Mothers leaped the flames with children held close in their arms, and a very old man crossed perched on his grandson's shoulders, whooping and waving his cane like a sword.

"Why do they do that?" Meg asked Gul.

"For luck, for health. To keep bad things at bay."

"Don't they get burned?"

"Not if they jump fast enough. Not usually."

Meg noticed that the hill seemed less crowded, and she caught sight of the May Queen and her captor slipping into the woods. "Is it over?" she asked, dismayed. "Is everyone going home?"

"Ah, not home . . . not quite yet. They'll be back when the fire's died down to coals, and march the beasts through 'em. The beasts need luck, too. Then they'll all take a coal from the fires to relight their own hearths. There's not a fire burning within twenty miles save the Beltane fires."

"But what is it all about? Just for luck? What about the Love Chase? What's that for?"

He grinned, then quickly sobered. "T'keep the fields fertile, and the trees fruitful," he said, turning away from her quickly. "Come, we shan't be wanted here, and there's naught worth seeing. But there's another sight to see, if you're up for it."

Of course they were—even Meg had by now overcome most of her trepidation. Her eyes were growing accustomed to the night, and she no longer started at every owl hoot or insect buzz. This place might be filled with mystery, she decided, but it could hold nothing dangerous. The brownie now seemed no more than a strange regional beast, like a hedgehog—a thing she'd never met before and found outlandish but, after all, perfectly harmless. As for the warnings, veiled and direct, from the Ashes and Bran, well, it was hard to heed these when there were so many other people going about at night, happy and fearless. If they could, why couldn't she?

"Come! Quick, now!" Gul started at a run, and the children, catching his sudden urgency but not knowing if they were chasing him or fleeing something, set off after him. But they did not go back through the ancient apple orchard, and though they ran on for many minutes along the uneven ground, they did not come to the Commons. Meg wanted to ask Gul where they were going, but she wasn't the fastest runner, and lagged behind with Dickie and James. At last Gul slowed his mad career, and Meg stumbled to a halt beside him.

"Are we in the forest?" It seemed a foolish question—the trees were thick all around them, and the earth was mossy and rich with violets and white-spotted toadstools. What else could it be? "We're not supposed to go in the forest. We promised! Auntie Ash said it was dangerous."

"Aw, it's not dangerous," Rowan said, thumping his sister on the back. "She's just afraid we'll get lost."

"Ye'll not get lost if you keep close by me," Gul said. "I've known this forest since the first acorn fell." To the children, it was no more than another queer country expression. "Come this way, and softly. I'll show you how another kind of folk spend Beltane Night."

Though she knew they were no more than a two-minute run into the forest, it seemed to Meg unfathomably deep. Her fear returned, but she discovered that there is a certain kind of fear that comes only with excitement and anticipation. She dreaded what might be in this forest, what Gul Ghillie was about to show them, and yet, even had the path homeward been laid clear before her, she'd not have taken it. It was a new feeling for her. She had to know what came next, cost her what it might, and so she followed Gul along with the others. But she did pick up James (tired from his run, and mercifully unprotesting) and let him wrap his legs and arms around her. Better, she thought, that he should be near.

As they walked, the night seemed to grow closer. She knew that, to see in the dark, you cannot look directly at the thing you wish to see—peripheral vision is better in the gloom. So she unfocused her eyes, and found that, though she could not look straight at any of her companions and distinguish them, she could keep track of them all out of the corner of her eye. Movement registered more clearly than shape . . . but as they walked, all about them seemed movement. The tree limbs danced, and even the bark on the trunks appeared to shimmy. It seemed at times that creatures moved beside them. But, no, when she looked there was nothing, only Gul and Rowan and Silly and . . . Where had the others gone? She could not find Finn or Dickie.

Serves Finn right, she thought as she hastened to keep Gul in view. But poor Dickie!

Not so very far off from the Morgans, Finn was following a sound and a light, and Dickie was trailing after him. "This way! This way!" a voice that seemed to be Gul's called from just out of sight. Behind the bracken, a golden haze shone, and Finn assumed Gul had lit a lantern. He quickened his pace, making Dickie run and wheeze after him, but he never seemed to draw closer to that glow, that call, that lured him onward. "This way!" Finn heard again, more faint this time, and he dashed ahead, stumbling over ground-growing vines and tearing his clothes on thorns. And then the light was gone, and no one answered his call. He was alone in a wood suddenly darker than ever. It was almost a relief when Dickie staggered into view, clutching at the trees for support.

"Where are the others?" Dickie asked, a tremor in his voice.

"Oh, they're around," Finn said. He was breathing hard, but he wasn't frightened. "Just playing a trick on us. Morgans thought they could lose us." Maybe it was rage that kept any fear at bay. "But I have a trick for them! Come this way, back to the Rookery. I'll get there first, and they'll find all the doors bolted. I'll be snug in bed, and they'll be locked out till morning, and the crazy Ashes will know what they've been up to."

He set out in what he was sure was the right direction. "We should try to find the others," Dickie said, sounding miserable. He had used his last Kleenex at the Red Hill, and now was forced to resort to his sleeve, which was already growing damp.

Finn only scowled at him over his shoulder and didn't

slacken his pace. Dickie took a few uncertain steps after him. He certainly had no wish to be left alone in the forest, but he felt an obligation to search for the Morgans. Surely they couldn't be far off. He'd tell them what Finn was planning, and with Gul to guide them homeward they could reach the Rookery first. Maybe then Finn would be the one sleeping in the garden or on the cold stone steps! Dickie ran in the opposite direction, calling out the Morgans' names. But though he shouted as loudly as he could, he never heard an answer.

Meg suggested looking for the others, but Rowan and Silly seemed glad to be rid of Finn, even at the expense of Dickie. Gul only laughed and told them again that there was naught to fear in the forest.

"A will-o'-the-wisp led them away," Gul said. "There's no real harm in a wisp, only fun. They lead folk astray, but seldom to danger." Meg didn't like the sound of that "seldom."

"We had to be rid of them. There's things to see that are only for those of your bloodline. We'll meet up with your friends later."

"Finn's not my friend," Silly insisted hotly. "More like an enemy."

Gul turned on her with a piercing gaze and asked her, "Has this Finn Fachan ever tried to kill you?"

"Well, no, of course not!" Silly said, looking away in some embarrassment.

"If you were hanging off a chasm's edge, would he pull you up?"

Silly spat on the ground and said, "I wouldn't ask him to!" But she found she couldn't look Gul Ghillie in the eye.

"Call no man your enemy until he has proved himself so, and

even then, you may have to change your mind. You are very young"—coming from one who seemed only a few years older than herself, this seemed too much—"and you are quick to anger, swift to resent, and slow to forgive. But, however strongly children hate or love, it is no more than play, though they always think otherwise." How strange it was to hear such words, which were better suited to old Uncle Ash, spring from Gul Ghillie's curling lips.

"There are greater things afoot this night than Finn Fachan will ever know," Gul continued. "Follow me another little way, and hide in the thorns as you did before, and you will see what it means to be of the Lady's line. She would keep all this from you, I think. Duty has always been an easy thing for Phyllida Ash when it concerns only herself. But she is too apt to take on burdens to keep them from others. You are children, but you are of her blood, the only ones, I believe—save Bran, her father, who longs only for what he has lost. Someday it will fall to one of you . . . or it will fall away altogether. But you understand none of this!" He laughed like rippling water, and skipped a merry jig. "And why should you? Not yet! Come, and see the wonder of the Green Hill!"

Meg heard bells from quite nearby, and she thought the May Day procession had regathered and looped back through the woods. But the bells sounded somehow sweeter, as though they had been forged and beaten out by hands that understood both precious metals and music, too. The children stepped forward, and this time Gul did not bid them crouch and hide. Rather, they stood, somewhat obscured by the boscage, perhaps, but in plain enough sight to any who cared to look for them.

For the second time that evening, Meg heard the clomping of hooves, muted now by crushed and rotting leaves, and the sound of a joyous company. They seemed to speak a strange language, in voices so sweet it was like singing, and Meg felt tears come to her eyes. Before them was another hill, washed in pale starlight and filigreed with dewed spiderwebs. Ringed all around with the forest, it rose more steeply than the broad, sloping Red Hill, and seemed more a crafted dome than a work of nature. It was bare of all foliage save low-growing herbs and grasses, as though the trees and vines did not dare intrude upon such a place.

And then the hill opened.

The Fairy Rade

A TRICK OF THE DARK, Meg thought, a play of shadows, for how could a solid hill open as though a portcullis had been drawn, as though the green sod hid a vaulted door? A great archway had opened in the Green Hill, and she could see a pale light emanating from within, and white columns that rose to unseen heights. Glowing balls like fireflies hovered about the door, and the singing grew louder.

The music changed, and from the hill came a fanfare of horns and flutes.

"My queen!" Gul breathed beside her, and Meg thought with some dismay that she'd be forced to hear the boys gawk and stammer over another May Queen of questionable beauty. But when the figure emerged from the Green Hill's heart, even Meg found that she trembled and her breath seemed to catch in her throat.

The woman, or the form of a woman, was mounted on a tall charger with a pale-gray dappled coat, a beast as much beyond the clumping plow horses of the May Day march as this woman was beyond the May Queen. Her mount was arrayed in jewels of white and green that seemed not merely to reflect light, but to give off light of their own. He pranced on legs that appeared too delicate for such a tall animal—he stood as high as a draft horse, with a broad chest and haunches that bunched with power held in check. He seemed aware of the value of his burden, and walked so lightly that his gilded hooves bent no grass, left no mark of his passing.

What can be said of the woman he carried? When the children spoke of her afterward, none could quite agree on her features. Her hair fell over her shoulders, and it was fair, but where Rowan saw spun gold, Silly saw cascading moonlight. Was she tall? She seemed a giantess to Meg, and yet the others said, no, she was no bigger than their own mother. Was she lovely to behold? Who could say that she was not, though each saw her differently. Meg felt no more jealousy looking at her than she'd feel looking at a bird of paradise or a tawny jaguar, and it was a beauty that somehow didn't make her feel plain in comparison. Rowan would have run to the peasant-girl May Queen's side if he could have, but had there been a sword at his back he wouldn't have presumed to take a step unbidden toward the Fairy Queen. She was clad in green and silver, with silver sandals on her feet, and jewels in her hair. At her side, depending from a belt of linked emeralds as big as walnuts, was a long knife sheathed in a jeweled scabbard. "Though why she carried a knife I don't know," Rowan said afterward. "There's no one in the world that would harm her—or could, I think."

Her gaze seemed to sweep over the children, and there was a

faint smile on her lips that looked as though it never left, but she gave no sign of having seen them. She rode on for a bit, then reined in her steed with the lightest touch.

A drum like a heartbeat sounded from within the Green Hill, and though it almost hurt the children to tear their eyes away from the woman, they turned to see a host of figures spill out of the archway. Many looked perfectly human, and rode on horses that were either gray, or cream-white with strange pointed red ears. They rode with dignity and looked out on the world like aloof nobles, upright and fair to behold.

But among them (and it was a wonder to Meg that the horses did not rear and bolt) capered such creatures as made the Rookery brownie seem quite natural by comparison. A few looked almost human, until you found a shocking grotesqueness—one arm alone, emerging from the chest, or a huge nose but no mouth. Still others had fur, as though they had only just missed being badgers or hounds. Some were tiny and squat, some elongated like a Modigliani painting, with spidery fingers and wild hair. Side by side were the unspeakably beautiful and the unutterably horrible—and, indeed, the children were speechless as they watched this company caper around the mounted lords and ladies. They seemed to be mad, dancing and pinching one another and swapping hats and pulling hair, a mass of terrible jesters to entertain the two dozen or so who perched on their horses in absolute dignity. Meg thought, though she wasn't quite sure, that some of the creatures were changing shape and size.

"The fairy rade," Gul Ghillie said, in a voice that surely must have been heard by the odd company, if indeed they weren't phantoms. "Tonight, while the land is ripe, the Seelie Court will traverse the forest and traipse across the hills, to revel in fruit and flower, in earth and stream. Let all see them who might! The glory of the queen, the fairness of her court, her prince and consort, who has stood at her side since the first wren hatched from the first egg."

The children saw no prince at her side, but again the queen's eyes seemed to pass flickeringly over them.

Gul lowered his voice to a whisper. "Tonight, my little friends, you have seen that which few others have witnessed, and kept their eyes after! A sharpened hazel twig would be the just reward of any who spied unwelcome on the queen and her court when they gather on such a purpose. Yet Phyllida Ash has seen this, and her mother before her. And Bran . . ." His voice grew tight, though they couldn't tell which particular emotion he was holding in check. "Bran once rode with this company, fair as any fairy lord, and well beloved. He will not return. And now you children have seen it. Look well, and remember, for this is but the beginning."

Was it sorrow in his voice? Meg placed a warm hand on his arm, as she would soothe James when he fell, or an unhappy kitten. The boy who had been saying such mysterious things looked at her, and for an instant he was a boy no longer, but a man, both young and old, with a regal bearing and a troubled face that was yet unlined by care or time. She blinked, and he was Gul Ghillie again, and his staring eyes were laughing and kind.

"It might well have been you, and not your brother," the boy said. "But he is the eldest, and it is his right. You are made for other things." She frowned at him in perplexity. Before she could ask him to unravel the riddle, there was a new disturbance on the Green Hill.

"The Host," Gul breathed. "The malevolent ones."

From out of the darksome woods came a shrill neigh that made the dappled horse toss his head and lay back his ears. Where Meg was sure there had been no one (for even the colors and cacophony of the Seelie Court could not mask such a horde) came a phalanx of fierce and beautiful men in steely black mail riding close abreast. Two carried scarlet banners, and the others held glinting pikes. They rode toward the queen, who seemed hardly more aware of them than she was of the children, and their ranks parted to reveal a single rider, a black-haired fellow with fine features who reminded Meg a little of Finn.

He sprang down from his horse and walked toward the queen. He drew a breath to speak, but before he could do so, the queen bent her head to him in welcome and said, in a voice as serene as snow, "Why do you come dressed for war on this night of merriment?"

He bowed to her, low, though his eyes never left her. "The Black Prince is always ready for war."

Meg, watching with the others, unseen, remembered the Black Prince of history. In her mind, he'd looked nothing like this.

From behind the martial men slinked shadowy shapes that refused to come within the space of light the queen seemed to carry with her. They were like the horde that followed the queen and her court—not men at all, and hardly beasts, but some creatures from nightmares. Hairy or scaled, massive, with clubs, or cringing and fanged, they seemed an altogether more unwholesome lot than even the most disturbing of the queen's court. They were fewer in number . . . or perhaps they only seemed so because they lurked on the periphery of the children's sight. But, unlike those of the queen's court, they soon noticed the interlopers, and from the darkness beneath the tree boughs the children saw red eyes squinting their way, and heard slimy sounds suspiciously like a creature licking its lips in anticipation.

"It is unkind to remind us of what is to come," the queen said softly. "There is time enough to gird ourselves for battle, and Midsummer is many days away."

"I come from idle curiosity, no more," the Black Prince said, bowing once again in his sinuous fashion. "Have you chosen your . . . sacrifice yet?"

Under his breath, Gul murmured, "Treacherous! Unfair! He knows she cannot lie, and thinks to profit by it!"

"The Seelie Court makes no sacrifice if it is victorious," the queen said. "But, yes, we have chosen." And her lovely gaze, so deep and old, like the distant sea, turned upon the children and Gul Ghillie. Only he wasn't Gul Ghillie anymore. Standing beside Meg was the man she'd glimpsed before, so regal that there was no doubt in her mind that he belonged at the queen's side. The dirty, lively brown boy was gone, and in his place a man in bright raiment walked to lay his hand on the dappled horse's flank. The queen smiled down at him.

The children stood alone now, huddled close and trembling

(save James, who seemed to think the whole night was no more than a particularly good play) as they watched their new friend become the prince of the Seelie Court. "They can all change shape," Meg whispered. "Bran told me they can take any shape they want. Gul was a fairy."

This time, Rowan did not laugh, and Silly did not think her sister a coward. They saw before them something they never would have believed, creatures that were born before time in the heart of England's woods and hills. Memories of fairy tales fell away, notions of Shakespeare's diminutive pixies crumbled to dust as they watched the two great trooping courts and their myriad minions meet that May eve. Here was something almost unfathomable, a power and a danger they had never imagined, but a beauty, too, that made them stay though they wished to run. For even when they looked upon the queen, surely the most beguiling creature they had ever seen, they were almost overwhelmed by a sense of their own peril, and some instinct told them to save themselves and flee. Yet even more powerful was the allure of the fairies, lovely and horrible alike, and they could not look away.

"Who is it you have chosen?" asked the Black Prince. His features had altered subtly upon Gul Ghillie's transformation, and now the shadows on his face shifted and contorted until he was as ugly as he had once been fair. He scowled at the man who had been Gul. "Who do you offer up in the War?"

"We have chosen our champion," the Seelie prince said. "On Midsummer Night, shortest night of the year, when the light rises to its greatest power before succumbing at last to the darkness, he will choose his weapon and meet your champion on the fell field of battle. He will kill . . . or he will die. So it has been. So it shall always be, every seventh year, while the leaves grow green in this land."

The queen spoke again. "We have chosen, but we do not know if the champion is willing." Slowly, her eyes swept to the Morgans, and Meg felt a chill run along her neck as the sea eyes lingered on her. Kill . . . or die. Under the spell of that gaze, she almost felt as though she could. . . . Then the eyes moved away, and rested on the one beside her.

"Rowan Morgan, propitiously named, child of the Guardian, whose bones will one day lie in this earth, will you be my champion?"

Aghast, Meg turned to her brother. He seemed to be in a trance, and stared unblinkingly at the queen. No, Meg thought. Not him. Not . . . not kill . . . or die. Then some tiny voice in her called out, Me! Let it be me! I will go in his stead! I am not afraid! But before she could speak, Rowan took a step forward into the pale halo of light. Though low growls came from the woods behind the Black Prince, Rowan never took his eyes from the queen. In a voice that seemed too deep, too grand to be his own, he said, "What you command, I will do!"

The queen gave a little laugh. "That I well know, for none can deny me! But in this alone I cannot command you. You must go willingly."

"No," Meg whispered to him. "You can't. I won't let you." She took a step forward to put herself between her brother and the queen's temptations, but he shouldered her aside almost roughly.

"I go willingly," he said, as if in a dream. "Wherever you bid me." As though he had been doing such things all his life, he bowed to her. Several half-seen things around the Black Prince stirred at the sight of Rowan's bent, bared neck.

"A child?" said the Black Prince. "The teind shall be easily paid at this rate, and the War will be done before I've had any sport. Is this how battles are fought? Mayhap I'll choose that little babe at his side, and hide him in a hollow log to prolong the fighting. A pretty scheme, this!" He scowled at the prince. "Will you sacrifice your own champion just to end the battle early? I want the fray to last long enough to slay you, and you well know once a champion has fallen the fighting ends. I mean to kill you, and make your queen my own. Will you buy yourself another seven years at the cost of this boy's life?"

But the prince didn't look at all concerned, and on the Seelie side, an impish green creature with long ears that pointed at the tips and lobes made a rude face at the Black Prince and gave a loud raspberry.

"We shall see how the child comports himself in battle," the prince said. "Choose who you think best, and we will meet at Midsummer."

The Black Prince leaped upon his horse and wheeled the beast around with a flourish. "We will meet!" he cried. "And the Host will win the field. Treasure these days until Midsummer, my queen, for soon you will have a new consort!" With a jangle of armor he galloped away, and his retinue followed. Great gashes were left in the turf where they had stood.

As soon as the forest swallowed them up, the Seelie Court

burst into a cacophony of song, dispelling the ominous gloom the dark company had brought. Then the queen held up her hand, and all fell silent.

"Children," she said, in a voice as kind as their mother's, "you have nothing to fear . . . though the things you have seen, and the things you have heard, are fearsome indeed. Be merry on this night, and on some tomorrow you will learn what is to come." She spoke a low word to her horse, and he pranced lightly off. Rowan made as if to follow her, but Meg held him back, and the prince who had been Gul Ghillie shook his head.

"This is not the time to learn more," he said. "Go, and follow the will-o'-the-wisp. He will lead you safe to the road. I will find you again. Farewell!" He mounted a horse held by one of the nobles and galloped off after his queen, scattering the romping hordes of his followers.

A moment later, the hill was sealed and bare, all traces of the fairy courts gone. The horses of the Seelie Court left no mark, and when they had passed over the torn earth the foliage healed itself. Meg, who had to be sensible because no one else ever would, immediately ran through the litany of disbelief. Had that miraculous crowd really been there? Had they said those dreadful—and yet oh-so-exciting—things? And in any case (she was clearer-headed than any of the others at that moment), shouldn't they be getting home before they were found out? She gave Rowan a shove, for he was still staring spell-struck at the green swath where the glittering company had stood.

"C'mon!" she said, gathering up James and pulling Silly by the arm. "We're not going to see anything else here tonight, and we can talk about it just as well safe at home." But, somehow, it seemed that nothing would ever be quite safe again.

Meg hustled and bustled her reluctant siblings home, finding refuge in her mother-ways when what she really wanted to do was shake Rowan until he admitted what a fool he was. Fight in a war? Was he mad? Yes, she decided, this was a night of madness. In the morning, she was certain, she'd be able to talk some sense into her fairy-addled brother.

Silly came along easily enough, albeit with a sort of bemused smile on her face. For the rest of that night, she reminded them of some of the odder fairies she'd seen (though Meg and Rowan had mostly looked at the more human-seeming mounted court), and pulled faces and capered in imitation of them. Rowan walked with the other Morgans back through the woods, following the dusty glowing ball that hovered ahead of them just within sight, but he seemed hardly there. His thoughts were all with the queen, and his heart ached with the desire to serve her. Boys, Meg thought.

They met a very cross Finn on the road, and found Dickie sleeping under the shrubberies at the front of the Rookery. Each group had its own secrets, and no one had a word to say as they made their way safely home. The crows in their high roosts mumbled and cursed at the children creeping into the house, then tucked their great beaks under glossy wings and went back to sleep.

Several Palavers

THE MORGANS, having added everything up and realized that their great-great-aunt and -uncle were not loonies after all, knew they should at once spill their strange tale to Phyllida and Lysander, who evidently knew all about fairies, and would no doubt have words of wisdom, or at least of comfort, for them. The Ashes knew the fairies, and the fairies, it seemed, knew them. Who better to consult when you have just seen the two great courts of English fairies, which few alive have ever seen, and your brother has been conscripted to serve in one of their wars?

But they did not tell the Ashes, not yet. They had known one another far longer than they'd known their English relations, and were more inclined to put their trust in their siblings. And it seemed to them, somehow, a very terrible thing to be found out. They had been warned not to go out that night, and promised to stay inside . . . and see what the consequences of their disobedience were! They weren't so much afraid of any punishment, for what could vie with the glory and the danger that had faced them that night? Could a chastisement, a grounding, or even a whipping make them regret the beauty they had seen, or save them from any of the peril that seemed to loom? Still, they had that universal dislike of an I-told-you-so, and, being young, they found it particularly disagreeable when an adult is proved to have known best.

As soon as they crept into the house that night, they went to bed. Even Silly had grown tired of imitating the fairy faces. A deep weariness fell over them all—which may have been part of the fairy glamour, though it might have only been that the hours of traveling, excitement, and sleeplessness finally caught up with them. In any case, they mounted the stairs in a stupor and curled up in their beds, where perhaps they dreamed of things nearly as wonderful as they'd beheld in waking life.

They woke up late the next morning to find someone had brought rolls and marmalade and orange juice on porcelain trays and placed them at their bedsides. The Morgans gobbled down most of it before they had any clear memory of the fairy court, and they nearly collided in the hall as the girls and boys dashed for one another's rooms at the same time. They collected in the girls' room, all finding cozy spots on Meg's bed. But for several minutes they just sat there, uncomfortable and almost embarrassed.

"Was it real?" Rowan asked at last.

"Do we all remember it?" Meg said breathlessly, turning from one to another. "The queen, and Gul turning into the prince, and . . . and what she said to you?" Her wide eyes settled on Rowan.

"I'm to fight for her, against some other champion," Rowan

said, though in the clear light of late morning he didn't seem nearly so sure of himself as he had standing before the lady on the edge of shadows.

"Why did you say yes, Rowan?" Meg said, wringing her hands. (Hand wringing is a very awkward thing to do. But perhaps when one is distraught, it feels more natural.)

"I . . . I don't know."

"He was trying to look brave in front of the queen," Silly said.

"No, it wasn't quite that," Rowan said slowly, still working things out in his own head. "I wasn't trying to look brave. I *was* brave, but only right then, when she was looking at me. For her, I could have done anything. That's how it felt. Not that I could have *tried* to do anything, but that I actually could have done it. I don't know why I felt that way. I certainly don't now."

"Well, you're not going to fight," Meg said with absolute finality. "We'll just have to tell them that. They can't make you fight. That's all there is to it." Though, somehow, she knew it wasn't.

"I guess so," Rowan said. "But if I promised . . ."

"It doesn't matter," said Meg, who in this case didn't have a very fine notion of honor or promises. "You're only a boy—you can't fight in a war. No matter who tells you to."

Rowan didn't look entirely convinced, and said nothing.

"Shouldn't we try to find them then?" Silly asked. "To tell them that Rowan won't fight? When's Midsummer anyway?"

Meg shrugged. "Summer's June, July, and August. It must be sometime in July. I'll ask Auntie Ash. But Gul—I mean the prince—said he'd find us, didn't he? We'll tell him then. It will be easier without the queen there." She looked archly at Rowan.

The matter settled, in Meg's mind at least, they turned to discussing the fairies themselves. They were all very much in awe of the lords and ladies, and even those on the Black Prince's side seemed chiseled by artists of exceptional skill. The queen was their chief topic, but Meg kept bringing up the Black Prince, wondering if he was as devilish as he seemed, and Silly was still entranced by the lesser fairies, with their odd forms and cavorting antics. They rehashed what they had heard, and what they thought they had learned from the conversations—that there were two courts of the fairies, the Seelie and the Host, and it was quite evident to the children which they preferred. They were still naïve in the ways of fairies, and they wanted to classify the two as either *good* or *bad*. They did not yet know that such words are laughable in dealings with the world of Fairy.

"They have a war, then, every seven years," Silly said. "And the Black Prince wants to kill the Seelie prince. But why did they want you to fight with them?"

Rowan didn't much care for the way she said it, but he took her point. Those of the fairies who looked most human were taller and stronger and more warlike (for all that they were beautiful) than any humans he had ever seen. And the others—why, even the tiny or comical ones looked intimidating to him, and if they could change shape, as Meg claimed they could, then there was no limit to their ferocity. What need had they of a human boy to fight their battles for them?

They talked on, and in the noise of their mingled laughter and wonderment they did not hear the bare feet that padded just outside their door. Finn Fachan, dressed in pin-striped pajamas, leaned against the wall and drank it all in. On any other morning, he would have thought all the Morgans either had gone mad or were playing an elaborate trick on him. But while wandering alone in the woods he'd seen something that made their overheard stories seem credible.

When he set off in the direction where he, in his foolish confidence, was sure the Rookery lay, he moved with no thought of wild beasts or brigands, and certainly no fear of fairies. He was a sensible fellow, a thoroughly modern boy who knew that such things as fairies could not exist, and the dark woods held no peril for him. If he didn't yet believe in them, however, they certainly seemed to believe in him, for, as he tramped his way through the vines and roots, squinting eyes watched him, and voices no louder than rustling leaves mocked him. Unseen by Finn, little pixies with grass growing out of their backs jumped under his feet, and when he trod on them the stray sods turned him in a new direction. He thought he was heading home, but others in the forest had plans for him that night, and they directed his steps.

Though he wasn't frightened, he was growing ever more angry. He cursed the Morgans in general, and Rowan in particular, spitting out oaths under his breath that even he wouldn't dare say aloud. Those who followed him, who guided him, listened with interest. Here is one who does not care for the Seelie champion! they thought. Now, what use can be made of this?

Finn heard another voice calling out to him, but this time there was no doubt that it wasn't one of the Morgans. It was a woman's voice, harsh and rasping as an old crow, and it grated upon him like a knife scraped over bones. Yet the words it spoke were perfectly calculated to lure him nearer, for Jenny Green-teeth always knows how to entice people to her shores.

"They lie to you!" she whispered from the tangle of willow roots where she made her home. "They keep secrets from you, boy! They run from you to see great wonders, and leave you to the darkness." Her lips were wide like the mouth of a catfish, and she gnashed a multitude of fangs as the scent of boy-flesh drew nearer.

"Who are you?" Finn cried as he stumbled toward the voice.

"The water murmurs its secrets to me, child. I hear them laughing at you."

"Where are you? Show yourself!"

Before him lay a dank and stagnant pond covered over in green slime. Bubbles rose from the murk, clearing circles in the scum to show black water beneath. The voice was very close now, but he could see no one.

"Come to the water's edge," Jenny Greenteeth said, and there was an age-old hunger in her voice. "Peer into the water, boy, and you will see what your enemies are about."

He was unable to resist that grating voice, or the promise it offered of secrets revealed. If there was one thing Finn hated, it was secrets—unless they were in his keeping. He knew the Morgans were plotting some unpleasantness against him, probably in league with their crazy relatives and that milquetoast Dickie. If there were secrets to discover, no force could keep him from unearthing them. He knelt on the mossy bank and immediately felt dampness seeping into the knees of his trousers.

"Bend over the water, boy! Do it now, before it's too late!"

That was enough for him. He lowered his head and with both hands swept away the slime that coated the surface. Beneath, the water was like a dark mirror, and he stared fixedly into it. For a moment he saw his own face, then the water clouded and cleared to show a gathering of outlandish people, some on horseback, some on foot (or paw, or hoof), dancing at the base of a hill. Among them was a woman so lovely it made his chest ache, and he bent until his face almost touched the foul water.

And then he saw in their midst the four Morgans. There was Rowan, speaking to that woman. There were the others, keeping it all to themselves, running away from Finn so they could laugh to think how he had missed out. The dawning realization that there were really fairies (for even to the jaded Finn, what else could such a company be?) paled beside his resentment that the Morgans had contrived to keep him out of it. But he had gotten the better of them! The voice had called him to the gazing pool, and he had seen just what the Morgans hoped to keep from him. Ha! Fool Finn Fachan? Not this time!

He stared and stared at the image in the pool, wishing he could hear what everyone was saying. They were probably telling the Morgans more secrets. Well, he was on to them now, and no secret was safe from Finn. He'd find out everything there was to know about the fairies. Already he'd forgotten how he'd scoffed at the Ashes, how he'd planned to step on ants, how childish all this fairy business had seemed just a few minutes ago.

Jenny Greenteeth had not hunted in a long time. All of the Gladysmere children knew to stay away from her pond, and it was only once in a great while that some disoriented traveler passed her way and was tempted to draw near to her putrid hole. There was a time when no one could come within the reach of her long sinewed arms and escape, be he child or man. (For, though she preferred the tender flesh of children, she would make do with adults, or rats, or frogs, when they came close enough.)

Now she was out of practice, and she found herself so fascinated by the nearness of such a tasty morsel that she took too much pleasure in stalking it, and did not strike in time. There were his soft white hands, still trailing in her pond; there his throat, where flowed warm blood. So delightfully near! So delicious to anticipate the feel of her hundred sharp teeth sinking into the place where his neck met his shoulder! She should have grabbed him with her crushing arms and drowned him, to be sure of her prey. But she could not resist the temptation to tear at him first with her teeth, and she crept up until she was directly below him.

Alas for Jenny Greenteeth, she forgot that she was no longer hidden beneath the floating verdure of scum. Her face revealed itself clearly from the depths, and Finn threw himself backward just as she sprang. For a moment her green body arched in the biting sting of the air, which burned her like fire, and then she sank back into her dank home, sulking and starving. She had a small hope that he would disbelieve his eyes and might creep closer for another look. Then she would snatch him and pull him under—she'd take no more chances.

But Finn, though he dearly wanted to see more of the Morgans and the fairy courts, had seen the flash of teeth, and took off at a run as soon as he could gather his legs under him. Within a few minutes he found the road, and shortly thereafter the Morgans. He was full of sour looks, and told them nothing of what he had seen.

When Finn lurked outside the girls' room the following morning, he couldn't hear every word they said—for who, talking of fairies for the first time, would speak above a whisper? He did not hear about the War, though he did catch a word here and there that told him Rowan was having closer dealings with the fairies than Finn liked. The Morgans described the very things he'd seen in Jenny Greenteeth's pool, and he smiled to himself to think what means he would use to find out more. Then he backed up a few paces, cleared his throat, and entered the room. The Morgans immediately fell silent, but he affected not to notice.

"Sleep well, kiddies?" he asked, yawning himself. "Aren't you glad you took my advice and went out last night?"

"We didn't go because you told us to!" Silly said. But she remembered Gul Ghillie's words, and didn't say any of the other nasty things that occurred to her.

"I thought you'd all be lost for sure when we were separated," Finn said. "I didn't know *what* I'd tell the Ashes. Did Gul show you anything interesting?"

"No," said Rowan smoothly. "We got separated from him, too."

"Hmm," Finn said, appearing uninterested. To himself, he was thinking how generous he was to have given them a chance to confess. "Well, what's on the schedule for today? Explore the house, or go to the village . . . or look for silly fairies at the bottom of the garden?"

The Morgans laughed nervously, except James, who said, "They're not in the garden. They're in the woods."

"Funny James!" Silly said, and dragged him off in a rush to get breakfast. Rowan had an impulse to put Finn in his place by telling him exactly what they'd seen the night before, but he caught himself in time. Meg suddenly remembered Dickie, and ran off to see if he was awake. She, too, was desperately afraid she'd say something, though it was more from an urge to impress Finn than to cow him.

Safe away from him, she rapped softly on Dickie's door. He let her in, and she sat on a flowered ottoman while he wrapped a robe over a long sleeping shirt that pulled tight at the buttons.

"Why are all your pillows on the floor?" she asked him. They were in fact shoved into the farthest corner.

"Down," he said. "I'm allergic."

"Oh. There are probably foam pillows somewhere."

"This doesn't seem like the kind of house where they'd have foam pillows," he said with long-suffering acceptance, and sneezed.

"Is it really that bad? Can't you take something for it?"

"I do. I have medicine for my allergies, and an inhaler for my asthma, and once a month I get shots. But it doesn't really help."

"Oh," she said again, "I'm sorry." She didn't really know what else to say. She was used to offering solutions to people's problems, but she couldn't see how to help poor Dickie.

"We were talking about what to do today. Explore the house, or the garden, or maybe go into the village. What would you like to do?"

"I don't know. . . . Anything you want."

Meg, who was used to getting an argument from her siblings about almost everything, was surprised to discover that this easy acquiescence and indifference were actually annoying. "Don't you have a preference?"

He shrugged. "I sneezed so much in the garden kitchen, I think the real garden would be worse. Would we walk to the village, or drive? Only, I got a blister on each foot last night. I'd like to explore the house, I guess, though it's pretty dusty."

Honestly, Meg found it hard to have the proper sympathy for poor Dickie. She tried to imagine what she'd be like if everything made her nose run, if she was shy and didn't seem to have any real friends, and then she felt more kindly toward him. She hadn't known him too well before the trip, but the few times she'd spoken to him, he'd come across as fairly bright. He was awkward, and seemed to have a hard time convincing himself to speak, though when he finally did it was frequently something clever (when it wasn't a physical complaint). Still, he wasn't quite up to her standards, and for the moment her friendship was based more on pity than anything else.

To shift the subject from his allergies, rather than from any real curiosity, she asked him how he'd fared after they were separated. To her surprise, he looked almost frightened—certainly uncomfortable—and he crossed behind her to shut and lock the door.

He said nothing for a long while, until Meg said, "Tell me!" very earnestly. Then, with nervous glances around the empty room, he began.

"I had the strangest dream. At least, it must have been a

dream. We were separated, Finn and I, from the rest of you. We followed a light we thought was yours for a while, but it disappeared, and we were lost. Finn said he was going to get back to the Rookery before you and lock you out, so you'd be caught when the Ashes came home. He went off, and I tried to find you so you could hurry back."

"Oh, did you, Dickie?" Meg cried, jumping up and giving him a quick little hug before she could stop herself. "That was swell of you!"

Dickie beamed and blushed, and it seemed to be easier for him to go on. "But I couldn't. I called and called, and no one ever answered. I thought you must have heard me—maybe you just weren't answering."

"We'd *never* do that to *you*," Meg said stoutly.

"Well, I walked on, but after a little while I didn't have any idea where I was going. I came to a stream, a tiny trickle, and I remembered that a bigger stream went by the road at the Rookery. So I thought maybe this one fed into it. I started to follow it, but it went in between some rocks. Big boulders, much taller than me. I didn't want to go around and risk losing the spring, so I started to climb over them, but it was hard with only the moonlight, and I stopped to rest.

"And then, while I was sitting on one rock and leaning against another, I heard a strange voice. It said, 'Thank you for visiting me. I have been so very lonely.' It startled me, but it was such a gentle little voice, so sad, and so hopeful, that I couldn't be scared. I thought it must be someone just behind the rock, and so I talked to him for a while. I asked him if he knew where the Rookery was, and he said he'd taken lost lambs there before. He told me about the stream, about the music it makes from day to night, and he sounded like it was almost all he knew of. He asked me about my home, and I told him about Arcadia. He seemed very impressed with it. 'Imagine,' he said, 'such a place in hills and woods, where people do nothing but learn all the livelong day!'

"And then he said that he had never met such a pleasant fellow as me, and he had to come around the rock to introduce himself properly and shake my hand. I must have been dreaming by then, though I don't remember falling asleep. He said, 'I'm a Urisk, and they call me Tim Tom.' Then he came around the rock with his hand held out. But it wasn't his hand I was looking at. He had a sort of skin tied around him—it looked like a fox—and his feet were like goat's hooves. But he didn't look like a faun or a satyr. I've read about those. He was very thin and very sad and kind of hunched in on himself, like he was afraid to be seen. And I . . . I stepped back, and I think I fell and hit my head, and I don't remember anything else. When I woke up, I was back here, and you were, too. Now I think about it, I seem to remember one other thing. A voice, it must have been his, sighed and said, 'Another little lamb for the Rookery, and no friends for Tim Tom.' "

"Are . . . are you sure it was a dream?" Meg asked him.

"Do you think it could have been real? It *seemed* real. Could he have been a fairy, d'you think? I didn't think your relatives were serious, but could there really be fairies here?"

She was tempted to tell him about her encounter with the brownie, at least (though last night was really too secret to spill easily), but something still held her back. Perhaps it was only that Dickie looked so pleased at having had an adventure, at seeing something no one else had seen. Learning that they had all done just the same, and better, would diminish it.

"I don't think Phyllida and Lysander would lie," Meg said, choosing her words carefully. "If people have believed in fairies for hundreds of years, there must be something to it."

"I'll ask your relatives!" he said excitedly. "I'll tell them what I saw, and they'll tell me about fairies. They must know all there is to know."

He had gotten no farther than swinging his legs over the edge of the bed when Meg sprang up and barred his way. "Are you crazy? Then they'll know you were out last night. And if they have any sense, they'll know the rest of us were out, too— you'd never go out alone." She didn't mean for that to be hurtful, and after all it was perfectly true, though it smarted just the same. Dickie knew he wasn't adventurous, but he didn't like it rubbed in.

"I have to find out some way!"

"You can ask them questions, just not all at once. And be careful. I'll ask them, too. I'll talk to them after breakfast." She had far more faith in her own subtlety than in Dickie's. But it wouldn't hurt for another person to be seeking out information. Even if Rowan wasn't going to participate in the fairy war, a new world had been opened up to them, and they certainly weren't going to let it slip away.

They all ambled down to the garden kitchen, and the cook brought them oatmeal and honey and eggs and grapes. Midway through, Phyllida popped her head in and told them that she'd decided breakfast and lunch should be informal meals, but that they'd all gather at eight for supper. "You no doubt have your own business to attend to, and don't need the responsibility of showing up at any particular hour to eat," she said. "And I don't want to have to worry every time you're ten minutes late—so better not to know at all. I'll take inventory at supper."

How marvelous she is, Meg thought. It would be just like living on their own, free to make their own decisions about practically everything.

"Meg," Phyllida said as she was leaving, "come and see me in the parlor when you've finished eating. Daisy will show you the way." Daisy was one of the housemaids (and also one of the cows, though in this case Phyllida referred to the former).

"I'll come now," Meg said, wiping the honey from her mouth and shoving her plate away.

This is it, she thought with foreboding. Meg was perfectly capable of holding her tongue, but if Phyllida asked her directly about last night, she didn't know if she could lie to her face—or if she should.

The Truth About Fairies

MEG HAD NEVER been in a room called a parlor, and thought this one perfectly charming. It was all done in soft pink tones, with overblown dahlia blossoms on the wallpaper. The chairs were very plush and comfortable, and there was a clever little writing desk that unfolded to reveal secret compartments. As in most of the other rooms of the Rookery, there were several vases of flowers, this time dusky-yellow roses mixed with trailing ivy.

"Bran tells me you've seen the brownie," Phyllida began as soon as Meg had settled herself.

"Yes, I . . . I saw him in the kitchen. He disappeared so quickly I wasn't sure I really saw him."

"And that's what Bran should have told you, no doubt. If he'd laughed at you, you'd have thought it all a trick of your imagination. That might have been for the best. But Bran is of his own mind on this, and I'm not sure that I don't agree with him, now that I've met all of you. I thought maybe you could come here and remain blind and stupid to what was going on around you. I see that isn't possible."

"I'm sorry," Meg said, which she often said when she didn't know what else to say.

"Nonsense, girl! No need to be sorry. You weren't stirring up trouble. It just happened. The brownie chooses who will see him, just as they all do. It was wrong of me, though, not to tell you—to tell all of you—something of what goes on around here. Of course, if I just sat you down and told you all of it, you'd never believe me. And there might have been better protection in that than in all the knowledge and precautions in the world. What you don't believe in cannot hurt you. Did you tell the others about the brownie?"

Meg looked down at the carved wooden feet on her chair, and finally confessed that she'd told her siblings.

"Ah well, you'd have to, wouldn't you? But not the others? Not Dickie or that Finn?" Meg shook her head. "Good, good. Best to keep it away from prying outside eyes. The less they know the better, though, living here, they're bound to see hints of things. Especially around this time of year."

"Why now?"

"Oh, it's a volatile time. The fairies get more lively as the season grows. They like the greenery, the blossoms, and the fruit. You hardly ever see the Neighbors in the dead of winter, except perhaps one of the Host. They're always on the alert."

"The Host?"

"The bad fairies would be the easiest way of putting it, though how much any of them can be bad or good I still don't know.

They're all of the same family, more or less, but there are two courts. The Seelie, they call the more benevolent of them. And the others are the Unseelie, or the Host, or the Strangers. But that's not to say you can trust the Seelie, or that one among the Host might not do you a great kindness someday. That's the thing about the world of Fairy, Meg Morgan—you can never be sure what to expect. I've known the fairies, in their good forms and their bad, large and small, fair and hideous, since I could crawl about the garden, and even I could never tell you more than a fraction of their quirks and freaks. Bran, now, he thinks like one of them. But that's another story."

Meg realized that she would dearly love to hear about Bran, but she didn't quite dare ask, and Phyllida went on.

"It's in my family, you see—in my family and yours. The tale is almost lost in the centuries, but I can tell you the heart of it. Long ago, longer than you can even imagine, an ancestor of mine was appointed to be the human guardian of this place. In those days, there were not nearly so many people in the world, and the influence of the fairies was more strongly felt. They would talk to herdsmen in the fields, teach women to weave, or give council in war. They would seduce men's daughters and sweethearts, and sometimes swear friendship with humans and offer them fairy hospitality. But the men grew stronger, and the fairies faded a bit. And they changed, too, for I do not think in those days there were such terrible members of the Host, fairies that hate humans and would cause them harm.

"There came a time when each grew apart from the other. Humans began to fear the fairies, and desired some protection against them. And yet there have always been those among the humans who still loved the fairies, and who know they must be honored and preserved. The fairies, too, needed protection, for they were being driven from their homes, and the old friendships were forgotten. There was a woman, an ancestor of mine, who was wise and kind—and beautiful, I suppose, for all women in old stories are beautiful. She was a friend of the fairies, and the men also trusted her, and both clans named her Guardian of this most sacred place."

"Here? This is sacred?"

"Aye, above all spots in England. There were once fairies everywhere, from Penzance to the frigid Scottish northlands. There still are a few remnants, in the wilder places, where people keep their old habits. But this was always their home—their capital, if you will—their palace and their sanctuary. Under the Green Hill is where their home lies, beneath the earth from which all things grow. The woods, too, are theirs, where thrive oaks that are as old as time, and stones that the years cannot eat away. Even when they wandered far afield, this was their holy place, and when they came home, it was to the Green Hill. You would not know it—and few have ever seen it—but inside the Green Hill is another world. Would that I could tell you the wonders I have seen there! The fairies are close with their secrets, and quick to resent any who reveal them.

"This, then, is their principal home, and, for all the power the fairies possess, it is a strange and misty power, and cannot stand against the determined might of humans. So they craved some assurance that this place would always be safe for them. My ancestor—Angharad was her name—took up residence here, and learned the ways of the fairies, and taught the people charms to keep them safe from the more malevolent among their neighbors. She was a mediator between the two peoples, so different, yet more closely bound to each other than either cares to realize. Her role is passed along the female line, and she taught her daughters, who in turn taught theirs, until my own mother told me all that remains of fairy lore."

"Why haven't I heard of all this before?" Meg asked.

Phyllida sighed, and when she spoke her voice seemed to come from very far away...or very long ago. "I had an older sister, whose lot it should have been to hold the place that is now mine. But this was when the world was changing. There were planes and motorcars, and wars that made the world seem much wider than Gladysmere and its woods and hills. Chlorinda would not stay. She ran away one day, and I...we...did not hear from her for years. Later, we got word that she was in America, married to a man named Robert Goodfellow. She had a daughter, Chloe, who married a Richard Tamlane."

"My grandparents," Meg interjected. "I only just remember them. They both died when I was little."

"Yes, I know. Fell into a volcano, didn't they? Blood will tell in strange ways. Adventure was always in our line, though it has usually been of a more local sort. Let me see, they had Glynnis Tamlane, your mother, who wed Tom Morgan and had all of you. And so the line split into a new branch that knows nothing of its heritage."

"Why didn't Chlorinda ever say anything? There isn't a single family story about it."

"She was desperate to get away, to forget everything about this place. It frightened her. Her father, our father, was gone then, taken, and we didn't think he'd ever be recovered."

"Bran, you mean?"

Phyllida laughed. "Strange, isn't it? Though no stranger than so many other dealings with the fairies. Yes, Bran is indeed my father. Don't ask me about that story now. I don't think I have the heart to tell it. All said, it's not surprising Chlorinda never spoke of any of it, and the tales were never handed down. Oh, perhaps there were some rumors. I know your mother didn't quite relish the idea of sending you here. She's uneasy about us, even if she doesn't know why. But you're safe enough, I think."

Meg was silent a moment, then said, "You don't have any children, Auntie Ash. Who will be the Guardian of this place when you . . . I mean, when you're not here?"

"You mean when I die? Don't be afraid of the word, child. And don't be afraid of death. It is only another change, and we are changing all the time. I don't know what will happen. . . . I suppose I should have planned better. But we are a long-lived people, at least those of us who don't traipse around volcanoes, and there is time enough to think about that. Eighty-four is no age." She chuckled. "I suppose to you it's old enough. Here, try one of these macaroons. You didn't half finish your breakfast."

Meg munched the treat and almost choked as she rushed to swallow it and ask more questions. "Where did fairies come from? And what are they, exactly? I mean, they're not all like the brownie, are they?"

"You ask things that would take a lifetime to answer, and even then I'd just scratch the surface, and likely be half wrong in the bargain. Fairies are . . . fairies. They have always been in England, a part of the land, like the dirt and the boulders. I don't know that they came from anywhere. Perhaps they once lived alone in this land. There are those who say they arrived—or were born, or created—at the very moment man set foot in England. They depend on humans in strange ways. I'll tell you more of that later. When the Christians came, they said fairies were fallen angels who were too good for hell, too bad for heaven, and lived a half life on earth. That's hogwash, of course. They were here long before anybody thought up Christianity. Some say they are old gods grown weak for want of worship, some that they are nature spirits, protectors. But I don't know where the fairies came from, only that they belong here, and if one day they are ever gone, this land will not thrive.

"As for what they are . . . why, they're everything you can imagine. They can be beautiful and kind, or beautiful and cruel. They can be fanged and horrid, but thresh your wheat for you. They change shape at will, and they change temper even faster. They have laws, but they can break them. You don't dare trust a fairy, of either court, and yet, if you do not trust them, they will never deal with you squarely. They have a society that in part mimics our own—they have a royal court, lords and ladies, and you may see them in clothes and fine jewels such as a human noble might wear, eating rare foods and sipping nectar. But those same fine fairies may on another day seem sallow and sick, clad in leaves and rags, and tearing at toadstools and moss. Which is the true form of Fairy? Both. Or neither."

"It's awfully confusing."

"Indeed. And sometimes dangerous. Most fairies won't want to hurt you, but their morals are not like ours. If they take a fancy to you, they might honor you by inviting you to dance with them. You'll step into a fairy ring—that's a magical circle of mushrooms—and they'll put a spell on you so you can't stop dancing. You'll dance until you're weary, and beyond. They'll take their merriment with you, and you will dance in that charmed circle until you die from exhaustion. Or they'll steal you away from your friends, your family, to keep you with them, and make you believe you're happy. You'll think you're just sitting down to a feast with them, but when you've finished eating and they let you go, you'll find sixty years have passed in the outside world. That's another fairy peculiarity—time moves differently for them. They hardly age at all, and don't always understand, or care, that our lives are so fleeting. Yes, there is joy beyond imagining to be found with the fairies, but sorrow and suffering, too, and you cannot tell which lot will be yours."

"Is that what happened to Bran? But he didn't grow old."

"Another perversion of fairy time. Hush, I said I would not speak of him now. Take another macaroon—they're good for the digestion."

Phyllida Ash stood up, and it seemed harder for her than usual. She crossed to the window and talked to Meg with her back turned.

"That is why I give you so many warnings, Meg Morgan. There is no reason to think the fairies mean you any harm, but it is best to avoid trouble. There are dangerous things that live in the pools, and creatures in the woods you ought not to meet.

Fairy food can make you a prisoner, and so I tell you not to eat the food of strangers. Even knowing your name can give them a power over you—though you knowing their names can give *you* a power, too. So promise me, child, and promise me again, that you will heed my warnings!" She wheeled around and held Meg in a gaze so powerful the girl trembled.

"I will! I promise!" Too late! she cried to herself.

Oh, how Meg wanted to reveal the truth! Maybe, she thought, Phyllida can fix everything. If she knows the fairies so well, surely she can keep Rowan from fighting. Yet she hesitated. She was ashamed they'd violated Phyllida's rules—Meg was no lawbreaker at heart—and what once seemed like a mild act of disobedience now seemed a crime tantamount to treason. I should tell her, Meg thought. But she didn't, not quite yet.

Phyllida softened immediately. "I suppose you'll tell all you know to the others?"

"I'd like to," Meg confessed. "I won't if you say I can't."

"You won't be able to stop yourself. I was a girl once, too. And it will help them understand how serious it all is. Perhaps you shouldn't tell Finn and Dickie. They have no part in all this."

"No," Meg said, "I won't tell them." She hovered in the doorway, unwilling to confess, unable to leave. "Auntie Ash, when's Midsummer?"

Phyllida looked at her sharply. "Why do you ask?"

"Oh, when I saw the brownie, Bran said Midsummer was dangerous. I just wanted to know when I should be extra careful."

"You should be extra careful all the time, but Midsummer is the twenty-first of June."

"Why is it so dangerous?"

"Oh . . . ," Phyllida began, and stopped as if she was sorting through truth and lies and evasions, deciding which would serve best just then. She settled on a vague version of the truth. "It's another holiday, like Beltane. The fairies have a . . . a ritual they do on Midsummer. Nothing you have to worry about."

A ritual? She must mean the Midsummer War for which the queen recruited Rowan. Meg's mouth gaped and closed as she tried to decide whether to tell Phyllida. I'll tell her, Meg decided. I'll tell her right now. Or in just a minute. She bought herself a more little time by asking, "Is the ritual very important?"

"Oh yes. Everything that lives depends on it. If something happened to interfere, nothing green would ever grow again. But don't you fret, dear. Things have gone on for millennia; I assume they'll go on a while longer. You children just be sure you stay inside on Midsummer Night and you'll have naught to fret over." She patted Meg on the head and sent her off with a fistful of macaroons.

As soon as Meg was out the door, she slumped against the wall and gulped, her hands tightening until the cookies crumbled. Nothing green will ever grow again. She was close to panic at the thought. She had no idea the Midsummer War meant so much. If something happened to interfere . . . Would it be interference to get Rowan to back out of the War? She remembered Phyllida's intensity when she talked about the fairies, and that deliberate carelessness even Meg recognized as evasion when she mentioned the War.

I'm afraid she won't stop it, Meg thought miserably. If I tell her about Rowan, things might be even worse. From what she said, it's her job, the job of all her ancestors, to see that things like the War happen as they always have. Maybe she won't help me. Maybe she won't let me interfere.

She wanted more than anything to tell Phyllida, for part of her trusted that she would be enfolded in her great-great-aunt's soft arms and told that everything would be taken care of. Another part of her wasn't so sure. She hadn't known Phyllida long, after all.

For now, Meg took the easiest and most dangerous route a person can take—she decided to decide later. There's more than a month and a half until Midsummer, she thought. Plenty of time to figure out if I should tell Phyllida.

Immeasurably relieved at deferring her responsibility, she ate her macaroon crumbs and went to find the others.

Around the Rugged Rookery
the Ragged Rascals Ran

THERE IS NOTHING quite so much fun as exploring someone else's house without the owner's watchful eye, and what is fun in six rooms is even more so in a hundred.

Whatever secrets the Ashes had were not concealed in the house, and they gave the children full permission to go through every room to their heart's content. "Just tell me if you find anything particularly good," Phyllida had said at dinner the night before. "I haven't been in half the rooms since I was your age, and for all I know, there might be great treasures somewhere about. Or skeletons. I don't know which."

"What'd she want you for?" Finn asked when Meg returned from her talk with Phyllida in the parlor.

"Oh . . . she wanted to see if we needed any more clothes." Meg was amazed at her own facility for lying.

They all trooped up to the third floor and began to open doors. The first few revealed nothing more exciting than bedrooms. These were good enough in themselves, with old tapestries covering the walls and grand canopied beds raised up on daises. They had their own curiosities, for those who cared to look—one had a chamber pot shaped like a fat carp's head, another held a peculiar mirror with etching on the back of the glass, so that, when you looked into it, it always seemed there was someone behind you, peering over your shoulder. At the moment, though, the children had higher hopes than mere bedrooms, and they sallied onward.

Meg had a great deal to tell her siblings, but there was never a moment when Finn and Dickie were out of earshot. She managed to tell them only that Midsummer was June 21, which was an innocent enough thing to say. Even at that, Finn sidled closer and wanted to know what was so special about Midsummer. "It's just another holiday, like Beltane," she said, as lightly as she could, echoing Phyllida's words. Finn, suspicious of everything now, and thinking every word held a clue to what he wished to discover, would have pressed her harder, but just then Dickie found the library.

There were actually two libraries in the Rookery, and they had already met one of them. It was on the first floor, a cozy, leathery place rather like the smoking room but without the billiard table, and lined all around with novels. Some were rare early editions from the days when people first realized they could write novels. On other shelves were books by the Victorians, with practically a whole wall of the prolific Anthony Trollope. They had a good selection of everything worth reading written before World War I, as well as a few pretty books about birds and plants. It was a fine library for any reader . . . but the third-floor library was another animal entirely.

Dickie could tell it was extraordinary just from the smell. An odor of knowledge permeated the air, ghosts of arcane secrets wafted about by the breeze the children made when they opened the door. Here were books more rare than any first editions. Many were bound in calfskin, and not a few had solid metal covers, so that they seemed more like treasure chests than proper books. Some were locked, and some placed so inconveniently high on the shelves it was obvious they were not meant to be disturbed very often. A large mahogany desk and a worn leather wingback chair were the only furnishings. The air seemed stale, as though no one had visited that room in decades. But, oddly, though there was dust on all visible surfaces, the library didn't make Dickie sneeze. Books have their own peculiar kind of dustiness, which didn't catch in his nose the same way cat's hair or thistle pollen might.

Even Finn was briefly impressed by this room, for it had a grandeur that would not be denied. He was particularly intrigued by a globe on the floor in the corner. It was as big around as his arms could reach, fashioned out of jewels and semiprecious stones. The Atlantic was lapis lazuli, the Pacific soft jade. England was a rough-cut emerald, and the fjords of Norway might have been crystal, or they might have been diamonds.

There was a scurrying behind the shelves, and Finn said, "Ugh, rats!" But Dickie, whose nose was as keen as a hound's when it came to allergens, could detect no trace of the ammonia smell that comes when rodents have made a place their home. Though the others, however much they liked the library, were eager to explore the rest of the house, Dickie said he thought he'd stay, and meet them later for lunch.

"One down," Meg said under her breath. "One to go."

Near the library was a room dedicated to maps, with canvases unfurled on the walls and scrolls nestled in umbrella stands. It, too, had a table in the center, and on this was a map of Europe with little red and blue pin flags piercing it, and tiny models of tanks spiked like thumbtacks. A long time ago, someone had followed the movement of troops in World War I.

A few doors down was a room filled with arms and armor— they would find several such rooms, each holding the weaponry of a particular period, as though a long succession of owners had prepared for a battle that never came, and at last put their martial gear into storage. This one had arms from the time of Napoleon— cavalry sabers and antique rifles and patinaed pikes. There were tricornered hats in glass cases, with plumes untouched by moths or rot. Uniforms on headless mannequins had fared less well, and their reds (and blues) were faded, their brass buttons tarnished by time. Finn and Rowan wanted to take the arced swords off the wall, but Meg flatly refused, and something in her tone stayed their hands. They had a fierce, brief bout with rattan practice sticks they found, but Meg put a stop to that after Rowan got a nasty bruise on his arm.

"Let's play hide-and-seek," Meg said at last, desperate to get Finn away so she could talk to the others.

"That's for kids," Finn sneered. Nevertheless, it didn't take much to convince him to play. Even when they agreed to confine themselves to the third floor, the possibilities for hiding were so vast that it promised to be a challenging game. Finn volunteered to be It, and went back to the library to count and see if Dickie would be in on the game. The Morgans dashed off, and Meg pulled them into a room they hadn't yet explored.

"We're not all supposed to hide in the same place," Silly protested, even after Meg started to reveal the tidbits Phyllida had told her. Silly had a very strong sense of fair play, and thought that if you were going to bother with a game you ought to do it right. But she eventually hushed as Meg recited as closely as she could everything that Phyllida had said.

"I really think we ought to tell her about last night," Meg said. "I wanted to—I almost did. But I decided I wouldn't unless you agreed." She didn't want to tell them how vital it was that the Midsummer War take place. This would only add to Rowan's stubbornness. If he thought the world might end if he refused to fight, he'd never capitulate.

"No!" Rowan said at once. "I don't want the Ashes to know."

"Surely we wouldn't get into any trouble. I mean, we're in enough already, with the fairies. Phyllida and Lysander wouldn't do anything else to us. They'd make sure we were safe."

"We'll be fine," he assured her.

"Weren't you listening to what I said . . . what she said? They're not tame and friendly, they don't have pretty wings and flit in flowers. They're dangerous! People have been killed by the fairies, or stolen away, or—"

"No," he said again, firmly. "We're not going to tell them. Gul will come back, maybe today, and we'll explain things to him. If we told the Ashes, they might send us away."

Meg didn't much like that idea—their parents would be disappointed in them, and, despite her growing unease about the fairies, she felt a compulsion to know them better, if she could. "But it's better than being forced to fight someone."

"No one's forcing me to fight," he said in a strange voice. "If we left, I'd never see *her* again."

"Her? Oh, you mean the queen? Yes, I'd like to see her again. Not at that price, though."

Rowan said nothing, but he looked as if even the price of his life might not be too high to pay. Meg frowned at him. "You're not thinking of doing what she wants. You wouldn't be that foolish, would you? Agree to be in their silly war just to impress her? You'd die, just for her?"

"Who says I'd die?" Rowan countered. "You have a pretty low opinion of me if you think I'd go in prepared to die."

Meg opened her mouth to speak, but she was so frustrated at his obstinate stupidity that nothing came out. It was simply against all logic for an untrained boy to agree to fight in a war, particularly one in which he had no personal stake. If someone had to fight, why not a grown-up, a soldier? And how could a battle have any effect on growing things? Yet, according to Phyllida, nothing would grow again if this ridiculous war didn't happen every seven years. It didn't make sense to Meg.

He can't mean to go through with it, Meg thought. He's talking big now because he doesn't want to look scared, but as soon as he realizes how real all this is, he'll back down. Seven weeks. I have seven weeks to change his mind. It was as reassuring as an eternity.

"Don't you think we should hide now?" Silly asked. Fairies

were all well and good, but there was a game to be won. The fairies, not so immediate a concern, could wait. Anyway, she thought it rather exciting that her brother had been chosen for battle, even if she was a little bit jealous. It never occurred to her that he might be killed. Death was for other people, people who weren't related to you, whom you didn't know.

They agreed to play the game a bit more earnestly, though Meg had half a mind to go off on her own until lunchtime, maybe to the garden, to think things through without a bellicose sister and fairy-struck brother distracting her. Her mind was so muddled—to trust Phyllida or not, to have faith in Rowan's good sense, or really to believe he would fight. She needed time, and, fortunately she had plenty, or so she thought.

Before they split up, Silly checked the room they were in for good hiding places. It was only another bedroom, if anything less promising than the others, but she was drawn to a large piece of furniture in one corner.

"It's like in *The Lion, the Witch and the Whachamacallit*," Silly said, opening the door.

"*Wardrobe*," Meg said.

"Yup, that's it. Look, it's full of furs, too, just like the one in the book. I wonder if there's a passageway to a secret world."

"We have enough to do here with the fairies without finding another world full of trouble," Meg said testily, and started to leave as Silly delved deeper into the wardrobe, crushing the furs against her cheeks. She almost ignored Silly when she said, "Wait! There *is* something back here." Then she heard the muffled click of a latch being lifted, and Silly's voice grew fainter, but echoed strangely.

Alarmed, Meg followed her, and in the dim light that filtered through the window and past foxes and sables saw a staircase rise from a narrow door.

"There's a secret passageway!" Meg called back, and James and Rowan joined them in the cedar-scented recesses. Mercifully, it wasn't a door to another world, but a hidden staircase was enticement enough.

The door was wood, the same sort as the wardrobe, but the steps were slate, scarcely more than two feet across, and the cold walls that brushed their shoulders were stone set in mortar. Though the light from the room didn't reach beyond the first few steps, Silly was undaunted, and how could the older ones be less brave than their little sister?

They felt their way slowly, not quite holding hands, but groping at one another's shoulders and backs to keep in constant contact. The stairs were steep, and seemed to skirt along the side of the house. At one point they turned sharply, and a second flight continued onward and upward. At last they came to a barrier, and a little exploration revealed this to be a door. "Probably locked," said Meg. But it wasn't—the latch shifted easily, and they were nearly blinded as the door swung open on smooth, greased hinges and they were awash in a wave of clear white light on the Rookery roof. Sleek young crows took flight at the disturbance, but grizzled, hoary old rooks only fluffed their feathers and gave gravelly caws. They had seen far stranger things in their long lives, and were not bothered by creatures as innocuous as children.

Five stories is not a great height, nothing compared with the buildings in New York City, or even the venerable stone structures of Arcadia. The Morgans often went to the top of the school's bell tower, up 201 steps, where, amid the deafening peals of bells taller than they were, they could see the spreading countryside of hills sheltering deep, narrow lakes. This height was nothing to that . . . and yet it seemed somehow a greater thing to stand godlike above the places they had ventured the previous night. There was the stream, a silver winding snake, and there the road overhung with limbs so ponderous and leaves so light. Green was all around them, until it met the piercing blue of the sky. They could see the tops of the tallest houses in Gladysmere (few rose above two stories), and beyond that a break in the greenery that must be the Commons. They could not see the summit of the Red Hill, though the breeze still carried a faint, acrid whiff of smoke.

"The Green Hill must be over there," Rowan said, shading his eyes. "But I can't see it." Its top did not reach beyond the highest trees, and, indeed, from their vantage point, they could see that the oaks seemed to grow more densely around the spot where the Green Hill lay, shielding it from the rest of the world . . . or perhaps shielding the rest of the world from the hill. Then, as if responding to their longing, the treetops shifted, as though from a high wind, and there, peeking between the gaps, the Morgans glimpsed a green as bright as new spring leaves, a green almost gold in the unforgiving noon light that made the oaks seem grim and gray. Then the trees closed in on their secret, and the Green Hill was again hidden from view.

Rowan leaned on his elbows in the trough of the dagged parapet, looking over the forest that hid the Green Hill.

Strange visions filled his head, visions of himself, clad in mail that chafed him under the armpits, with a close-fitting helm hugging his skull, and a sword in his hand. He saw himself facing an enemy who stood in shadow, unseen save for the outline of his bulk and the glint of his weapon. It was with some wonder that Rowan watched himself face this threat, saw his own legs stand firm, his hand brandish its sword unwaveringly at the foe. He was proud of that Rowan he saw, the one whose lip did not tremble, who didn't turn away from the challenge simply because he was no more than a boy. There was a version of himself who was brave, who was willing to face any danger, for . . . he heard the Fairy Queen's voice, low and rich, calling out to him from the Green Hill. *Rowan!* she called. *Rowan! My champion!*

And then Meg shook him, and he was only a boy again, staring at the woods from the Rookery roof.

"Are you all right? You looked like you might tumble over the edge."

He assured her that he was fine, and wandered off to see what was to be seen on the rest of the roof. But to himself he made a resolution, and swore that no wheedling words or good sense from his sister would sway him. He would do whatever the Fairy Queen desired. He would fight willingly in the fairy war and kill—or die—at her bidding.

After they all agreed not to tell Finn or Dickie about the stairs to the roof (for no real reason other than it seemed right to keep secrets from them), James, Rowan, and Silly went back downstairs to finish the game. Meg decided to stay on the roof. She had some thinking to do, and up there, in the bright sunlight and lively breeze, she could be reasonably sure of being undisturbed.

"The game will go on fine without me," she said in response to their halfhearted urgings. Indeed, it turned out to be a sorry game of hide-and-seek, for only two of the players ever hid, they were never sought, and no one was found until they all gathered later for lunch.

Finn was supposed to count to one hundred in the library. It was of course his intention to count to ten, slip out, and sneak back down the hall to see where the others had hidden, but, alas, his worst nature was checked so early that, instead of cheating, he never started playing at all. He found Dickie looking quite at home in the library, where he already had five books spread out around him. Before Finn could decide on the most effective way to tease him, he noticed what Dickie was reading. One of the books was entitled *Fairies and Other Queer Folk,* another *Legends of the Little People.* A book so big it was a wonder little Dickie managed to lift it was opened to a stylized illustration of a figure who looked, as much as any flat illustration could, like the hideous fanged woman Finn had seen in the scrying pool. Dickie seemed most interested in an old vellum-bound tome that was opened to a chapter called "Benign Solitary Fairies—Urisks, Pookas, and the Brown Man of the Moors." On the right-hand page was a sepia sketch of a shaggy man with hooves for feet.

Dickie looked up in some alarm. He'd become so immersed in his studies that he'd nearly forgotten about the existence of anyone else in the Rookery, and certainly never thought he'd be disturbed. He was immediately on guard, and rightly so, for at almost any other time Finn would have fixed on some vulnerability and pounced. Dickie expected to be tormented about avoiding the others, seeking out books, his paleness, his pudginess, his allergies—anything could have become Finn's target, and Dickie made up his mind to endure whatever came as best he could. It would be only a matter of time before Finn grew bored and let him return to his pursuits. Dickie closed the tome he was perusing, but Finn slipped his finger between the leaves and opened it again.

"What have we here?" said Finn.

It was probably surprise that loosened Dickie's tongue over the next few minutes. For Finn, who had always either been malignant or rudely ignored Dickie, was suddenly polite and interested, friendly, and even jocular. It was as though Dickie had really been his friend all along, and he'd teased and tormented him from high spirits, not malice. Finn had a remarkable way of turning course mid-stride. He had the gift of seeming sincere. When he was kind, it seemed that he would always be kind. When he was unpleasant, it seemed he could never behave otherwise. His true nature may have been somewhere between those extremes, perhaps nearer one side than the other. You'd not go too wrong with Finn if you remembered that he was never as bad, or as good, as he might seem at any particular moment. But the same might be said for all of us.

Finn perched on the table beside Dickie and spoke in such a way that one might think he had never disparaged the others for their talk of fairies, never scoffed at the idea fairies might exist. He was interested in what Dickie had uncovered, and Dickie found himself being spoken to as an equal. He opened up—slowly at first, but he grew more voluble as Finn continued to speak kindly. Dickie found himself telling Finn things he shouldn't. At last, almost against his will, he told Finn about Tim Tom.

"And he's here, right in this book!" Dickie said at the tale's end. He pointed to the sketch. "He looked almost exactly like this. It says the Urisks are shy and lonely, and live along rocky riverbanks. They're more common in Scotland, but they're found all over the isles."

"Amazing!" Finn said. "And the information's all there? Just like a field guide to fairies?"

"Well, I don't know if everything in the book's accurate," Dickie confessed. "But this part sure seems to be. This other one talks about water fairies, and this one is all about charms and spells for keeping fairies away."

"Is there anything about charms for *finding* fairies?"

"I don't know. I've only just started to read. Almost all of the books in here seem to be about fairies, in one way or another. Only . . ."

"Only what?"

"Well, I can't read many of them. Just these and a few more are modern, and written in English. A lot of them are in Latin, and I just know a little bit of that."

"More'n I know. Where'd you learn Latin?"

"My father taught it to me. My mother . . . my mother was a classics professor at Arcadia. She spoke Greek and Latin. He learned Latin, too, and it was like their secret language, before . . ."

"Your mother died, didn't she?" Finn asked softly.

"When I was very young. I hardly remember her. But my father taught me some Latin. He doesn't like me to speak it, though. I think it hurts him too much to be reminded of her." Dickie blinked three times, very fast, then went on. "The rest of the books . . . I don't even know what language they're written in. Old English, maybe? Gaelic? Nothing I've ever seen, and I certainly can't read 'em. I have a feeling the real secrets might be in those books. These . . . well, they're interesting, but they seem like just folklore, things people have passed on as stories. Not real knowledge, if you know what I mean. But I don't know if I need to bother looking everything up. The Ashes seem like they know all about fairies. I can just ask them. Meg said I shouldn't, 'cause then they'd know we were out. But I'm not stupid—I don't have to let them know we were out last night."

"You told Meg about the—what was it?—the Urisk?"

"Yeah, and she believed me, too, just like you do. I'm so glad you—"

But Finn interrupted him. "Then did she tell you what she and the others saw last night?"

"What they saw? No. She didn't mention anything. You mean after we got separated? She said they just found their way home."

"She didn't tell you about the fairies on horseback? Or the hundreds that gathered at the foot of the Green Hill?" He affected a look of utter amazement. "Of all the rotten, selfish . . . Well, *I* won't keep any secrets from you, Dickie. *I'll* tell you all about what I saw last night." And with some embellishment, he revealed to Dickie what he'd seen in Jenny Greenteeth's pond.

"They didn't tell me, either," Finn said bitterly. "They want to keep it all to themselves. You should have seen the fairies. The ones on horses looked like kings and queens, all decked in jewels. And the others, why, they were as strange a sight as your Tim Tom, if not stranger. I saw them as plain as day in the pool, though I couldn't hear what they were saying. But the fairies probably told them wonderful things, and gave them gifts, and those rotten Morgans want to keep it all to themselves! Isn't that just like them? We're staying here together, we're all strangers in this place—you'd think they'd want us to know, too. But no. The Morgans, and the Ashes, are all in a conspiracy to keep things secret from us."

Dickie looked horribly hurt, which was just what Finn intended. Dickie had thought Meg, of all the people here, was his friend. He'd told Meg his secret, and she hadn't reciprocated. Probably laughed at him the moment she left the room, and told the others as soon as she could. Everyone laughed at poor Dickie.

"I wouldn't even bother to ask the Ashes, if I were you," Finn said. "They obviously don't want us to know anything. *We're* not part of the family. Well, if they don't want us to know, they shouldn't have invited us here!" Which, of course, they hadn't.

He had Dickie right where he wanted him now, and he struck home. "But we can get the better of them! We can find the fairies on our own. Why, there's probably enough information here in these books to tell us all we need to know. You can do the research, can't you? You can translate the Latin. I know you can. And together"— for a lonely boy, that was a marvelous word— "together, we'll show those Morgans! They can't treat us like this! We'll teach them to try to keep secrets from Finn Fachan and Dickie!"

Dickie found Finn's voice and arguments irresistibly compelling. It was hard for him to think badly of the Morgans . . . but much easier now that Finn was egging him on.

"I'll do it!" he said, eyes aglow with a new fervor. "I'll learn everything there is to know about the fairies, and we'll find them. And we won't tell those Morgans anything, not a single thing. I'll treat them just like they treated me . . . I mean, us."

They spoke of their schemes for a while, and Finn thumbed through some of the books. But he didn't have the patience for serious research, and thought it best to leave the work to Dickie, while he reaped the rewards himself.

It was only as Finn left that Dickie felt his first twinge of misgiving. Standing at the door, Finn smiled at him. But it wasn't the affable smile he'd put on before. This was much more reminiscent of the old malicious Finn. Such a smile might a cat bestow upon a mouse with a limp. Not the most challenging prey, the cat thinks, but still useful for diversion in its own way. He slipped out the door, and Dickie, reminding himself of the Morgans' treachery, continued his studies.

Alone on the Rookery rooftop, Meg chewed thoughtfully on her lip. She had intended to do some real thinking, but if you've ever tried this you know the closest you ever get is daydreaming. Thinking happens on its own when you least expect it—you get good ideas when you really need them, not when you're just looking for them. Up in the clear air, caressed by sunlight, Meg found it hard to concentrate on any one idea for more than a few minutes, and eventually she gave up entirely and just stared over the grounds.

She didn't know anything about Rowan's resolution, or she might have found that thinking came a little more easily. Had she known he was going to fight—or, as she would have put it, get himself killed—in the fairy war, she'd have stopped at nothing to prevent him. She'd write to Mother and tell her . . . Well, she couldn't very well tell her the truth. She could say there was fever in England, in the countryside. She could say the Rookery had burned down, or that Silly had gone mad, or that James had broken fifteen bones, or anything that would get them all home.

But since she knew nothing about Rowan's thoughts, her musings were far less serious. She was still worried—oh, plenty worried, for that was a part of her nature. She didn't believe denying the Fairy Queen would prove all that easy. Yet, however hard, it would be done, and then . . . why, then they were left with a land full of fairies, beautiful and dangerous. Though she tried to do the sort of thinking that results in conclusions, she found that conclusions were impossible, and she contented herself with merely thinking *about* the fairies, which kept her occupied for quite some time.

She perched so quietly, for so long, that at last even the skittish young rooks returned to their favorite roosts, and the birds talked among themselves. Sometimes one would cock its head and fix her with a bright black eye, to make sure she didn't have food, but after a while they forgot she was there, and when, close to two o'clock, she suddenly leaped to her feet with an exclamation, even the staid elder birds took flight.

Meg was sitting at one end of the U. To her left were the trees that hid the Green Hill, and to her right, just below her, was the garden. The part near the house was quite civilized, with the kitchen herbs laid out in geometric beds that seemed designed to be viewed from above. As it sprawled away from the center of the U, the garden grew wild. There was still order to it, for it had been laid out by a skilled hand. But though the herbs were tended daily, the other shrubs and trees were left largely to their own devices.

There, where the garden was so thick and wooly that it could scarcely be called a garden at all, walked that familiar chestnut head. So Rowan didn't feel like staying in the game, either, Meg mused. She leaned over the parapet to call out to him, but some force stayed her, and instead she watched him from her eyrie. He took a few steps, then paused as if looking for something, or perhaps waiting for someone, then moved on a little bit more. Something about his attitude suggested he was talking, but no words reached her on the roof. He disappeared under the solemn branches of a yew, and she waited for him to emerge. But instead of seeing the top of his head come out, she saw the top of another head join him, a dark-brown blur that moved so swiftly she could not be entirely sure it was a man and not a dog. Again she almost called out to him, but thought it better to wait and see. A few minutes passed, and she saw a movement under the thinner branches at the yew's border. The brown head came out again, and this time it looked unerringly up at her. It was Gul Ghillie, and he waved at the astonished Meg before scampering away—or perhaps disappearing—into the greenery.

She was struck with a gripping dread, a dismay so crushing, so powerful, that if she thought she had any chance of surviving she would have leaped from the roof to get to Rowan a bit faster. She ran to the door and rushed down the secret stairs at such a frantic pace that it was probably only their narrowness that saved her from a serious fall—she scraped against the walls as she went, and they steadied her. Through the furs she thrust herself, out of the bedroom, and down more stairs, until she came to the garden kitchen. The housemaids stared at her, and Jack, the lazy, arrogant errand boy who was always chatting up the girls, said, "Coo!"

Meg ran up to her brother, who was standing in a daze, staring at the place where Gul Ghillie had been. There was a strange hollowness about him, the bewildered look of a man who has stared into the sun too long and paid the price with his vision. He seemed older somehow, more handsome, but hardly the same Rowan. Meg took him by the shoulders and shook him until his head lolled.

"What did he want?" she almost screamed. "What happened? Did you tell him you wouldn't fight?" She let go of his shoulders, but her hands, balled into tight fists, rested on his chest.

He looked down at her as if noticing her for the first time, and his smile was distant and condescending. "I gave him my life," he said softly.

She stared at him, bewildered. "What?"

"My life. I gave it to him. He placed his hand on my chest, just here"—he put his own fingertips on his breastbone, between her two fists—"and when he took it back there was an egg in his palm." He gave a little laugh. "A tiny speckled egg. That's how significant my life is."

"Your life? What do you mean?"

"My life. My soul. Whatever you like. I gave it to him, and he put it into an egg."

"But . . . but . . ."

"Because I am their champion. I am *her* champion. A bird will take the egg into the forest, and build a nest, and keep it warm, keep it hidden. When the Unseelie Court chooses its champion, he, too, will have his life placed in an egg. We will serve them till the end, in success or failure. There's no turning away now."

"But ... but ... it doesn't make any sense! How can your life be in an egg? You *are* alive. You're standing right here in front of me. It's a trick! He's trying to trick you into doing what he wants!"

Rowan gazed down at her with a certain sympathy. How could she ever understand? "It's no trick," he said, patting her dark-brown hair as though she were a frightened puppy. "This isn't something they could force me to do. They choose a champion every seven years, but he has to go willingly. I've pledged myself to their cause, and my life is theirs until it is decided at Midsummer."

"I won't let you!" Meg wailed. "I'll tell Auntie Ash! I'll call Mother! They'll drag you home, where it's safe. I won't let you do this!" But her heart cried out, Too late! You had your chance to tell someone.

"Don't you see, Meggie? I'm bound now. Unless I refuse, and another takes my place, I am bound to fight at Midsummer. If you locked me in my room, the champion from the other side would still seek me out. If I refused to fight but none took my place, it would change nothing. Even if you took me back to America, it wouldn't do any good. At dawn after Midsummer Night, one of the eggs will hatch, and that bird will push the other egg from the nest. One of us will die. And I promise you, it won't be me."

He straightened and stiffened, and looked so manly that Meg hardly knew him.

She grasped at the solution he offered. It seemed so clear to her. "You said you can get out of it if you refuse to fight? Then you have to refuse! You have to! Let someone else fight."

"No, Meg, I won't."

There was something about his tone that halted all argument. He sounded like a grown man.

"Oh!" she said, angry amid the tears. "It's all just so . . . so stupid! I'm going to stop it!" She ran away from him, from the house, her eyes so blurred that she stumbled.

"There's nothing you can do," Rowan called after her. But she paid him no heed.

She rounded the edge of the Rookery, crossed the road, and kept going. At first she didn't know where she was headed, just that she had to get away from the horrible things that were happening. How could he be willing to fight in the Midsummer War? How could they let him? He was only a child, scarcely older than herself. What confidence could they have in him? He was brave enough, as a rule, tall and strong for his age, perhaps, but certainly no warrior. It was as though everyone else had been blinded to some very simple truths that she saw all too clearly. In a way, she was right. For all that he believed himself a willing participant, Rowan was under a fairy glamour. And perhaps the fairies themselves lived under the veil of some illusions, for in Rowan they saw their champion. But did they care, Meg wondered, if he died? Auntie Ash said their morality isn't like ours. . . .

It wasn't until she was deep in the forest (did the Ashes' rules count for nothing?) that she realized she was going to the Green Hill. The enormity of her decision stopped her in her tracks. She was alone in the place where all of those . . . things . . . dwelled. And she was prepared to charge up the Green Hill and tell those fair lords and ladies that they could never have her brother. She gulped, and leaned against a tree. *I can't,* she thought. But then she steeled herself. *I have to. That's all there is to it.* And she set off again, at a slower pace, delaying the inevitable but pushing resolutely forward.

The Green Hill has a magic to it—not every traveler can find it, even if she knows exactly where it lies. Perhaps it was because Meg was of Phyllida's blood, perhaps because the fairies favored her. Or maybe when one traveled with an earnest purpose the paths became clearer. In any case, Meg's feet turned unerringly in the direction of the Green Hill, and once again she saw what so few others have seen.

The hill, brilliant emerald in the afternoon light, was bare and lonely. Whatever magic it possessed, it kept its secrets hidden that day. She ran around the base, searching for the entrance she'd seen so clearly the night before. But the hill was solid, and she found no levers or buttons, nor even a rock that might serve to open the Green Hill. At last she gathered her courage and climbed to the summit. Not one living creature beyond the birds and insects stirred in her sight. In a voice at first halting, she called out, "Where are you?" No one answered her call.

"I know you're here!" she cried. "I know you can hear me. You can't have him! You can't make Rowan fight for you! He's just a boy!" Still the hill was mute.

Meg stood on the top of the Green Hill for a very long time, railing against the fairies as few would have dared. At first she was angry, and cursed them with every oath she'd learned from Silly. Her voice grew hoarse from shouting, and at last she began to weep, hot tears falling into the green herbs. She sank to her knees, unable to go on, but she beat upon the hill with her fists until she felt near to collapse.

Finally, utterly worn out with emotion, she fell silent, and even her tears stopped. Her head sank until it rested on the turf, and she remained like that, with half-sobbing breath, until she felt a hand on her shoulder. She scrambled around (and it was very like Meg to realize, as she did so, that she was getting grass stains on her knees, and think what a chore it would be to get them out), and her puffy red face turned up to find the fairy prince gazing down kindly at her. He looked so noble and so gentle that she burst into hopeless, inarticulate sobs again.

The fairy prince, who had seen the world begin and would see it end, looked with pity on the little creature huddled at his feet. "Do not grieve for the warrior who is not yet fallen," he said, placing a hand upon her disheveled brow.

Sniffing loudly, she wiped her eyes and tried to steel herself once more into anger instead of sorrow. "You're sending him to his death," she said miserably.

"Oh, can mortals see into the future?" he asked her with a low laugh. "Because I cannot. I do not think my queen would have chosen your brother if she thought his chances so poor."

"He's just a child!" she protested. "Why would she choose him? He doesn't know how to fight." In fact, though Rowan was strong and agile, he'd taken pains all his life to avoid fights. Even the sore temptation of Finn Fachan hadn't made him bellicose, though with him Rowan had been pushed nearer than ever before. Rowan was a diplomat, a peacemaker.

"The queen chooses who she will. It was your brother's choice to accept."

"She put a spell on him!"

"She casts a spell on all who see her, even you . . . even me. But Rowan was not forced to agree, and only he can change his mind. There's nothing you can do."

"But . . ."

"And do not call him a child. He's older than you, Meg Morgan, and don't you think you're old enough to know your own mind about things? You're his sister, and would protect him if you could. Rowan doesn't seek your protection. If you want to aid him, help him train. Time grows short, and he has much to learn. Don't hinder him with your doubting words. Be his sister and his friend. Be a child of Phyllida's blood, and let the bones fall where they will.

"I will come to you tomorrow—at the foot of the garden, where the trees are thickest. There, Rowan will receive his weapons, and begin to learn to use them. Training is lonely work, and I think he would like his family there to encourage him. But keep the others away. They should not know." He turned and walked down the hill, and it was a moment before Meg had the presence of mind to go after him. There was so much more to ask him, and she still hadn't given up on finding a loophole, some way of keeping Rowan safe.

"Wait! Why do you fight a war, and why once in seven years? Does it really keep green things growing? And why does a human have to die?" But by the time she got to her feet and peered down the hill, it was bare of all save herbs and butterflies.

"Blast these fairies!" she mumbled, then called, "Come back!" She waited a while in the sun and the breeze, but no one came, and at last she made her weary way homeward.

Lemman's Woe

THE ASHES NOTICED that there was something going on with all their summer charges. Meg was silent through lunch, absent as the sun sank lower, and markedly distant over supper. Rowan had the sort of distracted, glowing look they mistook for young love, Finn's eyes shifted restlessly from person to person, Silly giggled unaccountably, and Dickie's brow was furrowed as he tried to assimilate the information he'd gathered and remember whether *ano* meant "year" in Latin, or something quite rude. James was the only one who seemed his usual self, and he sang little songs under his breath all through the meal.

That night they all had their own rooms, and Meg retired early to hers. Meg didn't think she'd be able to sleep. When our minds are so full and frantic, we think they can never find the peace of slumber. But our bodies know better what we need, and she only tossed on her pillow for a few minutes before she fell into a refreshing sleep untroubled by dreams.

For those first blissful moments on waking, she forgot all

about the previous day, and lay in cushioned comfort as the new light of morning crept past the half-drawn curtains. When her memory returned, it was like a physical blow, and she doubled over where she lay, clutching her knees to her chest. She meant to have one more talk with Rowan—she meant, in fact, to have as many as it took, despite the Seelie prince's advice—only this time she would be entirely calm and rational, and would reason her brother into agreeing with her.

That was her mistake, she thought. She had tried to appeal to him through emotion, and with what must sound to him like an insulting doubt in his abilities. Her new tack would be actually to appeal to his loyalty to the Fairy Queen. You want to serve her, Meg would argue. You want her side to win. But don't you see it would be ever so much better for the Seelie Court to pick someone with a bit more . . . experience? It will help the queen if you let someone else fight in your stead. Perhaps that tactic would succeed where a sisterly concern for his safety had failed.

But she was forestalled by the entrance of one of the housemaids, Rosemarie, who came with tea, and water for washing. She threw open the curtains and tidied the room a bit as Meg got dressed behind a screen. Meg had hoped to find Rowan before the others gathered for breakfast, but Rosemarie was of a mind to gossip.

She chatted blithely about an otter who was stealing chickens, a cousin with the mumps, and her aunt's rheumatism until Meg lost interest. It got a bit more intriguing when she turned to the exploits of Jack, who, it seemed, had been on the verge of being fired for four years.

"Never does a lick of work, and always after the lasses. If you ask me, Jack's days are really numbered now, or will be as soon as the lady finds out he's been pestering poor Lemman. Not that he'll get anything from her—he just likes to tease. Still, I think it mighty unkind, tormenting the poor wee beastie. 'E says she don't care, but I don't rightly know about that. She never talks, see, or even looks at you much. We don't bother her. She works the dairy, and I tell you, the coos never gave more milk than under her care. But she pays you no more mind than a cat at its cream."

"Can't she talk at all?" Meg asked, coming out from behind the screen.

"Ah, she used to. Used to sing something fine, too, though it were always unhappy songs. Least, they sounded mournful. She sang 'em in another tongue, and I never could make 'em out. That was before her man died. I never will know how such an ill-favored lout as Gus Leatherman got the hand of a girl like that. Have you seen her? She's a pretty little thing, the sort you don't see very often. Makes you look again, she does. Reckon I wouldn't like her much if she had more to say for herself," Rosemarie added with a laugh. "But I do feel sorry for her. Her man, he was caught in the mill wheel and drowned, 'bout three months after he brought her here. The Lady kept her on. Guess she had no place to go. If you see that Jack heading toward the dairy, you tell him to go . . . well, go do something. You can do that, you know, being the Lady's kin.

"Oh, I almost forgot, the Lady wants to see you this morning. Says you've done some exploring on your own, but there's a tuthree things she'd like to show you. Graveyard, likely. All your kin are buried here, going back hundreds of years. Quite a thing to think about, isn't it? I never heard of my own kin farther back than my grandmother, and I couldn't tell you where their bones lie for the very life of me. Well, go along to breakfast, and the lady will find you."

Phyllida joined them at their meal, and gathered up the Morgans. Finn and Dickie were told they were welcome, too, but Phyllida made it seem that it wouldn't be much fun, even for those who were obligated to go. "Moldering old gravestones," she said offhandedly, giving the others a perfect opportunity to decline. Dickie wanted to spend as little time in the pollen-y outdoors as possible, and was really eager to submerge himself under the dusty leaves of knowledge. Finn wanted to consult with Dickie on his progress before putting some of his theories to the test himself.

The Morgans followed Phyllida, and the excursion was really better than they expected. The graveyard, at the south side of the Rookery, was an extensive hilly patch full of odd monuments and crouching, leering gargoyles. Nearly every stone had a story attached to it—some maudlin, like that of Abigail May, who died in 1765. A graying statue of a dog lay on her sunken gravestone, looking mournfully at the inscription. "She had a little terrier dog she loved. A passing tinker stole it, and she followed him on foot all the way to London to get it back. She never did find him, but the story goes she came upon another dog that looked just like him near Blackfriars, and scooped him up even though he growled and bit her. She was that sure it was her own Bonnie Boy. Dragged him all the way home; then they both died of rabies.

Funny thing is, her own dog showed up after that, and he never would leave her grave. Sat there five years. They made a little hut for him, for the winter, but even in the worst weather he wouldn't leave. Always did his business on Samuel Greave's monument, which was fitting, because he was a notorious dog-hater."

Some plots held the remains of warriors, with strange or stirring tales. "This one is my great-great-grandfather Captain Horatio Berkeley, who sailed with Admiral Nelson. He was a teetotaler—a very unusual thing in our family—and every time he got his daily portion of brandy while aboardship (he was an officer, you see—the others only got grog), he stowed it away in a cask. He thought how nice it would be to surprise his fellow officers with all his saved brandy if the war lasted and provisions ran low. But then Admiral Nelson was shot and killed, and they were weeks from home. Well, he was a hero and a lord, and couldn't get a burial at sea like an ordinary sailor. All the same, he'd start to get pretty rank if they held him until he could be returned to the bosom of his family. Then Captain Berkeley had the marvelous idea of pickling the admiral in his conserved brandy. They folded him double and shoved him in the cask, and when he came out weeks later, he looked as fine as he did in life, if somewhat pruned."

She went from grave to grave, telling her tales, and the children forgot their preoccupation with fairies under this fascinating tutelage. They didn't realize it, but this was one of the oddest family graveyards in England, perhaps in the world. In most such yards, a single name predominates. A man founds the dynasty, and passes it on to his son. The line, the name, the property, and the titles run through the masculine descendants. The new blood in the family is all feminine. But in this strange family, tradition stipulated that all inheritance pass along the female line. Only a woman could be Guardian of the Green Hill, Gladysmere, and surrounding lands. And so, with each generation, a new name was brought into the family, as the daughters, heirs of great responsibility, took husbands to keep the line strong. There had been a caretaker or two through the ages who never wed, but even this was no obstacle to succession.

Phyllida Ash led them next to a hollow somewhat beyond the graveyard where grew nine elegant trees that looked like inverted hearts on slender trunks. Each leaf was a spearpoint. "These are your ash trees. Or, rather, the family ash trees," she said, walking up to one of the larger trees and patting its grooved bark.

"Oh, you mean because of your name?" Silly asked.

"No, dear, that's just a coincidence. The ash tree has long been a symbol of life, like Yggdrasil, the Norse world tree, which held all of creation in its roots and boughs. These trees don't go quite that far—they only hold the life of one person. When a member of our family is born, an ash tree is planted. Those who marry into the family get a tree somewhat later. This one is mine, more than eighty years old. This is Bran's, only a little older, because of course he didn't get an ash of his own until he married my mother. And here is Lysander's, which has grown nearly as tall as mine, though it was planted twenty years later. A very vigorous tree, his. This is your mother's—let me see, thirty-seven, no, thirty-eight years old—and your father's, just a year older than Rowan's."

The Morgan children saw four trees in a row—two quite robust, nearly the same height for Rowan and Meg, one somewhat smaller beside them for Silly, and at the end a healthy little sapling no more than four feet tall, James's tree.

"You planted trees for us, even though you never met us? Even though you might *never* have met us?" Meg was touched.

"Every member of the family—that I know about—gets a tree. And who's to say I didn't know you'd be coming, eventually?" She tapped the side of her nose in a gesture the Morgans had not seen before.

"But shouldn't there be more?" Meg asked. "Why aren't there trees stretching back as far as the gravestones?"

"The trees are each bound to a person's life. When he or she dies, the tree is cut down. Generally used to make the casket, though not always, and the roots are dried and put on a bonfire after the funeral. Many, many trees have grown here, and many have fallen."

"If the trees are connected to a person's life, what happens if the tree dies before the person?"

Phyllida looked at Meg sharply, but then said, "Why, I don't believe it's ever happened. Ashes are hardy trees, and of course we take care to keep them safe from rabbits and such when they're young. I doubt there are better-cared-for trees in the county than these. Sometimes the trees are omens, and wilt and droop when their person's death is near. It is said that saving the tree can save the person. But you certainly wouldn't want any harm to come to your ash tree." She gave a delicate shudder.

"Why plant the tree in the first place, if it would be so bad if it dies?"

"People with ash trees tend to live longer, and fall ill less. Trees are strong, and they don't suffer the same way humans do. They can withstand a great deal. It is sometimes helpful to have a part of your life bound up in something so solid, so enduring. It's a very old magic, and generally not spoken of, but, given who you are, I suppose there's no reason to keep it from you. It is said that if you hover at the very gates of death, if all hope is gone, your life can be saved by your ash tree. The tree is hewn, split straight down the middle, and you are passed through the cleft. Then the tree is bound up, and if it heals, and lives, why, so do you. But splitting a tree nearly always kills it. And what if you were wrong, and the person wasn't really about to die? Well, they'd die for sure once their ash was killed. So it could really only be done when there was no other hope."

Meg wasn't sure she liked all this. Her life bound to a tree she hadn't even known about until this moment? Rowan's life held captive in an egg? Was it in the egg, and the ash, too? How could life be separable from the person it belonged to? It had never occurred to her that our lives may not be entirely our own.

Phyllida took them next to the outbuildings: a stable that housed two lazy hunters, four pied carriage horses, a quiet saddle horse, and a cream-colored pony named Persephone; a henhouse that supplied the estate with eggs, though they bought their roasting chickens from somewhere else; a low red building that held tools, fertilizer, and assorted useful flotsam; and the dairy and cowshed, Lemman's domain.

The Rookery cows led a very comfortable life, rising late and breakfasting on succulent grasses and grains before offering up their milk, and then heading out, sometime around noon, to a nearby field to do a little grazing and chew their cud. Each of the twenty or so cows had her own stall with a low swinging gate, but each cow also knew how to open that gate, and when left to her own devices sometimes bunked with a friend or took a midnight stroll around the shed. The cows could also unlatch the main gate to the dairy, which the Ashes thought a good precaution in case there was ever a fire, but the conscientious cows never strayed when they weren't supposed to. Lemman, their caretaker, had an almost magical control over the beasts, and they always did her bidding. She slept in a loft inside the dairy, and rarely left its confines except to accompany the cows on their daily pilgrimage. When the children met her, she was milking the last of her charges, a shaggy red Highland cow.

I say "met," but though Phyllida offered an introduction, Lemman never looked up from her chore or offered any indication that she was aware of the Morgans. The steady sound of milk hitting the pail did not falter, and her cheek did not move from the cow's side. The cows, however, seemed quite interested in the newcomers, and lowed welcomes as they stretched their necks for a closer look. At Phyllida's urging, the children stepped hesitantly forth to pet them. It's more intimidating than you might think to make overtures to a cow. If you're not used to them, they seem awfully big. But these were kind cows, and very gentle, and though they crowded close to the Morgans they were careful about where they put their hooves and moved in an orderly fashion, each yielding her place to another when she had had a good sniff and gotten her ears rubbed. They were all the colors cows come in, some pure white, others brown, some calico or patch-work. One was brindled, one blue-ticked, and one, the smallest, was a pale dun that was almost yellow. Her left horn turned downward, her right one up, and something about her expression made her seem particularly intelligent. On some secret cue, she moved to the door and waited at the boundary, while the other cows lined up behind her.

Lemman, finished with her milking, took the bucket into the adjoining dairy, and returned a moment later to take her place at the dun cow's side. With one hand on the cow's back, she led the procession past the children, giving no sign she saw them. Rose-marie was right: Lemman was lovely, with a sort of wistful, dis-tant sadness in her large eyes. Her movements were very slow, like those of an old woman who must put a great deal of thought and care into each step. And yet she was graceful, as though per-forming in slow motion the steps of some inner dance. She was tall and lissome and fair, with hair the color of a wheat field under the sun.

"Well, that's Lemman," Phyllida said as the girl and cows trooped past. "I'd hoped she might pay you a bit more mind, but she's lost in her own thoughts, as usual. Once in a great while I'll get her to talk to me, and Bran sometimes spends hours with her. He does most of the talking, of course, but it's one of the few times she raises her eyes to look at any human."

"Why is she called Lemon?" Silly asked. "She didn't look sour."

Phyllida laughed. "Not Lemon, dear! Lemman." She spelled it for them. "It isn't really her name. It means 'sweetheart.' It's what that Gus Leatherman called her, while he lived, and it stuck with the rest of us. But it's like their kind not to give their proper names. He already had her in his power—she'd be a fool to offer him any more control."

"What do you mean . . . their kind?" Silly asked.

"Och, can't you tell to look at her? She's a fairy—or was, until that wretched man stole her away and bound her to a mortal life." Phyllida shaded her eyes and looked after the retreating figure at the head of the line of cows. "A few years ago, it was. We took on Gus Leatherman as a stablehand. Never did like the looks of that fellow, but he came on a high recommendation. So we kept him on, and gave him the little cabin just behind the stables. Did his job well enough, though none of the other servants ever took to him. He had a sort of greasy way about him, hard to put your finger on. A Dr. Fell sort. You know that rhyme? 'I do not like you, Dr. Fell, the reason why I cannot tell. . . .'

"Then, one day, he brings home a woman. Perfectly allowed, and in fact I was going to ask him if he'd like to move into a larger cottage down by the glade. Thought there might be more Leathermans on the way. But then I saw her, and there was no mistaking it. She was one of the fairy folk, and he'd somehow captured her.

"Now, that's no mean task! Some fairies are innocuous, and some are powerful, but if there's one thing they all excel at, it's keeping themselves out of human sight when they want to. It's well nigh impossible for all but the bravest and cleverest to capture one. And from what I could tell, Gus Leatherman was neither. But there she was, meek and submissive, sitting quietly in a corner, while he tried to tell me he'd met her at the harvest fair. I wouldn't have believed it even if she was human—he wasn't the sort to get a girl like that without some sort of strong coercion. And there might be times when a fairy falls in love with a human, but even then she generally lures him to her world, not the other way around.

"I badgered him for the story, but I suppose I wasn't intimidating enough. Lysander tried, too, but Gus Leatherman only laughed at his threats and said he'd earned his Lemman fair and square, and he meant to keep her. We were determined to find out how he succeeded in trapping her, for only then could we find a way to set her free. He was stubborn, and in the end we had no choice—we had to tell Bran.

"I've never seen him in such a fury. He...he hurt Gus Leatherman...badly. Lysander tried to pull him off, but Bran threw him aside like he was a sack of leaves. He would have killed Gus that day, I think. Finally—and perhaps Gus did have some hidden cleverness—he said something that cut through Bran's rage. He said, 'Only I know the secret. If you kill me, she'll never be able to go back to the fairies.'

"Well, those words saved his life, but they didn't save him from the next two hours alone with Bran. He got it out of him...in the end. That is, he found out how he'd caught Lemman in the first place. Some fairies take the form of animals. Oh, they all can, if they want to, but some spend most of their existence that way. There are swan maidens, and the selkies of the northern coasts—the seal maidens. These fairies sometimes spend time in human form, and when they do, they take off their feathers, or their fur, like unzipping a dress. If someone finds their pelt, they can't change back. They're prisoners in their human form, prisoners of the one who has their animal skin. Gus Leatherman happened upon Lemman's pelt, and she became his.

"Lemman was one of the otter girls. There are a few in these parts, where the stream grows wider and deeper. Marvelous creatures, always sporting and carefree. I don't know why they'd ever want to take on human form, as lovely as they are. Have you ever seen an otter at play? Can you imagine what a torment it was for Lemman to be trapped, bound to a low, coarse man, living behind dark walls, instead of swimming in cold, clear water? Unless her otter pelt is returned to her, she will always be human, and miserable.

"Gus Leatherman never told where that fur was hidden, no matter what Bran did to him. We searched his house, the grounds, we contacted his family and everyone who had ever known him, looking for that skin. Alas, he'd hidden it too well, and when he died a while later, drowned in the mill pond, he took his secret with him.

"Three years Lemman's lived with us. We thought she'd pine and die, but Lysander had the idea to let her work with the cows. Right about when she took them over, that little dun cow came from nowhere and joined the herd. One of the fairy cows, we think, come to keep an eye on her. After that, well, she's never been exactly happy, but she seems able to bear it better, even though she knows she'll grow old and die like the rest of us if her pelt is never found. We haven't given up yet, but who knows where it is? He was too cunning for us in the end, and poor Lemman has to suffer for it."

"Can't the fairies help her?" Meg asked. "Isn't there some way they can find her pelt?"

"The fairies live by strange rules, child, and even they can't do whatever they like. No, poor Lemman can only be freed by a human. There's nothing the fairies can do, short of comfort her."

Phyllida gathered herself up with a little sigh, and shook her head like a bird ruffling its feathers. "Go on about your business, children. That's enough tales for today. Stop to see Lemman when you've a mind. She may not look at you, but I think the company cheers her a bit. And she does hear everything you say, however silent she may be." She wandered off toward the house, leaving the young Morgans alone at the door of the dairy.

For a time, they spoke of the pitiable Lemman, and made resolutions to search for her otter skin. But with so much else on their minds, they knew it was little more than rhetoric of the moment. War was coming, after all.

Meg was still waiting for an opportune time to start her new tirade against Rowan's decision, and was debating whether bringing it up in front of Silly and James would work for her cause or against it. Would he see how horrible was the very real prospect of his death when he looked into his little siblings' eyes? Or would Silly's warlike nature only encourage him in his grim determination? Before she made up her mind, she saw a dark figure in the distance, moving swiftly and, she thought, furtively, away from the Rookery. Large and broad and, even in outline, wild-looking, it could be no other than Bran, and she directed their attention his way.

"Where's he going in such a hurry?" Rowan asked, narrowing his eyes suspiciously.

Meg shrugged. She was thinking of the tale Phyllida had just told them. It was Bran's role that most arrested her. She pictured him in that murderous rage, attacking Gus Leatherman, and the thought of it made her tremble. She was drawn to Bran, particularly as she learned more about him, but it dawned on her for the first time what a large and powerful man he was, how capable of violence. He was like a great dog that sits quietly by the fireside until roused by a threat, and then becomes all teeth and snarls.

Instinctively, all four sidled across the lawn to keep him in sight. His loping, wolfish strides skirted the garden and headed for the first thick stand of trees where the estate merged into the forest. There he stopped and looked over his shoulder, back toward the Rookery but not, to their immense relief, southward toward the dairy. Thinking that the way was clear, he stepped into the trees, where he was immediately met by another figure. The pair vanished into the woods. Meg had no idea who the other man was, but Rowan, whose vision must have become preternaturally sharp, said with a gasp, "It's the Black Prince! Bran is going off with the Black Prince!"

Inside the Rookery, Finn was grilling Dickie. "I've only been at it a day!" Dickie protested when Finn demanded concrete results. "I don't know how much of this is real, and how much is just made up. For all I know, these are bedtime stories."

"But have you learned how to find fairies?" Finn pressed, as though he hadn't heard a word.

Dickie waved his arms at the books spread a foot thick over the entire table. "This one says all you have to do is carry a four-leaf clover. But this one says a four-leaf clover is a surefire method to keep fairies *away*. One says primroses, another bluebells. Some say you carry 'em, some that you have to eat 'em, but I think they're poisonous. This one says to make a salve and rub it in your eyes. . . ."

But Finn didn't like the sound of these. He was too practical to think that merely carrying a flower would lure fairies, and a bit too cautious to risk imbibing potions . . . yet. "What else?"

"Well," Dickie said haltingly, flipping through pages, "there are a few other things, but the theme through it all is that you only see them if they want to be seen. They get angry if you intrude—"

"But I did see them, in the pool. They'll let me again. I just have to find them. They can't be that picky if they let all the stupid Morgans see them."

Dickie sighed. "Then why don't you just go out into the woods and look for them? If they want you to see them—"

"Just tell me what else you found," Finn said, rather too sharply for one who was pretending to be friendly.

And so Dickie told him about looking upside down between your legs at twilight, or standing upon the foot of one with the Sight, or binding about your waist a cord that has tied a dead man to his bier. He suggested that Finn could swim naked at midnight to find a water fairy, but Finn had had his fill of that sort of thing in his fleeting sight of the springing Jenny Greenteeth. Alternatively, almost any activity at midnight was apt to lure fairies, albeit of a more sinister kind. Dickie tried to tell him this, but for one so obsessed with discovering fairies, Finn seemed remarkably uninterested in knowing a great deal about their habits and ways. His understanding of the Seelie Court and the Host was that they were like kingdoms, or families—there was a division, but not along lines of character. And he paid scant heed to Dickie's warnings about the shifting, dubious fairy morality, and the dangers inherent in any contact with them.

"There's a story in *Old Wives' Tales* about seeing fairies through keyholes. But that only works if they come in the house. Oh, I almost forgot. Several books mentioned using a self-bored stone."

"What's that?"

"A river rock that has a natural hole in it, worn by the water. If you look through that, you're supposed to be able to see fairies."

"Where do I get one?"

Fortunately, Finn didn't see Dickie roll his eyes. "You *find* one. In a river."

"Oh. Well, I'll go get one, then." And he left Dickie shaking his head in astonishment. He really couldn't understand why Finn was so keen on finding fairies. What reason was there, other than curiosity? And if so, why wasn't he more curious about fairy lore in general? Of course, like Finn, Dickie felt the natural temptation to get back at the Morgans for keeping secrets from him. But he was used to being excluded, and it didn't have the same sting it had for Finn.

Then, too, he had an idea that there was more going on around him than he realized—or than he was meant to realize. His encounter with the Urisk had been tame enough, but even that frightened him somewhat in retrospect. Some of the things he'd read thus far scared him even more: captives in fairyland forced to serve all their lives. Monsters that would lure you in a benign form, then rend you in another more fierce. Human sacrifices every seven years. For every kindness a denizen of Fairy did to a mortal, it seemed one of its ilk did something wretchedly horrible. Dickie was seduced by the fairy glamour as much as the rest of them, but his instincts for self-preservation told him that it would be just as rewarding to study them in the safety of his cozy library.

With a sigh, he pulled a book from the bottom of the pile, but found, though it was titled, in plain English, *Mythology of Britain,* that it was written in Latin. He groaned audibly, then set himself to tackling the introduction. "I set forth here for the elucidation of my fellow man . . . Oh my, is that in the subjunctive?" He skipped that part and scanned down the line. ". . . strange beasts that dwell in . . ." In what? Dark something-or-other?

"Secret palaces," said a voice behind him in a whisper that was almost a hiss.

To read about strange beasts is one thing. To be accosted by one in what you consider your own private library is quite another, and Dickie must be excused for screeching and scrambling up onto the table. He had never particularly liked snakes, and it didn't help that this one was largeish, had stubby wings behind its head, and was coiled around the back of the chair he'd been sitting in.

Then the snake fanned its wings, peered at the pages, and recited the line in flawlessly accented Latin.

Somehow, this evidence that the beast was learned comforted Dickie. A snake that could speak English was a terror, but a snake that spoke Latin must be civilized. All the same, from the dubious safety of the tabletop, he insisted, "Snakes can't talk!"

The creature's hiss rose in a teapot whistle—he was laughing. "Of course snakes can't talk," he said.

"But you're . . ."

"You insult me if you think I'm a snake," it said, rising by several menacing inches but utterly destroying the effect when it tried to scratch the top of its head with its right wingtip.

"Then what . . ."

"I," the creature said grandly, "am a Wyrm."

"A worm?"

"I can plainly hear the 'o' in your voice. I said 'Wyrm,' not lowly 'worm.'"

"Are . . . are you dangerous?" Dickie asked meekly.

"If it is true that a little knowledge is a dangerous thing, what might be said of a great deal of knowledge?" the Wyrm quizzed him. "I have spent my life learning the tongues of men and beasts, and the wisdom each has accumulated. And I have been alive a very long time indeed. I know I don't look it." He turned his wedge head down modestly, and his scales darkened in what might have been a blush. "Periodic shedding is very good for the complexion. For three thousand years I have been studying, to learn all there is to know."

"And have you?" Dickie asked politely.

"Yes, nearly four hundred years ago. It was something of a letdown, I must say. Nothing left to look forward to. So I came here to forget everything. It's funny, but forgetting seems to happen much faster than learning in the first place. Already, I've forgotten more than half of what I once knew. Used to be able to do calculus with my wings tied behind my back. Now I couldn't tell you what happens as x approaches infinity if my life depended on it. Ditto for the dynasties of China, or the Akkadian warlords. Go on, ask me what the difference is between an arquebus and a blunderbuss. Couldn't tell you."

"But you remember Latin."

"Oh, I remember a great deal. Half of everything there is to know is still nothing to sneeze at. Someday, though, if all goes well, I will have forgotten everything, and then I can have the fun of beginning again. Are you a scholar?"

"I . . . I . . ."

"I see you speak only one tongue, and that badly. Come now, you are here, surrounded by books, interrupting my nap. It appears that you are a scholar. Do appearances deceive me?"

"No . . . yes . . . I'm studying fairies!" He blurted it out, and the odd thing was that he half thought a talking worm (I beg your pardon, Wyrm) would laugh at him for believing in fairies.

But the Wyrm uncoiled its sinuous body and flapped its leathery wings to rise, its body dangling beneath it, until it hovered at the level of Dickie's eyes. "A noble pursuit indeed!" he said.

"Though one not generally undertaken in such a comprehensive manner. The lore of the secret people is, sadly, so often confined to apocrypha, rather than methodical scholarly pursuit. Tell me, do you intend to include practical experimentation and field observation in your studies, or rely solely upon literature? And, nonsequitorially, do you intend to perch upon that table all day?"

The Wyrm's conversation put Dickie at ease. It was, at any rate, better than talking to Finn. At least the Wyrm seemed to have a genuine interest in what he'd discovered. And perhaps he might be willing to help. To his own surprise, Dickie clambered down from the table and once more took his chair, while the Wyrm, panting a bit from the effort of levitation, eased himself to a comfortable coil on top of the books.

"I thought I'd learn all I could here," Dickie explained. "I don't know if I really want to see any more fairies."

"Well enough," the Wyrm said, nodding his head in approval. "Some of the greatest discoveries have been made by sifting through the labors of others. Standing on the shoulders of giants, as it were, the better to pick at their brains. There is no shame in synthesizing, as long as you have wit enough to separate the intellectual gold from the dross. In any case, fairies don't lend themselves well to systematic practical study. They are found by serendipity, not effort, and their secrets uncovered at great personal peril. Yes, confine yourself to books, young scholar, when you delve into the ephemeral and infinitely vexing world of fairies. What have you discovered so far?"

With great enthusiasm Dickie revealed the fruits of his studies. The Wyrm listened attentively, occasionally interrupting to dismiss some tidbit as drivel. "Bend upside down and look between your legs? Nonsense! Why, then, everyone on earth could see fairies, and they'd never be safe!" He seemed to approve of some of the information. "A self-bored stone. Hmm . . . yes, that sounds right. But it only works in the general vicinity where the stone was found. You couldn't see Dorchester fairies with an Edinburgh stone." But the Wyrm seemed strangely perplexed by some things.

"There are so many gaps!" he said cheerfully. "Do you see how much I've forgotten already? At this rate, I'll be able to start learning again in only a few more centuries. That business about stray sods—never heard it before in my life. I still remember some things about the fairies, but, by gum, not near as much as I used to. Isn't this marvelous?"

But to the Wyrm's surprise, Dickie didn't seem too pleased. "I was hoping you could help me. If you could tell me what you know—"

"What would be the fun in that?" the Wyrm asked him. "Where's the joy of discovery?"

Dickie thought the joy would be just as good if the Wyrm told him everything he needed to know, but he kept this to himself. The Wyrm did offer him some assurance. "I still remember Latin, though. And the strange and melodious Gaelic tongues. I suppose, if you really have your heart set on it, I can help you translate these tomes. It goes against my inclination, for, after all, it means I'll be doing a bit of learning again. But I suppose, weighed in the balance, it won't compare to my rate of forgetting. Very well—you may count on my assistance." And he nosed himself into the pile of books and emerged a moment later pushing a slim volume with his snout. "We will begin with this, a treatise by the Venerable Ecclectus." Dickie rested his chin on his hands as the Wyrm declaimed upon the nature of subterranean mining fairies.

Slings and Arrows and Swords

FINN CAME LATE TO LUNCH with soggy trousers, and Dickie never showed up at all. Finn waited expectantly for the others to ask him why he was wet—he had a brilliant excuse prepared—but they never did. He had searched all morning, and finally found a smooth oval stone with a hole in its center. He'd tried it straightaway, but when he held it up to his right eye he saw nothing more than the predictable beauties of southern England in the weeks before full summer.

But just because no fairies lounged in the shade and no pixies danced on the banks, this didn't mean that his seeing stone was a dud. It only meant that there didn't happen to be any fairies in the immediate vicinity, and he determined to continue his quest after lunch. The one thing that marred his pleasure at the prospect of the afternoon's discoveries was the Morgans' singular lack of interest. What fun is keeping secrets if those you're keeping them from display no curiosity? Well, just wait till he had something really worthwhile! He'd make sure they knew he had a secret, one more massive than any they sought to keep from him. And he'd just laugh in his lonely knowledge, and look down on them, and make them wish they'd been more open themselves in the first place.

Finn, as you can see, had a rather inflated idea of his own importance, and he might have been disillusioned had he realized that the Morgans almost forgot about his existence on a regular basis. Rowan and Silly had expected to despise him actively, but as each hour wore on, they found him fading further and further from their thoughts. At breakfast the Morgans and Finn remembered to say nasty things to each other, but for the rest of the day they were apart, and except for Meg, the Morgans never thought about him.

Finn, on the contrary, devoted a good deal of his time to contemplating the Morgans, and each discovery he made seemed that much sweeter for the knowledge that the Morgans weren't sharing it. It was perhaps a nasty, bitter, lonely sort of pursuit, but it gave him immense satisfaction nonetheless.

He slipped off to search the forbidden woods for fairy spoor, and the Morgans gathered in the far reaches of the garden, safe from prying eyes. Almost at once they were met by the Seelie prince—in the form of Gul Ghillie. It was quite an effort for them to remember that the merry, scampering brown boy was in fact one of the grandest men they had ever beheld. On that afternoon, his carefree gait was somewhat curtailed by the burdens he carried. Across his shoulder was a tall, strung bow, and at his back a quiver full of arrows fletched in shimmering golden pheasant feathers. From a belt girded tight around his narrow hips hung two light swords, one long and fine, the other more like a knife, with a tine on either side of the blade. On one arm he carried a small round shield charged with a foxglove sprig, and in both hands, awkwardly, he held a sheathed broadsword. Diamonds of perspiration fell from his brow as he bent and unceremoniously dumped his cargo to the grass. He stood and unfastened the various buckles and harnesses that held the other weapons in place, and laid them beside the sword and shield.

"I think I chose the wrong guise for this day!" Gul said as he readjusted his clothes. "A man carries weapons better than a boy."

"That's why it's so stupid to ask Rowan to fight," Meg said hotly. "He's just a boy!"

"If you wish to argue later, I promise you'll have your chance. First hear me out. Perhaps you'll think differently in a moment."

Meg wanted to argue, but she was arrested by the pile of weapons. They were strangely alluring, and, almost against her will, her hand reached out toward one keen, shining sword edge. She snatched it back just before she was cut.

She remembered the prince's advice about giving her brother support instead of hindering him with criticism. There was a peculiar light in Rowan's eyes, such as seasoned warriors have on the eve of battle, and she felt again that vague jealousy she'd known at the Green Hill, when her heart called out, *Me! Let it be me!*

For a fleeting moment, she wondered whether she only meant to protect Rowan, or if there might be some other motivation for her determination to keep him from the battle. When she looked at the weapons, she felt her pulse quicken in excitement. She longed to hold them, to use them to some noble purpose.

Soon, she thought, I will try again to convince Gul and Rowan to end this foolishness. Her hand crept out unbidden once more, this time toward a bow half buried by the swords. Soon, but not yet.

Rowan's first task was to select his weapon.

"In the Midsummer War you may carry only one weapon into battle," Gul explained. "These are the relics of the Seelie Court, forged in ancient times of rare metals, heated in the furnaces of the earth's core, cooled in the snows at the crown of the world. From these three weapons the Seelie champion has chosen over the centuries. Each has slain foes without number . . . and each has been hewn from its master's lifeless hand. The weapons do not promise victory, but, wielded properly, they will serve you better than any human-crafted arms. Take them up, and learn their weight, their feel. I will show you each on this day, and you will make your selection."

Rowan knelt before the weapons laid out on the grass and looked at each in turn. His hand hovered for a moment, and at last came to rest on the broadsword. He picked it up, and found that, despite its size, he could lift it with ease. It was four feet long, grooved at its center ("for the blood to flow along," Gul told them later). But, for a relic of the fairy court, it was surprisingly simple. The blade was somewhat dull, the hilt unadorned by any jewels. There were rough engravings along the haft, symbols that Rowan didn't recognize, but no other ornamentation. The pommel was a half-moon knob, and a length of leather cord twined around the grip. And yet, the moment he touched it, Rowan felt a new energy surge up his arm. Already, he felt master of the sword, as though he could plunge into battle that very moment with supreme confidence.

"This one," he said, rising with the sword before him.

Gul laughed. "I thought it might be! But, come, you can't make your decision without giving the others a fair chance. They are all fine weapons." Reluctantly, Rowan agreed to test the others, but not until Gul had told him about the broadsword.

"Its name is Hagr, which means 'ugly.' None of the Seelie Court think much of it, and when it was first made they almost sent it back to the dwarves who forged it. They believed it an insult to have such a homely creation given to them, and wanted it fitted with gems and precious metals. But the dwarves refused. Take it as we give it to you, they said, or we'll cast it back into the molten furnace where it was forged. It remained unchanged, and it has proved to be the doughtiest of weapons. Hagr has won more battles for the Seelie Court than the other two weapons combined."

He picked up the round shield and fitted it to Rowan's left arm. "This is Tew, which means 'fat.' This was fashioned by the Old Man of the Hills. He lives where the wind never ceases to blow, an open, craggy place in the north where the trees are beaten down even as they try to grow. In his domain, a tree may be five hundred years old yet stand no higher than a child. It is from the wood of these ancient, stunted trees that Tew was crafted. Again, the Seelie Court was dissatisfied. How can a man fight with that heavy lump of wood strapped to his arm? But every man who lifted it has found it to be as light as a piece of balsa, and in all its battles, not so much as a chip has been cut from it. At least the Old Man of the

Hills had no objection to our decorating it. Tew's sturdy wood has been covered with the hide of a white hart, and the foxgloves on its face were made by the queen herself." Rowan stroked them reverently.

"There they are, Ugly and Fat, at your service! May they serve you well, Rowan. But, here, lay them aside and meet the others, that you may be sure beyond a doubt that these are your chosen weapons."

Rowan next took up the pair of slender swords that had hung at Gul's belt. They had jet-black handles with inlaid silver scroll-work, and their blades shone like mirrors in the sun. "The elder one is Hen, and the younger is Brychan. With them you fight in the Florentine style, more akin to fencing. The short sword stands in place of a shield, and the tines are meant to catch your opponent's sword . . . if he has one."

"What weapons will the other side be using?" Meg asked.

Gul looked on her with approval. "Their champion will also select among three weapons—a longsword, a pike, or an ax."

"And which has he chosen?"

Gul didn't know. "To my knowledge they haven't chosen their champion yet. But that doesn't concern you."

"Of course it does," Meg said hotly. "He'll be better prepared if he knows who he's to fight against." Gul seemed to think the identity of Rowan's opponent a trivial matter, and returned to the weaponry, showing him how to strike with Hen and parry with Brychan. Rowan found the technique awkward. It was hard to keep track of the two blades, and he felt he'd be just as likely to wound himself as his enemy.

He reached for the bow, and Meg felt a sharp sting of involuntary jealousy. *Don't touch it,* she wanted to snap. But he only plucked the taut string and set it back down—it held no appeal for him, and he immediately snatched up Hagr again. His choice was irrevocably made, and Gul took him a bit apart from the others to review the rudiments of stance and grasp.

Silly looked on with undisguised envy. "Just because he's the champion shouldn't mean we don't get to learn anything ourselves," she said, in that sort of voice that pretends to be low but is meant to be heard. "Why does the champion have to be a boy, anyway?"

"It doesn't have to be a boy," Gul called as he adjusted Rowan's shield arm up a few inches. "And there's no reason you can't learn to use the weapons, too. Pick yours, and I'll give you a lesson later. I'm sure you see that Rowan's training has to take priority." Somewhat abashed, Silly bowed her head, but an instant later dashed to the remaining weapons and scooped up Hen and Brychan.

"I want these!" she said eagerly, then cast a sly, sidelong glance at Meg. "You don't mind, do you? You can have the bow."

Meg didn't mind in the least, and finally succumbed to the temptation to pick up the five-foot recurved bow. It was made of a pale, gleaming wood marked all over with spots like a leopard's, like bird's-eye maple. The grasp was ivory, carved with the figure of a seated man with deer antlers. In one hand he held a torque, and in the other, a horned snake. She twanged the string and leaned close to it, smiling, as the vibrations spoke to her.

What Meg felt now that she held the Hunter's Bow was almost a deep and passionate and totally unexpected first love. Yet the emotion wasn't completely real—all the weapons were touched with the fairy glamour. The bow, almost sentient, spoke to her soul. When she held it, she felt stronger, braver than her usual self. She began to see, dimly at first, but growing clearer all the time, that there might be sense to fighting a war. She felt a thrill rise up her fingers as she stroked the string, and desired more than anything to shoot at something.

Meg was less susceptible to fairy glamour than most, but she was not immune. In one way she felt at peace—nothing could go wrong while she held the bow—and in another way she felt a sudden agitation, a desire to devote herself to her weapon, to training, to helping Rowan prepare for the Midsummer War. Beneath it her fears still lurked, and, almost like a memory, she told herself, I'll still find a way to keep Rowan from fighting. But she felt half drugged, and though the sensation lessened later on, it never left her so long as she possessed the bow. Though she hardly noticed it herself, under the bow's spell she almost completely stopped nagging Rowan, didn't bother to argue with Gul, and simply waited for the War.

"Don't try to use them on your own," Gul said to Silly and Meg over his shoulder. "I'll be with you in a while, to make sure you do it safely."

But the while grew longer and longer, and Silly and Meg sat in the shade of an elm, impatient yet fascinated, as they watched their brother practice throughout the afternoon. James, interested for a few minutes, soon turned to higher pursuits, like digging for grubs among the tree roots, and (though they weren't near the water) making little boats from twigs and leaves. Silly cradled her two swords in her lap, as another child might hold dolls. Meg's bow lay at her side, and one hand rested on the curving wood as she watched Rowan parry and slash at empty air. He swung the blade until his arm ached and his shield drooped low. Time and again Gul would step forward to correct him or reposition his arms or legs, moving back to watch Rowan repeat the same motion once more under his critical eye. It was grueling work, particularly because he didn't have the stimulation of an opponent, or even a wooden stock to strike. To send out blow after blow and make contact with nothing is both wearying and frustrating. But Gul (who had been training Seelie champions for centuries) worked him at this until Rowan felt ready to drop, and finally gave him permission to rest. Rowan collapsed under the elm tree, exhausted but happy.

"I'm ready for more," he said only a moment later.

Gul laughed. "Rest, lad. The girls have watched you long enough—they need their own work to keep them content."

At these words, Silly sprang up, clutching her swords. Meg wasn't sure if it was her imagination, but it seemed as if the swords had diminished. Both Hen and Brychan looked shorter and lighter, more suited to her sister's hand. "The Sister Swords for you, is it?" Gul said. "But Meg takes precedence, being the elder."

Silly made a face. "You don't mind if I go first, do you, Meggie?"

Perhaps she did, and perhaps she didn't. The bow was begging to be drawn, the arrows were crying out for flight. But Silly looked so eager that she yielded, and soon Silly's blades were flashing.

"Very good! Better than I've seen in many a year. Your blood breeds a bellicose progeny! Perhaps the queen chose amiss in your brother, young wildcat." Silly beamed, and he left her to practice rapidly drawing and sheathing her weapons.

"And what of you, Meg Morgan?" Gul asked, kneeling at her side. As before, she found that she could see a bit—just a bit—of the Seelie prince in his aspect. He was still Gul Ghillie, but for some reason, when he looked at her, he became older, more solemn, much more like the royal than a boy. And so each saw something in the other that the rest didn't see.

"I'd like to learn to shoot this bow," she said, almost meekly.

"Do you know who made it?"

It was on the tip of her tongue to say acerbically, Of course not, how could I? But she only shook her head.

"It is strange. Though it was crafted by so great a force, this weapon has only been chosen once before to take part in the Midsummer War. It was a very long time ago, and she . . . But in any case, the bow was made by one who is older and greater than any of my people. Older, and we have been here since the beginning. The tree it is carved from has not grown in millennia, and the beast whose horns lent that ivory died before humans walked this world. There, see, the craftsman's image is carved on the grip. He is the Hunter. But he is also the Protector. When an arrow finds its target, he is the one behind it. Yet, when you miss, and your prey is spared, this is also his doing. It fits your hand well. Now let's see if you can draw its weight."

She held the bow before her in her left hand and with the first three fingers of her right pulled back on the string. For the first few inches it seemed impossible, but, as if the bow read her ability, she found that as she drew it became easier. "How far back do I pull it?"

"As far as you like. To wherever it's comfortable. Some draw to their lip, some to their jaw. But keep your right elbow down, parallel to the ground. That's it. And bend your left arm, just slightly. Enough to make sure your elbow turns out, and not down. Come over here. There's a clear alley between the trees, and I brought a bale of hay for a target."

Before she followed him—she couldn't resist—she sighted down the place where the arrow would have been, picked a tree as a target, and loosed the bowstring.

"Ow!" she said, though what she really wanted to say is unprintable. She rubbed her left arm in misery where the bowstring had snapped against it. Already the skin was swelling, and a purplish bruise crept across her inner arm.

"That's two lessons for you, Meg Morgan," Gul said. "I told you to keep your arm turned out, and now you know why. And you should never shoot the bow without an arrow in it. If you do, all the force goes into the bow spine, instead of the arrow shaft, and that weakens it. Not that anything could weaken the Hunter's Bow, I think. But it's best to learn things the proper way. That bow won't always be yours."

He set her before a tightly compressed rectangular bale of hay with a feathered popinjay affixed to the top. She hit the target on the first shot (albeit on the edge), and as she found her stance, her arrows came ever nearer the center, until she was a dead shot. The bow seemed to thrill with each arrow launched, and Meg was filled with a wild joy.

While the Morgans were taking such pleasure in the fell arts of war, Finn was forcing his way through the forest, trying both to walk and to look through the self-bored stone at the same time. This proved harder than he had thought, and the forest took advantage of his distraction to help protect its denizens by reaching up with roots and vines to trip him. At last he gave up the trying task of attempting two things at once, and concentrated on finding a likely spot for fairy-watching. His goal was to approximate the same route they'd taken on their first night, to find what he reasoned must be the Green Hill. He remembered the chambermaid's allusion to this place, and it struck him that the emerald tumulus he'd seen in the pool must be no other. He didn't know its significance, of course, but, being a clever boy, he found it logical that such a monument, hidden in the middle of a wood, might hold some meaning to the fairies. The rotten Morgans had seen wonders there—why wouldn't he?

He came at last to a place where the stream snaked through the woods. At first he was wary of approaching the water, for well he remembered that glimpse of fangs in Jenny Greenteeth's wide, gaping mouth. But even to Finn, who was not particularly sensitive, that pond had seemed a noisome, foul thing, a place well suited to a monstrous inhabitant. Here, where the water trickled melodiously through rocky crevices, the environment was too pure to house anything dangerous . . . not to mention too shallow. Silver-sided minnows might live there, and the fierce larvae of dragonflies, but nothing more treacherous. Perhaps a clever fisherman might catch a tiny Asrai, a harmless water fairy. But she would melt away into a puddle if kept in the air for more than a moment.

Finn took up position in a likely-looking spot along the bank and sank down to his stomach, propping himself up just enough so he could hold the stone pressed to his eye. But he had nothing of the naturalist in his makeup. He was restless, always craving activity, and he found it impossible to focus his attention on anything as unrewarding as a lovely landscape for more than a few minutes at a stretch. For some it is an easy matter to sit and stare; for them it is not a wait for something to happen but, rather, an experience in itself. But Finn soon grew bored, and then impatient.

First his feet began to twitch, and then he found the ground ridiculously uncomfortable, and had to shift position every few seconds. His movements were enough to scare away any of the shyer inhabitants of the wood. Birds took flight for more serene habitats, and an otter who had lately been patrolling the region performed a graceful underwater turnabout and retraced its path when it heard Finn's twitchings. It was only the overwhelming desire to get the better of the Morgans that made him stay, until the sun fell a little lower and hovered between two trees, casting its heat directly on him. It is funny how fast restlessness can change to sloth, particularly in the hazy heat of afternoon. In a while, Finn dozed off, and his self-bored stone, clutched in his hand, fell from his eye.

The more wary creatures of the wood had fled, true, but others who lived in the forest thought they had no need to be particularly secretive. When you believe yourself invisible, you travel with complete freedom. Within a few moments of Finn's falling asleep, three strollers passed by on the opposite bank of the narrow stream.

The trio were as like as brothers—small, lean men with thin bandy legs, dressed in smart green suits and tricorner hats, each with a feather in it. Their shoes had gold buckles, and they smoked pipes of fragrant herbs far sweeter than tobacco. They chatted about this and that as they walked—loudly, for the Good Neighbors can't be heard without craft any more than they can be seen, unless they wish it. As with many human men, their talk consisted of bawdy jokes and tales of their drinking exploits, of brawls they had won and bets they had lost, and their rich laughter could be heard, by the right ears, for a league in all directions. Finn slept soundly through it all, his cheek resting on the grassy bank.

"What ho!" cried one of the little fellows, stopping short. "What have we here?"

"It's a log," another guessed.

"A lump," said the third.

"You're both right," said the first. "But it's a boy, too. And look at the crop he's grown for us!" With a skip he leaped over the stream and drew from the back of his waistband a sickle-shaped copper knife. The other two followed eagerly. The first little man crouched beside Finn's head, and for a moment the wickedly curved blade hovered menacingly at his nape.

"What's this?" he said, spying the stone in Finn's hand. "Oho, so you're out for a bit of tricksy fun, are ye, lad?" He reached for the stone, but his friends stopped him.

"Are ye mad? Do you mean to wake him? If he stands we'll never get his hair, and look how fine it is, like a raven's breast. It'll make a grand bit o' goods for some wee lassie."

For these little men garbed in green were Weavers, and they roamed in search of material with which to make their cloth. Though they sometimes used wool or linen or hemp, like the human craftsmen of those parts, they loved variety. These fairies would shear the tails from horses while they slept, or comb the fur from a kitten's belly. They spun spiderwebs into fine silken threads, from which they fashioned a lace that was invisible in all but moonlight. At times they even captured the moonlight itself to incorporate into their garments. But what they loved best to work with (perhaps because it was so hard to come by) was human hair.

They thought Finn's onyx hair particularly pleasing, and faulted only its shortness. Still, the strands that flopped about his face (of which he took such care, and which he thought so fetching) were long enough for their purposes, and while he slept the Weavers sheared him of his locks.

Their touch was gentle, and the knife so sharp it sliced effortlessly through his silky hair. Their barbering never would have woken him, but just as they were finishing, a woodpecker landed in a nearby bough and, looking down, found the spectacle so amusing that he trilled a chuckling song. Finn jerked awake while the sickle was hewing its last stroke, and felt a little tug. Thinking a beetle was crawling on him, he swiped at the air and thought he heard "Damme!" muttered near his ear. Thinking even more quickly (and more cleverly) than usual, he slapped the stone to his right eye and caught a fleeting glimpse of three figures tripping away, black tufts clenched in their fingers. His own fingers went to his head, and he gave a cry of rage to discover his cropped hair. He hurled his only weapon—the self-bored stone—at the retreating trio, but it didn't find its mark, and he spent the next ten minutes grubbing through the shrubbery to find it again, muttering curses all the while. The stone was gone, perhaps carried off by the Weavers, and after kicking a few trees and spitting into the stream, he headed home.

It is good to remember that, no matter where you are, there are always eyes upon you. Oh, very often they are not human eyes, and even more often they care less for you than the man (or woman) in the moon. But there is no deed on this earth that goes unnoticed, and nothing is ever forgotten. Ghosts of old gods will know if you violate their deserted temples, and a forest will remember the hands that set fire to it. A great many things watched Finn as he slept, when he woke, and while he made his growling and cursing way back to the Rookery.

He did not travel long before he felt a stinging impact on his calf. He slapped at it, thinking it must be a wasp. (No one had ever told him that this was the worst thing you could do if under attack from wasps, hornets, and their kin. The scent of an injured comrade drives all others in the vicinity to madness, and instead of one painful wound, you'll have a hundred crippling stings.) Near his leg he saw a stone the length of his finger, chipped in roughly the shape of an arrowhead, though the point was far too dull to tempt any respectable archer. Finn pocketed the stone, thinking to show it off later, and walked on, making no connection between the pain and the piece of chert. But a few paces later, he was struck again, just below the shoulder, and when he rubbed the spot there was a smear of blood on his palm.

This time, he had seen the missile ricochet off him and bounce to the ground. He whirled around wildly, looking for the person (as usual, he suspected the Morgans) who had presumed to attack him. He heard a high-pitched laugh from the trees, but saw no one.

"Come out, you!" Finn called, searching the greenery. His only answer was another manic laugh, and another stone. This one hit him in the rump.

"Stop it, you coward! Come out and fight." But his attackers had no intention of being seen. More stones flew, with an accuracy that would have been deadly had they been sharper, or hurled with greater force. Soon Finn had no choice but to make a run for it, and took to his heels with stones still pursuing him. He thought he caught a glimpse of a squat figure in the crook of a tree, holding a Y-forked stick.

"Elf-shot," Dickie told him later, when Finn, hiding his cuts and bruises, showed Dickie the stone and asked what might have made it. "The fairies use them to harry people who bother them. Sometimes they throw them, sometimes they use a slingshot. People who find elf-shot always think it's nothing more than flint tools from extinct tribes. Did you get hit with this?"

"No, of course not. I just found it on the road and was curious."

When the children met the Ashes and Bran for dinner, Silly took one look at Finn's head and burst out laughing. Meg, more tactful, said, "Oh . . . you cut your hair," in a tone that sounded as if it could be either an insincere compliment or commiseration.

"I didn't cut it," Finn said sourly. He'd thought long and hard about lying and saying he cut it himself, but he couldn't think of any way to tell it that didn't make him look like a fool. The Weavers hadn't taken as much as they could have—there weren't actually bald spots on his head—but his hair was cropped much closer than he liked, and the locks were uneven. Though he didn't look all that bad, in his own eyes he looked horrible. "I went to sleep . . . in the garden." After all, a story must have some untruth to it. "And *somebody* thought they'd play a joke on me." He looked the Morgans over one by one, as if to imply that any of them, even little James, might be capable of such infamy.

"You weren't in the garden," Rowan said. "We were there all afternoon, and we didn't see you."

"Well, I was obviously in a different part of the garden, wasn't I? Was it one of you, then? I'd think you'd at least pretend to have an alibi."

But Phyllida Ash said, "Tut, tut," and rose to have a look at his shorn head. "Looks like the work of the Weavers to me. Let me get my shears. I'll have it neatened up in no time." She slipped away, and Finn kept scowling at the Morgans. When covering up your own secret, it is good to imply that others have secrets, and turn the attention their way.

Then, from the far side of the table, Bran spoke. "You werena shorn in the garden."

Finn managed to look at him levelly, but there was something about the man that made him quail inside. "I think I know where I was," he said haughtily. He still didn't believe that business about Bran's being Phyllida's father, and felt inclined to treat him as an elevated sort of servant.

"The Weavers dunna come on the Rookery grounds. None of the Good Folk do, unless they're given leave. I make sure of it."

"You mean the fairies did this to me?" he scoffed, keeping up a good act. "Humph! I doubt it."

"If 'twere on the grounds, it weren't the fairies. If 'twere the fairies, it weren't on the grounds. That's all." And he lowered his head and glared at Finn with his peculiar orange-gold eyes until Finn looked away.

"And you!" Bran snapped, suddenly turning on the Morgans. "What were you doing all day?"

"Just playing," Meg said. "Out in the garden."

"You didna go in the woods? You didna leave the grounds?"

"No," she said, feeling herself start to tremble.

"Then remember not to."

Silly couldn't resist. "But we're *allowed* to leave the grounds, right?" She looked to Lysander. "We can go on the road, or to Gladysmere, can't we? You said so!"

"Wouldn't be wise," Bran said gruffly, looking at the children each in turn, his mouth twisted in a scowl. "There've been strange things afoot." His gaze flickered to Lysander. "Keep them close. Don't let them leave the Rookery."

Silly raised her voice in protest, but Lysander lifted his hand and called for peace. "We'll discuss this later. For now, I trust it will be no dire hardship to have your liberty curtailed for a few days. I have seen the signs, too, Bran, though no one reads them as clearly as you. Later, you must tell us, Phyllida and me, what you know."

"I know nothing!" Bran almost shouted, darting a quick and, Meg fancied, menacing look at Rowan. "Nothing!" And he shoved back his chair and stalked from the room, just as Phyllida came back with the scissors.

She took Finn aside near the light of the fire and snipped deftly at his hair until the strands were even and he looked as though he'd intended his hair to be that length. It was another silent meal, with many under-table nudges and questioning looks. After supper, the Morgans gathered in Meg's room.

"What I want to know is, why did Bran meet with the Black Prince?" Rowan said straightaway, curling his legs under him as he sat on Meg's bed.

"We don't know that he *met* him, exactly," Meg said. "You heard what he said at supper—the fairies aren't supposed to be here without leave, and he makes sure of it. Maybe he was just driving the Black Prince off."

But Rowan wasn't buying it, and Silly didn't seem convinced, either. "He was looking all around when he went to the woods. He didn't want anyone to see him." Silly had done the same thing herself plenty of times, and knew well that furtive look of one who is up to no good.

"And he didn't just run into the Black Prince," Rowan said. "It was a rendezvous. He knew the prince would be there."

"It still doesn't prove anything," Meg insisted.

"No," Rowan agreed. "It certainly doesn't. But it does offer up one possibility. I think they might have chosen Bran to fight for the Host. Why else would he hold a secret meeting with the Black Prince?"

"But it can't be!" Meg cried. "Bran's good. He's Phyllida's father. He wouldn't be the Black Prince's champion. He wouldn't fight against you."

"He might not know it's me he's to fight. And yet . . . did you see the way he looked at me over dinner? When he shouted to the Ashes that he knew nothing? I don't know . . . but I think we should keep an eye on him."

"Can't we just tell Phyllida? She could help us. She could clear everything up."

But Rowan had a lingering fear that, somehow, Phyllida Ash would have the power to keep him out of the war. Now that he'd swung Hagr and hefted Tew, he was more determined than ever to hold his place as the Seelie champion . . . the queen's champion. "No," he said sternly. "This is my task, not theirs. You will not tell them."

May Dwindles

THE DARLING BUDS OF MAY had blossomed, ready to welcome June, and the Morgans' secret still remained their own. They practiced their martial arts almost every afternoon at the foot of the garden, and at odd hours or in foul weather would sneak off to the Rookery's more obscure rooms to hone their skills with the collection of weapons scattered as ornaments throughout the estate. (Each evening, Gul Ghillie would collect the Seelie relics and return them to their home under the Green Hill.) Rowan never bothered now with the rattan practice sticks, but would engage in fierce battles with live steel against Gul Ghillie. Time and again, sword would clash with sword—or pike or ax, to prepare him for whatever his opponent might have in store. And Rowan practiced with diligence, performing the same sequence in endless repetition until the movements were second nature to him.

Silly practiced with an almost equal fervor, and sometimes the two would battle. Rowan had the advantage of height and strength, but he was a contemplative fighter who would defend patiently against his opponent's strikes, waiting for a lapse in judgment to give him an opening. Silly was quicker with her lighter weapons, and a very aggressive fighter, which was sometimes her undoing. When she struck home, the blow was telling, though when she missed, she would overextend and sprawl forward on her face. Then Gul or Rowan could declare victory merely by stepping on her back and plucking Hen and Brychan from her hands.

Meg always watched these battles between her siblings with half-averted eyes and her nails digging into her palms. She was sure that one of them would come to grievous injury. For all that they wore mail and steel helms, the danger of serious wounds was very real. But at the end of the day, when they stripped off their armor, they were never marked by anything worse than bruises. Perhaps there was a magic in the weapons that kept them from harming a friend.

It's surprising their secret wasn't discovered sooner, for the Morgans' physical changes were quite apparent. Never unhealthy or weak, they suddenly began to look like what they were—warriors in training. Rowan's shoulders broadened and his arms thickened, and Silly's coltish movements began to reveal a real power. Even Meg, who, with her bow, got the least exercise, began to look a bit more rugged, and her dresses pulled across the shoulders and chest. Their bearing, more than their physique, should have given them away. Rowan looked impossibly noble, more and more like a member of the Seelie Court himself than a mere boy. They all stood more erect, walked with more grace, and seemed suffused with a higher purpose. Though Meg was still fundamentally against this whole business, she had been almost completely converted in all the ways that matter. She didn't want Rowan to fight, but if there was no way to stop him, well, she wanted him to win. She was liberal with her encouragement and praise, and though she never picked up a sword herself, she watched him so closely that she could often detect his mistakes, and coached him in Gul's absence.

Nevertheless, she had moments of depression and heartache, when visions of her brother's failure and death would torment her. Then she would retreat through their secret passageway to the Rookery roof, and seek the solitude of her lofty perch and the comfort of the rooks. She would look to the Green Hill, and rack her brain for a way to save Rowan. She would gaze down on the flashes of steel at the end of the garden, where he sparred with Gul, and tell herself that there was really nothing to worry about. Of course he would emerge victorious.

What troubled her most was that, as the Midsummer War crept closer, the identity of his opponent was still unknown. Bran had given them no further proof of his treachery—nor had he given them any assurances. His grimness increased by the hour, and he growled obscure warnings to the Ashes and barked threats at the children. Many times each day, he warned them not to stray from the Rookery—which was quite all right with the Morgans, since all their business could be done on the grounds.

And he took to following them. They'd be chatting away happily over breakfast in the garden kitchen (though never about Serious Business, which they'd agreed not to discuss save in absolute privacy) when, suddenly, it would seem that a cloud descended over them. They'd fall silent, look up, and find Bran peering at them though the window. Caught, he never seemed disconcerted, but only frowned and moved on, to reappear later in the shadows of corridors, where he looked like an inanimate suit of armor until he sprang at them and asked where they were going, what they were doing. It became ever more difficult for the children to practice in the garden. Gul could hear, or perhaps sense, Bran approaching from far away, but there were still a few near-misses. At last Meg agreed to act as a sort of watchdog and tail Bran whenever the others practiced outside, ready to give a signal should he come too near their battleground.

And so, through the merry, merry month of May, she became Bran's shadow—albeit a timid and distant shadow. She watched him as he labored, chopping wood or mucking out the henhouse (for, whatever his relation to the Lady, he worked like a hired man), and found it no uncongenial task. He was silent and solitary, and when he worked, he did so with such utter absorption that it made Meg's job easy. It was like studying a wild animal from afar. As long as she was quiet and didn't get too close, he didn't seem to know she was there. Sometimes he'd catch her, and shout at her to get inside (or go out and play, if they were in the Rookery). But, like a wild animal, he seemed to grow accustomed to her perpetual presence, and there were times when she snapped a twig or sneezed, only to find that, instead of chasing her off, he continued with his work, an odd smile touching his lips.

Occasionally she would seek him out openly, bringing him refreshment while he worked (and claiming that Phyllida had sent her with the fruit juice or muffins), and then sitting some-where near him. Only rarely did she try to engage him in conversation—and even more rarely did he respond. She was al-most afraid of broaching the topic of fairies, lest he get some whiff of the Morgans' secret. She soon comforted herself with the realization that it would seem more suspicious not to speak of the fairies, for what child would see a brownie and then not be tempted to talk of it later? And so, tentatively at first, she began to quiz him. Generally he refused to answer, telling her such things were none of her concern, and sometimes it was like a game of twenty questions, only worse—he would volunteer no informa-tion himself, but reply to her queries with ambiguous grunts, the meaning of which, positive or negative, she was left to decipher herself. She got little information out of him, and she always had to be careful lest her questions reveal too deep a knowledge of the subject. Then, one morning, on the last day of May, Meg heard more than she'd bargained for.

There are those who will tell you England has very few perfect days. Too often it is cold, or windy, or rainy, or all three. Depressed Londoners will flee the dull, smoggy skies and river fogs of their metropolis for the seaside resorts on the southern coasts of Torquay or Penzance, only to find a sunless shore and uninter-rupted sea wind blasting its bitter breath across the strand. Or so the stories go. That season, however, the children were privileged to know England at its best. The days were bright and warm, full of the scent of flowers, breezy but not blustery. It was just cool enough to make it pleasant to work up a sweat with sword train-ing, just warm enough that, if you liked, you could wear short sleeves and short pants without getting goose bumps.

It was on just such a day that Meg brought Bran a tray bearing a tall glass of milk and a pretty nosegay of yellow primroses around a spike of drooping foxgloves. He took the milk without thanks and drained it at one go. Whatever food she brought, he always consumed it quickly and perfunctorily, as though he couldn't taste it or thought food a waste of time. The part of Meg that wasn't very good was tempted to bring him unsweetened lemon juice just to see if his tastebuds were in working order, but so far she'd always mastered that impulse.

A thought occurred to her, and she asked him, before she lost her courage or the moment slipped away, "What was the food like . . . while you were there? With the fairies, I mean."

For a long time, Bran was silent—so long that she thought perhaps he hadn't heard her. Then there came slowly over his face an expression she'd never before seen. She saw bliss, an unadulterated happiness, a face such as a lucky man might wear in the last few moments of a long life, as a monk might have when, after decades of meditation, the answer comes to him, and he finds that it is very simple. But it was not a peaceful bliss. There was about Bran at that moment an aura of ecstasy, vital and violently transcendent. Nor was it the innocent utter happiness of an untroubled baby. No, this was the sort of joy that comes after a lifetime of suffering, a paradise discovered after a journey through hell.

Meg looked at Bran in astonishment. She had never seen an emotion stand so brazenly naked on any man's face, and he was the last she suspected of being capable of such a display. He was lost in memory of a dream, of a time far better, in his mind, than any waking reality. Since his return from under the Green Hill, Bran had struggled like a man addicted to leave those years behind him. And though he managed to maintain a front of recovery, there was not a moment of his life when he did not think of, and then force himself not to think of, his time with the fairies. So frail were the barriers, so strong was his desire to relive the past, that the question of a child was enough to plunge him deep into the drowning currents of reminiscence, and for one heavenly, hellish moment he was back in that twilight world of sweet voices singing through an endless day.

Frightened that he had fallen into a trance, Meg laid a cool paw on his brow, and in an instant he jerked back to the moment and, teeth bared, grabbed her hand and her other shoulder with bruising fingers. "It was poison!" he growled savagely. "Poison and bile! Toadstools and wormwood and rue!" And he shoved her violently aside and stalked into the dairy.

Stunned, she gathered herself for a moment before moving to follow him. The door was ajar, and she slipped silently inside. The dairy was warm from the score of milling, mooing bodies waiting for their morning exercise, and the pungent but oddly pleasant smell of fresh cow dung filled her nostrils. The cows looked up at Meg, then told her plainly by their anxious glances where Bran must have gone. She went into the annex, where Lemman turned the cows' produce into cream and butter and new country cheeses.

He was on his knees with his head in Lemman's lap, and from the movement of his shoulders, it looked as though he might be crying. Lemman stroked his hair and sang a low song under her breath. She raised her eyes to the interloper, and greeted her with a strange, sad smile.

Several times before in her weeks at the Rookery, Meg had gone to see Lemman, though it might be better to say she'd gone to see the cows. She always greeted Lemman as if she might answer at any time, bidding her good morning or asking how her day had gone, or whether the cows were well. But though Lemman sometimes consented to look at her (which Phyllida said was more than she did to most), she never favored Meg with a reply. Still, she didn't seem displeased with the girl's presence, and where there was not absolute rejection, Meg was always game to persevere.

She told Lemman once how sorry she was that she'd been stolen from her home, and promised to look for her otter pelt. Lemman had glanced at her, then turned back to her task. Another day, she told the captive otter girl about her first encounter with the brownie. (She'd seen him several times after that, and took to leaving the heel of a new loaf on the table for him after each breakfast . . . though of course she never indicated by word or gesture that it was intended for him, lest he take offense and leave the Rookery.) She chatted to her silent and unresponsive audience about household gossip, what trees were blooming, what she had had for dinner, and though she never received any sign that her efforts were appreciated, she had an idea that Lemman enjoyed her company.

She knew that Bran visited Lemman often, but had never seen them together. When the song ceased, Meg was about to ask if Bran was all right, but Lemman held a finger to her lips and motioned for her to sit on a bale of hay pushed against the wall. Silently, Meg sat, behind Bran and out of his sight. After a time, he raised his head and pushed at his eyes with the heels of his hands, as if trying to contain something that was about to escape. He looked up at Lemman.

"Do you remember the drink they served under the Green Hill?" he asked her, a catch in his voice. "It was like water, cool and pure, but with such subtle flavor. It tasted of every rock it had flowed by, every speck of earth that had touched it. And how it made me feel! Like the very springwater itself, as though I was welling up from the earth's heart to gush free into the air and sunlight. It invigorated my body, it opened my mind. Why is it that all water tastes like dry ashes to me now, Lemman? Why is the world so dull and flat and colorless?"

Lemman lowered her head to his, but Meg couldn't tell whether she kissed him or whispered something in his ear.

"No," Bran said, "not even for her sake. Alas, Lemman! For us the world is empty and cold. But you will return someday. Never lose heart, *leanan sidhe*. The Lady will never cease in her search, nor will those who follow her. Midsummer comes, and my time draws near. If anything could turn me from my course, it's the thought that your grief might be heightened by my absence. What a comfort you have been to me! One who knows what I have lost, because she has lost it, too! Now the sun grows stronger, the nights grow shorter, and soon my pain will be ended. On Midsummer Night, I will know if such a price can buy me peace at last!" With that he rose and, without seeing Meg, left the dairy.

When the gate slammed behind Bran, the little dun fairy cow squeezed through the annex door and looked at the bewildered Meg with deep-brown sentient eyes, and she found that she addressed her incoherent questions to the cow as much as to Lemman.

"Does he mean . . . Midsummer . . . he *is* going to fight against Rowan in the Midsummer War? But why? How could he?" And then she remembered his beatific face when he recalled his time with the fairies. *What I have lost . . .* Phyllida said that Bran had been taken, and eventually recovered, stolen by the fairies and then saved after many years' imprisonment. Meg had accepted the story. But what if that wasn't quite the case? What if Bran had gone willingly under the Green Hill, so that his supposed rescue tore him from the place of his bliss? What if he felt as much a captive in this, the real world, as poor Lemman?

Meg recalled the words of the Seelie prince when in the guise of Gul Ghillie: *Bran once rode with this company, fair as any fairy lord, and well beloved. He will not return.* Why he could not return, Meg did not venture to guess, but she knew enough about the peculiarities of fairies by now to realize that associating with them involved all sorts of rules and taboos and prohibitions. Though he longed to return, for some reason he couldn't. Well, what if the Black Prince offered Bran his fondest wish? Would Bran kill Rowan if in reward he regained his place in the fairy kingdom?

"Lemman, you have to tell me—is it true? I won't believe it unless I hear it from you. It's too terrible! Is it true?"

Lemman stared at her unblinking, and then, very slowly, both she and the dun cow nodded. With a sob Meg ran from the dairy and set off in search of Rowan. As she rounded the Rookery, she collided with Phyllida and almost knocked the octogenarian off her feet. Had she had the presence of mind to apologize, however briefly and insincerely, the Ashes might never have discovered the Morgans' secret. As far as Phyllida was concerned, a child in rash high spirits could break fourteen of her old bones, as long as it was an accident and much regretted. Such misfortunes are all a part of the joyful, heedless carelessness of youth. But she did expect contrition, and when Meg ran on without so much as a "sorry," Phyllida knew either that Glynnis Morgan had brought up a very impolite child, or that something was dreadfully wrong. In either case, the matter must be dealt with. So, you see, instinctive politeness frequently pays off, and you should learn to apologize for almost everything you do, whether you mean it or not, just in case.

Phyllida tailed Meg at a clip that would have surprised the girl: Though she didn't actually run, she moved with a sort of sporting scamper that allowed her to travel quickly, even with a sore hip. Thus, under cover of Meg's own noisy steps and sobs, Phyllida came upon the practice session without even Gul Ghillie's being aware of her.

At first, she wasn't quite sure what was going on. It never occurred to her that her great-great-nieces and -nephews could so far disobey the rules she'd laid out as to become embroiled in the Midsummer War. She had spent the past weeks drifting along in complacent satisfaction, thinking that perhaps she should have been a mother after all, if children were as easy as this. They had shown little rebellion when she and Lysander declared that they shouldn't leave the grounds, and she thought that they must respect a firm but kind hand. She did not know that Finn regularly sneaked out to the woods to try his latest charm or potion for fairy-spotting, or that, with the Morgans, all the damage had been done the very first night, and they were in trouble aplenty without ever setting foot off the grounds again.

It certainly didn't enter her head that Rowan might have been chosen for the Midsummer War. She'd been well aware of the dangers inherent in living in a place so fraught with fairies, but her imagination only stretched as far as entrapment in fairy rings, or perhaps being torn apart by the skinless Nuckelavee, a horror roughly in the shape of a centaur. Those hazards, though daunting enough to the untutored eye, were easily avoided with just a few precautions, and the children had seemed tractable enough to take them to heart.

When she saw Silly, Rowan, and little James in the company of Gul Ghillie, she instantly recognized Gul as one of the fairies. How, exactly, I cannot say, for he certainly looked like any village lad. But she knew at a glance that her wards were consorting with a fairy, and she charged out of the bushes and spoke a word or two of powerful banishment that even the prince of the Seelie Court could not deny. He vanished with a laugh and a defiant snap of his fingers, but her banishment did nothing for the Seelie relics—paired Hen and Brychan, mighty Hagr and his ally Tew, and the leopard-spotted bow of the Hunter.

Had it just been Gul Ghillie, Phyllida would have thought it no more than relatively harmless fairy trickery that one of them should take on human guise, curious to find out about the Lady's heirs. Once she sent him away, the children would have received a stern lecture on the error of their ways, and been kept under much closer scrutiny for the rest of their stay. But as she stood in the children's midst, arms akimbo and eyes aflame, she spied the treasured weaponry and her heart sank, for it could mean only one thing.

I won't delve too deeply into the hours that followed. Lysander was summoned, and there was a great deal of yelling, threatening, and beseeching to be heard before the sun had set. In the end, all except Rowan had tears in their eyes. I really must say that on this evening, more than ever before, Rowan justified the Seelie Court's choice. It is hard to be brave and dignified under the rantings of a great-great-aunt and -uncle who can swear as creatively and unceasingly as the Ashes, but Rowan stood his ground.

They said things to him that would make grown men break down and promise to mend their ways. They told him to think of his mother, his poor mother, who would be bereft when he fell in a battle she could never hope to understand. They described, in vivid and painful detail, what his body would look like when it had been pierced by a sword or hacked with an ax. They told him they'd tie him up and ship him back home if he didn't put a stop to it. And through it all he looked at them like a serene young prince and said, quite calmly, that there was nothing they could do—his life was pledged to the Fairy Queen, his service to the Seelie Court, and fight he would. And the Ashes *knew* there was nothing they could do. But that didn't stop them from trying for many hours more to change his mind.

Phyllida was furious with Rowan, and called him a nasty, spoiled, stubborn brat who didn't have the good sense to do what his elders told him ... and then she pulled him to her breast and squeezed him as though he were going off to die that night. She was even more furious with herself, and called herself a doddering, blind old fool at least as many times as she called Rowan a green, senseless one.

At the beginning of the bootless arguing, Lysander had been sent to fetch Bran. Phyllida thought he might be able to talk some sense into the boy where she had failed. After all, he knew the fairies better than anyone. He might even be wise to some tricksy way of getting Rowan out of it. Maybe if he cut off all his hair, or wore an iron horseshoe on a gold chain, or set a fire on the summit of the Green Hill.... She didn't hold out much hope. She knew the old lore almost as well as Bran, for though he had lived with them, she had been raised with the accumulated knowledge of generations upon generations of her foremothers. Bran might understand the fairy ways, but if there was some spell to bind them or ritual to summon them, she had it locked away in her memory. She knew well that the rules governing the Midsummer War had been long established: Mortal blood must be shed every seven years, but no human would ever be an unwilling sacrifice. Only one whose heart was dedicated to the task would do battle. And, despite her best efforts, Rowan was stoic in his determination.

But Bran was not to be found. No matter—Phyllida and Lysander still had plenty of steam of their own, and began a fresh assault on Rowan, and to a lesser degree on his siblings for letting it happen in the first place.

"And we don't even know who he's to fight!" Phyllida went on, rolling her eyes to the heavens. "Trust the Host to choose someone particularly loathsome or daunting. They've had their eye on the Gladysmere blacksmith for the last three Midsummer Wars, and he'd make six of you, Rowan, my boy."

"Auntie Ash," Meg began, but Phyllida didn't hear her.

"Or maybe some treacherous Gypsy or tinker. They'd promise him gold and mislead him about what he'd have to do."

"I know who . . ." Meg tried again, to no avail.

"Just like the Seelie to pick a stupid noble boy for his ideals and his bloodline and then try to train him up at the last minute. Blast the Strangers, but they know what they're about! Probably picked some soldier, some big strong ambitious man who can knock the snot out of you blindfolded."

"It's Bran!" Meg finally shouted.

Phyllida turned toward the house. "Where? Has he come at last? He'll talk some sense into that brother of yours. Bran! Come here at once!"

"No, I mean they chose him. Bran's the one who will fight Rowan."

Phyllida refused to believe her at first, but after hearing Meg's tale she wasn't so sure. When she returned to the Rookery to search for Bran, she found that he had left. He was not seen again until Midsummer Night.

Bran

FINN AND DICKIE found themselves alone at supper that night, which so discommoded Dickie that he left to seek the sanctuary of the library and his constant tutor, the Wyrm. But it pleased Finn's sense of self-importance to have an entire table set with succulent dishes just for his benefit, to have three servants awaiting his pleasure and his alone. Feeling grandiose, he ordered every candle in the room lit and picked like a jaded aristocrat at each dish, finishing the meal with a call for pears flambé and a glass of brandy. The latter was ignored, but the server complied with the flambé, setting the fruit afire with a flourish, though he would probably have preferred to try his technique on Finn's head. Finn supped on in blissful ignorance, propping up his feet and imagining that he'd have an establishment like this one day, albeit with electricity and something a little sportier by way of transportation.

He was in a good mood. His efforts to uncover fairies had hitherto met with little success (other than an occasional pelting with elf-shot or shrill mocking laughter from just out of sight), but he'd consulted with Dickie, who revealed, it seemed somewhat reluctantly, that he'd discovered the formula for a seeing ointment. Finn had initially been reluctant to try any draughts or philters, for he was fastidious as well as timid about things that smacked too strongly of medicines and doctors. To make an iffy ointment of possibly toxic plants was a last resort. But all other methods had failed, wholly or in part, and as June neared, he was determined finally to one-up the Morgans.

As well as he could ascertain, the Morgans had had no further truck with fairies of any sort, though of course his spying could not pierce Gul Ghillie's disguise. Finn remained oblivious of the training that was happening practically under his nose, and he still thought to impress the Morgans with the discoveries he might make.

Now, with the help of his friend the Wyrm, Dickie had concocted a formula that made the invisible visible, and had gone so far as to try it on himself. He didn't report seeing anything (which wasn't quite true, for with the ointment Dickie saw not only the Wyrm, who slept, invisible, on a thick volume called *Things That Don't Exist,* but also a map painted in invisible ink on the curtains, and the passing shade of Harold Halberd, one of Phyllida's ancestors who fought in the Crusades, who nodded politely to him), but, more important to Finn, Dickie's eye didn't burn or sting or fall out. He snatched up the ointment and determined to try it himself in the woods the following day. He considered trying it that very night, but quite sensibly decided that things that choose to be invisible in the dark are probably worse than things that choose to be invisible in broad daylight.

Phyllida left the Morgans around sunset, having accomplished nothing. She and Lysander conversed well into the night, and eventually reached the conclusion it had taken Meg much longer to reach—that no force of their will could sway Rowan. Their only task now was to encourage him, and strengthen him in what ways they could.

More grievous to Phyllida was the knowledge of Bran's role. She was still incredulous, but Bran's apparent flight did nothing to exonerate him. She thought she knew too well the pain he had suffered after his restoration. Since the moment of his rescue from the fairy lands, he had longed to return there as a drowning man longs for one last breath of sweet air. But she'd never thought he'd pit himself against one of her own heirs. He was, you must remember, her father, and though she seemed the elder, she relied on him, now as in her childhood. Her first responsibility, as summer caregiver, must be to the boy under her guard, the innocent who had come to this grief (she told herself) through her own carelessness. But she had known Rowan a scant four weeks, and when she wept into the night, after Lysander had finally fallen asleep at her side, she was in truth weeping for Bran, her father, who seemed lost to her again.

In the morning, though, when the roosters, crows, and larks all sang in cacophonous chorus, she emerged from her room dry-eyed and clear-headed, and coolly gathered up the Morgans, directing them to bring their Seelie weapons to the practice grounds. She leaned against a tree, arms folded, and put Rowan through his paces with much the same critical eye as Gul Ghillie.

"When I was seven, I stood at my mother's side to witness my first Midsummer War," Phyllida said when at last he stopped, hardly winded, and sheathed Hagr. "The human Guardian of the Green Hill is always called to be an observer, and my mother took Chlorinda and me to stand by her side. That year, the Seelie champion was a fine young man from the village, the baker's son. He'd long been a favorite of the Seelie Court, and they had groomed him to the task since he was a boy. His opponent had once been a boxer in London, but when he passed his prime, he moved into his father's cottage, outside of Gladysmere, and turned to drink. He was still a tough one, however, and cruel . . . and many's the time cruelty has outweighed high-handed skill. He fought with the long pike, and the baker's boy with Hen and Brychan. A mismatched fight if ever I saw one, finesse against brute force. All around the Green Hill they fought, through the night, until the morning star peeked over the horizon, until one fell." She was silent for a moment, seeing the carnage through seven-year-old eyes again.

"And every seven years since then, I have stood at the foot of the Green Hill and watched a battle rage above me. I've seen great fighters fall, and feeble men rise to victory. I have seen base treachery and nobility beyond imagining. And every seven years I have seen some mother's son die at the hands of another. But never, my boy, have I seen a man hold his weapons with such skill as you. A month only you have been training? I would not believe it possible. And yet the fairies are fully capable of bestowing great gifts on those they favor—skill at arms, luck in love, gilded fingers, and honeyed tongues. If you stood against any save my father, I would give you victory this minute. But Bran has a soldier's heart, and his years with the fairies have given him skills beyond those of mortal men. The fairies, Seelie and Host alike, are all great swordsmen, for they, too, will all fight in the Midsummer War.

"Know this, Rowan, my child: Bran will kill you if he can. I do not know what force compelled him to fight for the Host, but now that he is committed, he will come at you like a dragon spitting fire. I had thought him too strong, too good, to buy his happiness at such a price. Now that he has turned, he who should have been your greatest protector has become a deadly foe."

How it pained the poor woman to speak those words! How old she suddenly felt as she said them, how crushingly heavy was the burden of her eighty-four years. That I should live to see this day, she moaned within. That such a thing should ever come to pass.

"You may yet prevail, child, though it is by no means certain. You have three weeks, three weeks only, to save your own life. Never cease in your training, and never forget how daunting is your . . . enemy." She could hardly say the word.

She took a deep shuddering breath and went on. "To better fight your adversary, you must know what lies in his inmost heart. Come, children, sit around me here, among the worms and the roots. I find this tale too heavy to tell standing." Meg noticed that Phyllida's joints creaked as she lowered herself to the ground, and for the first time, she seemed thin and fragile.

"My mother was the most beautiful, brilliant, kind, loving person in the world. Everybody's mother is, of course, but she was like one of the old Guardians incarnate. She would walk through the woods, almost a fairy herself, singing in their secret tongue. She tried to teach it to me—I only know a few of the words now. It has a way of slipping out of most people's minds, so only a few can ever learn it properly. Fairy music is like that, too. Try as you may to remember the melody, you can never quite catch it again. When she sang, the woods would come alive. And some evenings, the trooping fairies would come at her call and ride past us on broad-chested horses, with packs of milk-white, red-eared hounds baying beside them.

"My father . . . Bran . . . I've always felt sorry for the men who marry into our tribe. How like outsiders they must seem, and yet how privileged, to be drawn into not only the happiness of love but an enchanted world. Lysander had an easier time than most—he grew up in the village. But Bran loved my mother first, and learned the consequences of his love later.

"I think perhaps Bran's downfall lay in taking to it all too well. From the moment he set foot in the Rookery, I'm told, the Seelie Court swarmed around to greet him. That day is still remembered in legend, the day the fairies marched visible for all to see. From that moment on, Bran was swept up in his new life— the mystery of it all, the beauty, the danger. He plunged right in, learning everything my mother could teach him, and discovering on his own even the things she refused to reveal—things reserved for her own daughter only.

"He was a remarkable man—as you see him now. So handsome that all eyes turned to follow him when he rode about the countryside. My mother loved him as she loved this land, making him a part of her. And I loved him. He was like a mountain to me, an unmovable strength, a reassuring colossus. He used to take me on his shoulders when I was a little girl, and I swear that I could see over the treetops to the Green Hill itself. He'd walk in the woods with Lysander and me, teaching us all the plant lore he'd only just learned himself, and when I got tired, in the evening, he'd carry me home, with a fairy light leading us through the gloaming."

Meg didn't know which was harder—picturing Bran as a loving father, or Phyllida as a young girl.

"There came a day when he no longer took me for walks in the forest. Oh, he'd still go himself, but when I tried to follow he'd grow cross and tell me I had better help my mother. I was almost nine then, and it had begun to be apparent that Chlorinda wasn't suited to be the next Guardian. So it was true that my own lessons became more urgent. Still, I was hurt that he seemed to have no time for me. I cried in my mother's arms the first time he forbade me to follow him. She told me not to worry, that he was only concerned for my studies and just doing what a good father had to do. I saw something strange in her eyes as she said it. Have you seen it, when your parents lie to you in order to protect you? From that moment, I knew something was wrong, though I couldn't say what.

"My father was home less and less. Business, my mother told me. He came home before dawn and fell into bed without seeing any of us, without speaking a word, and slept the day away. Then he'd rise after dusk and set out again, and be away through the night.

"What does a child ever know of the things that drive adults?

To them the world is simple, and secrets are only petty things we keep from our parents, not they from us. I knew that things were changing—that my mother was unhappy and my father ever more distant. At that age I only saw how it affected me. My father didn't play with me anymore, my mother looked always with her far-seeing eyes into the forest, toward the Green Hill, and hardly seemed to see the child who stood before her. And Chlorinda, well, by that time she was always half angry, half frightened, and I did my best to stay out of her way.

"One day, my father set out on his nightly journey a bit earlier than usual. Dusk was just settling around the Rookery, and I was at play in the garden when I saw him striding toward the wood. I called out to him, but if he heard me he didn't turn around. I wanted to go with him, though I knew he'd send me back if he saw me, and I couldn't bear that. So, though I knew my mother would soon be ringing the supper bell, I followed him into the deepening darkness. I had never been alone in the forest after sunset before, and even with my father only a few paces before me, oh, how alone I felt! I think in truth I lost him that night, and not the next, which was when he vanished from this world for seventy years.

"I was a little thing, and used to the woods, so it was easy for me to hide. By then he wouldn't have paid any attention to me even if he'd caught me. His thoughts were already with the fairies, and I no longer existed to him. He came to a glade near the Green Hill, a bluebell meadow that opened to the starlight. There he met a lady of the Seelie Court. She laughed and took his hand, and he followed her like a man bewitched ... which I must tell myself over and over again he was. 'Come to the feast with me, and sup upon honey and sweet nectar,' she said to him. But even under the enchantment of his glamour, he'd been too well schooled to partake of fairy food. It is the first thing every village child learns at his mother's knee—that a single taste can make you a captive and slave forever. She laughed at him again. 'So many nights have I tried. . . . Soon you will yield. Very well, if you will not feast, at least you must dance.' And she drew him to her and whirled him about.

"Soon they were joined by others, stately couples of the high court, and dervish dancers, who seemed mad. The glade was filled with bodies, twirling and swaying, pressed close together in the crowd. The sound they made! Sometimes it was like the most beautiful music, with pipes and choruses. Then it would change, and sound like the wailing of tortured souls. Sometimes my father laughed, sometimes he seemed to scream, but while I watched, he never stopped dancing."

The children listened, spellbound.

"I ran home and . . . I never told my mother. I don't know exactly why. Perhaps you do. I composed myself and went in to dinner late and never said a word to show I knew where my father was going every night. He came home the following morning, but when he went out the next night, he never returned.

"I don't know how my mother got through the next few weeks. She blamed herself, you see, not my father. The temptation of the fairy court had been too much for him. I don't know if the man lives who can resist their call, once they've set their cap at him. *She* could have, no matter how hard they tried to lure her. Women can always pierce the fairy glamour far more easily than men, and are not nearly so subject to their tricks and wiles."

That's why they picked Rowan, Meg thought. If the queen had picked me, I'd have had sense enough to say no.

"When a person has been imprisoned by the fairies, there's always a way to get him back. The trick is finding it. Sometimes there's just one day each year when the captive's freedom can be won. Or you have to play a certain melody on a fiddle at midnight, or beat the fairies in a game of skittles, or trick the prisoner into wearing some piece of clothing inside out. The method is never the same. Mother did everything she could, racking her brain for lost memories from her ancestors, scouring our library for some text that might hold a clue. She followed the fairy rade when it trooped at Beltane, and though she saw my father riding among them, he didn't know her. Many times over the next seventy years, I saw him with the Seelie Court, dressed like them, proud and laughing, in jewels, amid the fairy ladies. But he did not hear me when I called out to him, and if I tried to touch him the whole court vanished.

"While my mother lived, she did all she could. She climbed to the top of the Green Hill and set it on fire. She threatened to renounce her Guardianship, sell the Rookery and the land on which the Green Hill stood, and let developers tear the whole forest down. It was only bluff, and the fairies knew that. However much she loved my father, however she yearned to have him near her again, she couldn't betray the obligation she'd inherited. She was the Guardian, mother of the next Guardian, and that was her first duty. It could not be set aside even for the sake of love.

"Chlorinda ran away when it seemed certain our father would never be saved. Mother hardly seemed to care. . . .

Chlorinda had her own destiny. We heard from her a time or two, but she never returned to England. My mother—she died when I was twenty, made old before her time by loss and grief. I became the Guardian, with Lysander to aid me. And never, as seasons waxed and waned, as fields grew ripe and quick and barren winter followed harvest, never did I cease searching for a way to bring my father back."

Phyllida looked at her hands where they lay in her lap. She was thrust back so far in the past, her own old body was a shock to her. Why, a moment ago, she'd been a girl, then a new bride. Now she stared at hands that could not possibly be hers, dry skin and gnarled knuckles, marked with spots and scars. How had they grown so old, when she could slip so easily back into the mind of her youth?

"How did the fairies capture him, in the end?" Meg asked, mercifully shattering Phyllida's reverie.

"Ah, that I never knew until five years ago, when he was returned to us. He said it was a trick, though I'm not so sure he could be tricked against his will. When he visited them that final night, the Seelie lady asked him once again to feast with her, and again he refused—for a man may pursue his pleasure without wishing to give up his freedom, his life. This time she did not draw him into the wild dance. She led him to a cave, a moldering, wet place with a carpet of moss and mushrooms growing out of the walls. 'If you will not eat,' she said to him, 'at least you can help prepare the feast.' She set him before a huge, deep cauldron that bubbled over a fire. 'You must stir this, never ceasing, until I return,' she said, handing him a wooden spoon. 'Then we will dance and make sport?' he asked. 'When I return,' she replied, and left him.

"So he crouched before the cauldron and stirred the brew. He was sorely tempted to taste it, for it smelled at times like rich lamb stew, then like May wine with sweet woodruff and honey. But he didn't dare put the spoon to his lips. Yet, for the lady's sake, he stirred for what felt like forever, and the cauldron bubbled on. The pot was deep, the spoon short, and as he stirred he scalded his fingers in the boiling brew. Without thinking, he sucked on his fingers to cool them . . . and he was caught. It might have been an accident, though who can tell if a moment of carelessness is not in fact surrender to one's deepest desire? My father was gone, my mother's love was gone, and he lived with the fairies for seventy years. The rest of us grew old, but he existed in unchanging limbo in a land where the sun never rises, the moon never sets. The Green Hill was his home, the fairies were his companions, and we no longer mattered to him."

"But you got him back," Silly said cheerfully. To her it was just an exciting story. She couldn't fathom any pain that had happened decades before she was born.

"Aye, we got him back in the end, Lysander and I, thinking it wise. Seventy years to ferret out the secret, to discover the night and time when he would be vulnerable, when we could bring him back to his home. I learned the way from a creature who lives in a pond in these parts, a horrid, foul thing called Jenny Greenteeth. She lives alone in her murk, waiting for prey to come too near her shore. But though she is a lonely, wretched, bitter thing, she knows all the secrets of the wood. The water whispers them to her. She wanted me to bring her a child—she dearly loves to eat a child, but they all know by now not to go too near her pool. That I wouldn't do, even for my father's sake. In the end, she agreed to tell me if I brought her a lamb, a kid, and a calf, no more than a day old."

Phyllida closed her eyes, remembering their screams as they were pulled into the water and devoured. "But she was true to her word—the fairies have to be.

"On the appointed night, Lysander and I waited at the crossroads for the fairy rade to pass. There were three fairy knights on horseback, each looking exactly alike, each with the face of my father. But Jenny Greenteeth had warned us about that. 'First let pass the black,' she said, 'and then let pass the brown. The man you seek will ride the milk-white steed.'

"We had only an instant as his horse went through the crossroads. We pulled him from his mount, and the two of us, old as we were, hardly had the strength to hold him down. He fought like a madman, calling out to the queen and her court to aid him, as though we were strangers to him. Perhaps we were strangers—how could he see the children he had known, through the cloak of years that had fallen on us? He wept and pleaded with us to let him go, then cursed and threatened us. He changed shape—for as the fairies' companion he had their powers. He changed into a serpent, and still we held strong, for we knew he couldn't harm us. Then into a bear he turned, grim and savage, and next to a snarling lion. He became a red-hot iron poker that seemed to burn us, but still we held, until, with sorrow in their faces, the fairies rode away, looking over their shoulders at the one they had loved.

"My father changed one last time. Gone were his fine clothes and jewels, and in their place moss and dried, crumbling leaves. For the fairy glamour had evaporated, and the illusion would not hold. That is the secret of the fairies, children—nothing that you see is as it appears. Nothing is real. For seventy years he had supped on toadstools and acorns, and thought them ambrosia. His silk and brocade garments were no more than tatters, his jewels bits of coal. And yet he had been happier there than as a mortal man. My father had been happy in that twilight world.

"With the glamour gone, he was a malnourished, ravaged carcass of a man, his hair tangled and his beard to his waist. I'd half expected him to crumble into dust, or have his years catch up with him all in a moment, like Oisin when he touched the ground after leaving Tir Na n-Og. But, no, my father stayed young, to all appearances the same man who had left his wife and children so many years ago."

"His wife was gone," Meg said, feeling Bran's pain with a pang that caught at her heart. "His little girl had grown old. How did he bear it?"

"When the fairy glamour had left him," Phyllida said, "he fell into a stupor, and we carried him home to nurse him. It was ages before he spoke. At first he would take no food, and even the taste of our purest springwater made him retch. But he had been a strong man once, and even if he had no wish to live, his body took over and saved him although his mind preferred to drift away into nothingness. For weeks he lived as if this reality was no more than a dream, or perhaps a nightmare, and one day he would find himself again in the world of the fairies. Then there came a day when he was lucid, and knew me for his own child.

And then he wept, and tore at his hair, and called out for his wife, who was so long dead. 'Seventy years!' he lamented to the deaf heavens. 'It cannot be. Just a few hours . . . I was only there a few hours. . . .' Such is it always to the captives, that their bliss, however long, seems no more than an instant.

"When he was able to walk, and take a little nourishment, he went to my mother's grave and knelt there for an hour. Chlorinda was dead by then, too, though buried in America, and he had a horde of great-great-grandchildren—you four. He recovered fast enough, it seemed, and threw himself into work around the Rookery. Soon he looked just like he did when I was a child, handsome and robust. But he was a man out of his time. Though the Rookery was largely unchanged, all around him the world was a different place, with fast cars and computers and space flight. He's done his best to shut it out, but sometimes young Jack plays modern music on his radio, or a jet plane passes, and Bran will actually cringe, as though he was just waking from his seventy-year trance.

"He was so full of remorse for what he did to me and to my mother. For a time I tried to get him to talk about his years under the Green Hill. He's told me a little bit, though it pains him too much to talk about it. At first I believed this was because it was so terrible to him, that he should have been enjoying himself, all oblivious, while those who loved him suffered through his absence. I suppose that was part of it. But those few times he did speak of his captivity . . . his eyes glazed over, and his entire body would tremble with the memory of it. You cannot imagine the pleasures the fairies can bestow on those they favor! To go from that blissful world to this real one must be almost more shock than the mind can bear. Though to my face he curses the day he was carried away from his family, there are times when he will fall into a reverie, and I see that he would do almost anything to return to the fairies."

Meg understood a little better that tearing bitterness of loss she'd seen in Bran in the cow barn. What's more, she realized what a dangerous opponent he truly was. He was fighting for something dearer to him than anything on this earth.

"Did he try to go back?" Meg asked.

"I thought he would, and I almost regretted bringing him home in the first place. After so many years, is it not more a punishment than a reward to fetch him back to a strange world—home, and yet not home; family, and yet not the family he remembers? Would it not be better, at this late stage, to let him languish in his sunless world, where, however false is his happiness, at least he is happy? Maybe I was selfish. All my life I longed to have my father restored to me. When I finally got the chance, I did not think I would be doing him a grave harm.

"He never returned to the fairies, and I think now that he couldn't. At least, not to the Seelie Court, where he made his home. Perhaps they viewed his return to me as a kind of betrayal, and this is his punishment, to be trapped in this world against his will, as I thought he was in the fairy world. Over the five years, the desire to go back under the Green Hill has become stronger. Oh, he won't confess it, yet I've seen him go to the woods, searching, no doubt, for a fragment of what he's lost. Since Lemman came, it's been even harder. When I asked him, he always swore he'd not go back even if he could. But now that the opportunity has been granted him, now that the bliss, or something like it, is again within his reach, it seems the temptation was too much. It is within the Black Prince's power to take Bran into his court. Whether he will or no, I cannot say. His offer must have been sweet enough to Bran's ears that he'd shed his kinsman's blood to win it."

She sighed deeply and took Rowan's hand in her own.

"That, Rowan, is why you must be on your guard with him. He fights for a treasure no man has ever tasted, to regain that which must be dearer to him than life—his own or another's. You fight for honor, and to live, but in your heart you have no wish to kill him. He will not be fighting under such a handicap. The lure of the fairies made him forget his loved ones once before, and now it has happened again. Be wary, Rowan, and be strong. If you would live, you must show him no mercy. He will have none for you."

Interlude

No one can know how Rowan spent the next three weeks as he prepared for battle. Oh, as far as his superficial actions, you can guess them fairly well—he trained and swung his sword and stretched his tendons, perfecting the skills that had come so easily over the preceding weeks. Every day Gul Ghillie met with him, only now, to help Rowan grow accustomed to fighting a grown man, he appeared as the Seelie prince. At first this threw Rowan completely off, for not only did his opponent strike from two feet higher than he was accustomed to, but he had a bearing such that Rowan felt constantly tempted to lay his sword down at his feet and swear his allegiance to the prince instead of fighting him. This, too, was a vital part of his training—to come at full force against someone whom he really didn't have any grudge against, whom he would befriend and admire if only circumstances were otherwise. It was indeed diabolically clever of the Black Prince to choose Bran as his champion.

This is all certain. What no one will ever know is what thoughts bounced around in Rowan's head those three weeks. Just what does a man feel when he knows that he will go marching forth against a formidable foe, that there's a very good chance he'll be killed, and, if not, that the only other outcome is that he'll have to kill someone? It is a situation many soldiers have found themselves in, and they get through it as best they can by a mixture of bluff confidence, joking bravado, and working their bodies so hard that their minds never manage to think too clearly or too long about what is to come.

These soldiers prepare for battles that are at once more uncertain—they don't know what will unfold, or whom, precisely, they will have to fight—and safer, for they are not the only combatants. Gul Ghillie had explained the Midsummer War in a bit more detail, and though it was true that all of the fairies would participate, Seelie Court against Host, the fairies would fight one another, leaving the field clear for the two humans to battle without interruption or interference. Whatever the fairy courts might accomplish among themselves, the ultimate victory would not be determined until one human lay dead.

One soldier among many usually expects to live. One man, fighting alone, is not afforded that luxury. Still, Rowan did not expect to fail. He was young, and youth can never brook defeat. Whether through wisdom or the callousness and confidence of youth, he thought only of the battle to come, and not its final moment.

Meg, on the other hand, waffled constantly between pride in her brother's obvious prowess and a terrible fear that always stalked her, and pounced, gripping her in its claws, when she least expected it. Ever since she'd first held the Hunter's Bow and felt the calmness of the glamour descend on her, she'd almost entirely given up trying to talk her brother out of the war. All the same, she could not quite shake the conviction that she should do something to stop it. Yet if she breathed so much as a word of opposition, Rowan only looked at her with a lofty sort of condescension, and Silly called her an old-lady worry-wart and told her to stop being such a girl. And so Meg, cowed by her siblings and swayed by the charm of her bow, held her tongue. But that did not stop her mind from silently reaching out for some opportunity to keep her brother from harm.

Occasionally she practiced with Rowan and Silly, though her archery had progressed so rapidly that hitting targets was tame. Gul Ghillie offered to take her hunting for waterfowl some morning, but this she steadfastly refused. Gul Ghillie had started to let the Morgans keep their weapons. Frequently, after a few minutes of shooting, she'd wander away from the training grounds, the Hunter's Bow unstrung and hung over her shoulder, where it bumped against her quiver, and find some sanctuary to pursue her fruitless musings. Most often she sought the Rookery roof, taking the secret path through fur coats and stoles, up the narrow blind staircase into the brilliantly illuminated crow's nest—or, rather, rook's nest.

The others never bothered with the roof anymore, and she was guaranteed to have it to herself. The morning before Midsummer, she was sitting there, safe above the world, lofty in the dread concerns none seemed to share. As she grew browner and more freckled in the noonday sun, she went once more over the possible solutions, dismissing each one in its turn, as she had before. She felt as frustrated as she sometimes did during math tests. She knew no new trick to solve the equation, and in desperation she revisited all those tired old failures just to see if she'd missed anything the first (and second and third and hundredth) time around. But she always arrived at the same unpleasant conclusion—unless Rowan changed his mind, she was powerless. Then she would fondle her bow, and forget for a time that she was worried at all.

She watched indifferently as, below her, Finn traveled (with many backward glances) toward the woods. She'd almost forgotten that he was a Rookery resident. He made himself scarce during the day, and when in the house he was often to be found in inexplicable confabulation with Dickie. When she bothered to think about either of them, it was with some wonder and vague satisfaction that they seemed to be friends. But she had so much else on her mind that neither Finn nor Dickie was a high priority.

She might have been dragged from her reverie if she'd known that Finn had been regularly spying on fairy life for the past few weeks. The seeing ointment worked like a charm, and Finn used it daily.

Now, if you or I had such a thing as a seeing ointment, we might be tempted to introduce ourselves pleasantly to all the fairies we met. But for all his faults, Finn was occasionally a very clever boy, and from what Dickie told him, and what he had gleaned himself from his bruising encounters with elf-shot, he had the notion that the fairies wouldn't be too pleased to find him spying.

Finn was an expert eavesdropper, and back in Arcadia he was

as up as any local gossip on who was spending evenings away from home, or had just received a Mercedes from the parent of a failing student. And he knew without a doubt that the key to successful spying is remaining unobserved. He learned to be stealthy, to lurk behind doors and quietly lift telephone receivers and, yes, even crouch below windows.

In the fairies he was presented a unique and amusing opportunity. With the help of the ointment, he could see them, and even hear them, when they imagined themselves concealed. If they suspected he could see them, they'd pelt him with elf-shot or worse. But if he traipsed his merry way through the woods, seemingly oblivious of the assortment of fairies around him, they'd act as though he weren't there.

It was difficult, especially at first, to see green-skinned bogies and winged sprites and not react. It was even worse because they constantly mocked him, calling him unpleasant names and making rude faces. (They thought they were invisible, of course, but I think they would have behaved just as uncouthly if they'd known he could hear and see them. Some fairies have no manners.) He kept his countenance blank through the worst insults, and fixed his right eye, in which he'd daubed the ointment, on the heedless creatures, sucking down all he could learn.

Thus, he came to know more about fairies than the Morgans did. Though they were favored by the Seelie Court, they saw none of its inhabitants other than Gul Ghillie in his two guises, and occasionally the Rookery brownie or a passing diminutive garden-variety fairy. Finn, on the other hand, saw schools of Water-Leapers (rather like bat-winged tadpoles with scorpion tails and sharp teeth) splashing in the pond, with little blue women on their backs. He saw a line of red-capped Knockers marching off to some distant mine, and spied a trio of Kobolds tramping down a barley field. The hideous but harmless pig-faced Jimmy Squarefoot picked his nose unself-consciously under Finn's stare, and an itinerant hag gave him the evil eye as she passed. He saw tiny golden fairies fly like bees through blankets of St. John's wort, and watched a willow with a woman's face in its rough bark wade across the stream, its weeping branches held delicately up above the ripples. Through it all Finn kept silent, and never showed by any sign that he could see the fairies with one eye.

He heard marvelous things, too. One morning, as he sat on the rocky stream-bank, a fairy lady and gentleman passed him. Except for their rather archaic clothes, he'd have thought them as human as he was. But when he closed his right eye and looked only with his left, they were gone. The fellow wore snug breeches and hose, the woman a high-waisted dress of dotted muslin and a quaint little bonnet. They walked arm in arm, and as they drew nearer, Finn heard what they said.

"The brewer's wife has been delivered of a strapping wee laddie," the fairy man said. "Bonnie gray eyes, I'm told, and golden curls."

"Ah, it will be good to have a young one about the hill again. How long has it been since a fairy child was born here?"

"Nigh on three hundred years," the man replied, then took the lady's hand and kissed it lightly. "You shall have your bairn, sweetheart. Tomorrow's new moon . . . I'll take him then. Have you fashioned the stock?"

"Aye," she said, and pulled from the folds of her garment a wooden figure carved in the likeness of a newborn with a pained expression on its scrunched face. "Like the bonnie boy it will look, but seem to wither with illness in three days, then seem to die. The parents will bury no more than a lump of wood, while the babe thrives under the Green Hill." The pair wandered on, and so Finn learned how fairies sometimes steal human babies, leaving the parents none the wiser.

On June 20, when Meg Morgan from her high perch spied him going off into the woods, Finn saw only two fairies, very small and unassuming, and to his mind not very interesting. At least at first. They were not beautiful, as were many of the flowery fairy maidens he saw, nor were they hideous enough to be fascinating. No, these were three feet tall and plainly dressed, except for a row of white feathers they'd attached in a line all along their sleeves.

Finn almost let them pass. This game, though enjoyable enough, was beginning to wear thin. He'd just about had enough of hobarts and hobgoblins, of pixies and sprites, and was considering whether he ought to tell the Morgans gloatingly about the fairy ointment, and maybe, after letting them beg for a week, consent to share a bit—only a bit, mind you—with them. A great secret unshared can only hold its appeal for so long.

As far as he knew, they hadn't seen any fairies since that fabulous first night. He wasn't sure exactly what they got up to all day, but it seemed that they never even left the grounds. Apparently, that one night of disobedience had been enough for them, and they tamely heeded the Ashes' injunction against leaving the Rookery.

Finn's only grounds for complaint—and, indeed, the thing that had kept him from telling the Morgans about the seeing ointment weeks ago—was that in all his spying he had never laid eyes on that fabulous creature, the Fairy Queen. Several of the lesser lords and ladies of her court had on occasion passed through the woods, but he wished more than anything to behold that vision he'd glimpsed dimly in Jenny Greenteeth's pool. Each day, he searched for the Green Hill he'd seen in the vision, but the sacred tumulus remained steadfastly hidden even from his magically seeing right eye. Though he was still hoping for a sight of her that day, in the end he decided that two drab fairies were better than none at all, and he followed the feathered pair along a deer path through the forest.

When the fairies go about their business, it is almost as if we humans are the invisible ones. Perhaps they really can't see us unless they put their minds to it. In any case, they often don't pay attention to humans at all. Which is fortunate for us, because most fairy attentions are hazardous one way or another. These two didn't seem to notice that Finn was following them, and if they did, they were too secure in their invisibility to worry about him. Finn wandered down the deer trail at a leisurely pace, as though he were out taking a casual stroll, all the while keeping the fairies just in sight ahead of him. As he traveled, he fingered the jawbreaker candies he carried in his pocket as provender. The fairies walked for a few minutes, then stopped at the base of a papery-barked white birch.

One of them looked up into the tree's upper branches and called, "Stay yer hand, old lady. I'm a-coming up!" The tree seemed to shimmy in answer, and the other boosted his friend up to the first low branch. With some difficulty—for birches are not the best climbing trees—the fellow pulled himself into the canopy, where Finn, pretending not to look, could see the branches rustle. A while later, the feathered fairy slid back down the trunk, sending out a spray of silvery shreds of bark.

"Still up there, all right," he said to his friend.

"Both of 'em?"

"Ye think I'd be so calm if they weren't? Two millennia, and I've never lost a life-egg yet."

"Two little eggs in the woods . . . What if a polecat et 'em, eh? What if a storm blew 'em out o' the nest? What would happen in the Midsummer War then?"

"Micawber, ye daft fool! D'ye think the White-Handed Birch Lady would let man nor beast near the eggs? Why, I'd like to see the polecat that's man enough to climb 'er, that I would. She's only safe with the likes of us. Didn't I tell her I was a-coming up? She'll be quiet for a few minutes now, but woe to the soul who tries to climb her if she's a-riled. Don't you fret, Micawber. Them eggs is safe enough. Least, until tomorrow night. Then one of 'em's doomed, Birch Lady or no."

"Have you caught sight of the Black Prince's champion? 'E's that fox-eyed feller as used to ride with the court. Never thought I'd see the day. His egg's the blue un."

"Haven't seen him. Don't see much of the court these days, what with . . ." Here he lapsed into a long and not very interest-ing account of his journeys to the Fens, the rheumatism he got there, his cousins who dwelled there, and his very tedious trip home. Finn almost left, but he guessed that the fox-eyed feller must be Bran, and stayed to hear more.

"Tomorrow night I'll be in for a treat to be sure," the Fenland traveler went on. "That other one he's fighting—'e's no more'n half his size, but to hear them tell it, he's twice as fierce. Should be a Midsummer War to remember."

His friend agreed, and patted the birch's trunk in farewell. "S'long, old girl," he said fondly.

"Are ye sure we shouldn't bide a bit, wait till she's her old fierce self again?"

The other fairy didn't think so. "Folks in these parts know to be on guard around her. They won't know she'll be harmless for a few more minutes. Them two eggs, and the lives they hold, are safe enough without us. Step smart, now, Micawber. I've got a barrel of last year's cider ready to be tapped." They marched away to their drink, and Finn took their place beneath the birch.

Now, Finn knew nothing whatsoever about the Midsummer War, and it never occurred to him that a person's life force could be held in an egg. But he did know from the fairy conversation that the eggs were supposed to be closely guarded, and so must be precious. And he knew that one of them, the blue one, belonged to his instinctive nemesis, Bran. Though he really didn't see how a birch tree could do him any harm even on her best days, he knew that, whatever her dangers, she was no threat for the moment. So, as soon as the fairies were gone, he hoisted himself into her slippery branches and took the two eggs, the blue and the speckled, and put two jawbreakers in their place.

It was a precarious trip down the boughs, and thrice he

almost dropped the eggs (and you know what would have happened to Rowan and Bran then), but in the end he touched ground safely, and headed home just as the Birch Lady came awake and shot a twiggy fist after him. He never realized how lucky he was to escape the birch's white hand. If it touches your skin, it sears a white mark and frequently brings madness. If it touches your heart, it brings death. Not to worry—most birches are kind, and dream their lives away. Very few of them are the deadly White-Handed Ladies.

Finn wrapped the eggs in a sock and tucked them in a mousehole he found in a fourth-floor garret, where he was almost certain no one would venture, and went to sleep satisfied. He did not know exactly what he had gained by stealing the eggs, but if he could in any way get even with Bran for his imagined slights and insults, it was a day well spent. Perhaps the eggs would have their uses, and at the very least, they might hatch into something interesting.

The Ashes made everyone go to bed early on the night before Midsummer Day—and of course most of them didn't sleep at all. James, sulky at being sent to bed, picked his scabs, his nose, and all of the embroidered ivy out of his pillowcase. Rowan stayed up late alone in his room, practicing sword strokes and blocks with his shield. Silly grumbled and read fitfully alone in her room for a while, then tried knocking on everyone's door. Rowan ignored her, Meg whispered shakily for her to go away, Dickie really was asleep, and Finn, rehearsing exactly how and when he'd reveal his intimate knowledge of fairies, told her testily to take a hike.

Meg finally fell asleep near dawn, but was awakened first by a dream of Rowan being killed by Bran, which was terrible, and later by a dream of Rowan killing Bran, which was nearly as bad. The world seemed to be out of its proper and logical alignment, and Meg felt younger than she had in a very long time.

The Longest Day of the Year

THERE ARE SO MANY WAYS in which we can divide up our world. We set people apart by their ages or faces, so that a man of fifty sees all boys of ten in a certain light, and all women of ninety in another. We cut the world into halves, and the northerners laugh at the southerners, and vice versa, while those in the east often cannot fathom those in the west. We call some animals elite— ourselves—and dismiss the personal lives of squirrels and fruit flies as inconsequential. We use time to divide the vastness into more manageable chunks, so that when one day ends we can let ourselves sigh with relief and prepare for a fresh one; each year is over and done with the moment it passes, and the past and the future have nothing to do with each other. For as long as there have been humans, the world has been temporally divided into discrete blocks by which we reckon our existence. For much of our history, the sun's cycle has been one of the most pronounced of such divisions.

As summer draws nearer, the sun rises earlier and sets later, so lengthening each day before Midsummer. After the Midsummer turning point, the sun wakes a bit later and goes to sleep a bit earlier, and so the days grow shorter, the nights longer. Midwinter, which is just before Christmas, is the shortest day of the year and the longest night.

Now, the people who figured all this out thought about the world a bit differently from you and me. We might celebrate the long days before Midsummer and the long (though declining) days after it with equal fervor. After all, the amount of sunlight at the beginning of September is roughly the same as that at the beginning of April.

But the ancients, and their descendants who still have fragments of the old ways in their lives, whether they know it or not, saw that boundary, that marvelous longest day of the year, Midsummer, as the beginning of a decline, the first sneeze as the year sickens and falls toward winter's death and darkness. You'd think Midsummer would be a time of unalloyed celebration, but, no, it is always tinged with the poignant realization that the best is over, the bloom has reached its fullness, and the rest is all downhill. A depressing lot, those ancients, though pragmatic. No matter that the rich bounty of harvest time still lay before them, or that harsh winter was still many months away. The longest day was passing, and the days would shrivel and shrink for the next six months. Contrariwise, though Midwinter has the longest night, the briefest day, it heralds the year's rebirth, and so that holiday is often a more hopeful celebration.

The Ashes were very businesslike about it all. They had some role in the village's Midsummer rituals during the day, which they accomplished without betraying to anyone that their relatives would fight to the death that very night. You might think that this was a strangely cold indifference, but for those who are accustomed to fulfilling obligations and steadfast in doing their duty, such mechanical obeisance to what is required is often the only way of fighting back emotion.

And also, you must understand, this ritual of the Midsummer War had been a part of Phyllida's life since her earliest years. She might not like seeing a young man die every seven years, any more than the shepherd likes selling his lambs for chops. But that was the natural order of things, and Phyllida told herself she'd be a terrible hypocrite if she suddenly protested against it just because two of the people she loved best in the world were involved. It *was* different—how could it *not* be different—but she made herself act as though it weren't. It had been going on for centuries, and there was no stopping it unless the participants themselves chose to.

Already Phyllida was in a state of mourning, for one or for the other, and somehow that made it easier. If you see your friend struck down by a bolt of lightning, the grief is so sudden, so shocking, that it can cripple you. But if you see your friend fall sick, and nurse him through the weeks before his end, why, you've spent those weeks already crying for him, and when the end does come, the sadness is somehow quieter, and the rawness of the grief has already been covered by time.

To keep them occupied and oblivious, she gave Finn and Dickie permission to attend the Gladysmere Midsummer festival on their own. Finn strolled to the village in the afternoon, but didn't see anything particularly interesting about a straw man covered in flowers, so he went back to the Rookery to amuse himself. It would just be another bonfire and a bunch of carousing peasants, he thought, neither of which held much appeal for him. Dickie likewise declined the offer, preferring to stay immersed in study with the Wyrm. If Phyllida hadn't had so much on her mind, she might have worried about his being cooped up so unsociably, away from his friends and the fresh air. But as long as he was comfortably out of the way, she didn't much care what he did on this day.

In the painstakingly planned ritual of the Midsummer War, the spectators—the Guardian and her associates, who served as official witnesses—were to arrive an hour before sunset. The reigning fairy court, the Seelie, would emerge from the Green Hill as the sun touched the horizon, and the challengers, the Host, would ride out of the woods at the moment the sun set. When the last rays hurtled through space, a few minutes after the sun himself had disappeared, the two champions would declare themselves, and the battle would commence. It would last until one of the humans had fallen, his blood shed on the Green Hill.

Meg emerged from her room late on Midsummer morning. She'd finally managed to snatch a few hours of sleep after the larks began their matins, but her eyes were red and her face was puffy from more than want of sleep. She walked despondently downstairs and found her siblings already gathered in the garden kitchen, talking furiously. Unnoticed, she stood in the doorway and silently despised Silly for being so callous, James for being so young, and Rowan for being such a fool, before she drifted away. She had virtually given up hope, and now only longed for it all to be over.

She wished she had someone to talk to, someone who might offer some words of comfort, or advice she'd be more willing to heed than Gul Ghillie's or the Ashes', who only told her again and again that she was powerless. But there was no one. She knew beyond a doubt that Finn was not one to offer her succor in this crisis. Dickie might have kind words, but when she sought him out in the library he looked so startled at the company that she could do no more than stammer a few senseless phrases and beat a retreat. Better, she thought, not to burden him with her troubles. Let him stay with his studies while she was left to deal with the painful reality. It never occurred to her that he might have uncovered something useful in the pages he perused.

Next she sought out Lemman, but the girl wouldn't even stay in the same room with her. No doubt she knew it was Midsummer. Did she grieve for Bran? Meg wondered. Or did she only wish that she were back with her own people on this, one of the fairies' most important days?

Eventually, in the afternoon, Meg went back to the kitchen, to find Rowan and his entourage gone. She forced herself to drink a glass of milk, which calmed her somewhat, then automatically poured a bowl for the brownie and left it on the counter. Much to her surprise, he appeared immediately and took a deep swig before settling down on a stool to wind a bundle of spun hemp into a ball.

"Here," Meg said, "let me help you with that." She took the

bundle and began to untangle it as the brownie wound the free end with his long, clever fingers. There is a magic to working with fibers. It is said that weavers see visions, and spinners will go into trances if they spin too long. Meg realized that convincing the strands to untangle helped to untangle some of the turmoil in her own mind. She found herself telling her troubles to the brownie, who through the tale said nothing, only wound the cord with hypnotic concentration.

"And I can't stop him," she said at the end. "I've tried every way I can think of to change his mind, but he insists on going through with it."

Brownies are as a rule taciturn fellows, and loath to speak. They only bother when they have something profound to say, so when they finally talk you'd be wise to pay them heed. The Rookery brownie said, "There's never a man changed another man's mind, nor one who controlled another's actions. All ye have charge of is yerself. Yerself and no other." And with that he tossed the now completed hemp ball into the air, and disappeared before it hit the ground.

"Fat lot of good that does me!" Meg called into the emptiness. When he started speaking, she'd felt a delicious glimmer of hope. Surely the brownie, one of the fairies, would know some way of keeping Rowan out of the Midsummer War. But no—just a trite homily on self-reliance. Disgusted, she decided to boycott the entire affair. She couldn't bear to see Rowan fight and perhaps fall, so she would hide away until it was all over, and learn how fate unfolded once it was too late.

When the Ashes began to call for her as evening came

creeping, Meg went to her favorite hideaway. Past the thick, luxurious furs of all the hunted animals, up the pitchy stairwell to her bird's-eye view of the declining orange sun. They'd be leaving any moment: the terrible Ashes who had let this happen though they should have known better; poor, stupid little Silly, who knew nothing of death, and had no idea this was anything more than an elaborate game; James, poor James, who would probably be playing with grubs and spiders in the dirt while his brother was being slaughtered; and Rowan himself, thinking he was an unconquerable hero, whereas she knew full well he was no more than a skinny, foolish boy. Let them go! Her grief had turned almost to anger now, and she hated every one of them for being so blind, so idiotic. Let Rowan go off and get himself killed like the poor misguided fool that he was....

She burst into tears she'd thought were long spent, and ran to the parapet. There were the Ashes, and Silly with James in her arms. She called out to them, but they were already specks on the road and couldn't hear her. Rowan! Had he left yet? No—he was supposed to go later, on his own, to the Green Hill. She had to find him. She didn't hate him. She had to tell him how much she loved him, tell him to be careful, remind him not to drop his shield too much in an overhand strike, as he was so apt to do. She wouldn't see him fight, but it became suddenly vital to see him before he left. He could not go off without her cautions, her advice, her love. It would be bad luck, tantamount to a curse.

"Oh, Rowan, where are you?" she whispered.

From her vantage point, she scanned the grounds, but Rowan was nowhere to be seen. In a frenzy she tore down the stairs, bruising her elbows on the cold stone walls. Furs tumbled to the floor as she pushed her way past, and when she struggled to be free of the fox stoles and beaver coats it seemed that some little animal sank its teeth into her shoulder. She wrenched free, and pulled with her a short cloak of deep scarlet with a collar of thick dark fur. She threw the cloak violently to the ground.

Two empty eyes looked forlornly up at her. Two limp paws trailed over the cloak, and a soft whiskered nose with a creamy chin rested against the ruby wool. It was an otter pelt, whole from tip to tail, fastened like an inconspicuous ruff around a forgotten cloak in an abandoned wardrobe. She told herself that it couldn't be. Surely they had searched the entire house? But even inanimate, the otter fur was somehow unnaturally alive. The holes where its eyes had been pleaded with her, and she'd almost have sworn that there was warmth from within that empty pelt. Rowan was momentarily forgotten. With awe she picked up the otter skin and cradled it in her arms, then went to the dairy.

Meg Morgan charged through the dairy doors, where she was at once confronted by the solemn face and unyielding bulk of the dun cow. She blocked Meg's path and refused to budge, looking at her in that particularly cowlike way that says, Sorry, but I really know best.

"You have to move!" Meg cried, shoving against the cow's bulk with her shoulder. But the cow knew that Lemman could bear no company that night, and would protect her against all unwelcome intruders. "Let me by!" Meg said, and then revealed the otter skin she held crushed to her chest. "This is it—it's been found at last!" The dun cow's eyes grew even larger and wetter, and with a grunting little moo she stepped back a pace and made a gesture like a bow. Meg rushed past her to the dairy annex, where she found Lemman in the company of a black-and-white kitten. She was holding it up to a large vat of milk so it could drink, and the ripples from the kitten's tongue were joined by others made by Lemman's falling tears.

"Lemman!" Meg called.

With infinite slowness, as though her slight form was bent under a grave weight, Lemman turned. Her fair hair hung lank in her streaked face, but still she was lovely . . . all the more so for her wretched sorrow. Meg held the otter fur out to her.

It was as though an incandescence suffused the dark dairy, and it washed over them both. With steps at first halting and heavy, then lightening as she came nearer, Lemman approached Meg and her pelt. Their hands touched, and Meg felt a warmth course through her veins. Then, before her eyes, Lemman changed. For an instant she seemed still a girl, but how altered! Her hair was billowing and clean, bright as a field of mustard flowers. She stood more erect, so lissome that her limbs seemed to float up— gravity and weight were nothing to her. A radiance emanated from her center, and she seemed more beautiful (and yet less terrible) than the Seelie queen herself.

And then she was a girl no longer. She dived into the pelt as though she was putting on a shirt, and as the thick, silky fur fell over her body, it became a part of her. There was an instant when Meg saw an otter head with bright, dark eyes atop human shoulders, and then the transformation was complete. Standing at her feet on splayed webbed paws was a very large, very joyous otter, its sharp white teeth bared in something like a smile.

Have you ever met an otter? Otters—even ones who aren't fairy girls in disguise—are the most carefree, happy beasts on this earth. Everything is play to them—the world was created solely for their enjoyment. The otter at Meg's feet shook itself from snout to tail in one delicious shiver, then (as the kitten watched uncertainly from the floor) leaped lightly to the rim of the vat of milk. It wasn't quite the quartz-clear waters of her natal river, but after years of being trapped in a human body, it was close enough. Lemman the otter dived into the vat with a milky white splash and swam in tight circles. She leaped and sported in her sleek, rediscovered body. At last, the first of her exuberance spent, she pulled herself out and jumped back to the dairy floor, shaking every last drop of milk from her coat (which the kitten, brave again, lapped up).

Meg, amazed, was laughing and crying all at once, and her vision was so blurred she missed the remarkable transformation back from otter into girl. When she could see clearly again, there was Lemman, barely recognizable as the poor pathetic prisoner who had worked the dairy. There was no denying she was a fairy now—no human ever looked the way she did. She might take human form, but no instant of carelessness would ever deprive her of her freedom again. Meg found herself somewhat in awe of Lemman now, and she bent her head and shifted from foot to foot nervously.

Lemman lifted Meg's chin with one alabaster hand and looked sweetly upon her. When she spoke, her voice was low and melodious, like a flute in its deepest tones. "My little savior!" she said. "My little friend. Always you have been kind to me, and now you have done me the greatest kindness of all. You have set me free, Meg Morgan. What a human stole from me, a human has returned. But for that, I'd have . . ." And for a moment Lemman's features shifted to a grisly mask of menace, and Meg fancied she saw sharp otter teeth between those human-seeming lips. It occurred to her that it was a very lucky thing Gus Leatherman was already dead, and beyond any vengeance.

Then Lemman's face softened again, and she was once more benevolent and beautiful. "Now the humans have my gratitude, and you most of all, little one. Friend to the fairies, friend to me . . . as long as you live, I will do everything in my power to aid you. Anything, that is, which does not cost me my freedom again." She gave a musical laugh. "What would you have, Meg Morgan? Riches? Your true love? A life unblemished by sickness or sorrow? Now that I have been restored, very little lies beyond my power."

"Please," Meg began, hardly tempted by those lofty offers, "my brother Rowan. He goes to the Midsummer War tonight."

Lemman looked as though she was retrieving a distant memory. "Ah yes. Your brave brother, and poor Bran, who longs for what is lost to him." All that had happened in her mortal years was rapidly fading away. Humans' cares were not hers, their fears and sorrows did not touch her anymore. Bran had offered her a measure of solace in her torment, but now even his life meant very little to her. She was immortal again, inhuman, and as far removed from them as a chilly mountaintop. But kindness always has a stronger hold than cruelty, and though she would shortly forget whatever pain and indignities she might have suffered at the hands of Gus Leatherman, her jailer, she could still feel a vague interest in the fleeting lives of Meg and Bran and those they loved.

"Please . . . Lemman . . ." She did not know if she could still call her that, now that she'd reclaimed her glory. "Can you keep him from fighting? Is there any way you can keep him safe?"

"Child, you know the laws of the Midsummer War. He is bound to fight unless he refuses to come and a willing substitute takes his place. The Seelie queen's power is such that he will never deny her. And who will stand in his place?"

"I will!" Meg said impulsively, though in truth the thought had been building within her ever since that night at the foot of the Green Hill when that little voice inside her cried, *Me! Let it be me!*

The epiphany was as shocking as diving into a glacial spring—her entire body seemed to gasp, and she trembled in astonishment even as her eyes opened with a startling new clarity. *I want to be the Seelie champion,* Meg thought. It was what she had wanted all along, not just selflessly, for Rowan, but selfishly, for herself.

The fairy looked down at her skeptically. "You would deny him his right, as the chosen champion, to fight, to kill or die, with honor?"

"I would protect him!" Meg said grandly.

"You would kill Bran, beloved of the fairies, your own ancestor?"

Meg gulped. She'd hardly considered that. At last she said, "If there is a hard thing to be done, I'd rather do it myself."

Lemman smiled at her. "Yes . . . after all, you are a woman, however young. Would it stop you if I told you I believe your brother will prevail in this battle?"

"Do you know that for sure?"

"I know nothing for sure," she said. "I do not know if the moon will rise tonight, or if the world will end tomorrow. But I believe your brother will take the field for the Seelie Court."

"That's not good enough. I have to protect him." She squared her shoulders and said again, resolutely, "I will fight in his place. Can you help me?"

"Call it not *help*, child. Call it merely granting your wish. I fear I do you harm in this, but, yes, I will do as you ask. I will keep Rowan from the fighting, and let you take his place."

"But can you really?" Meg asked, assailed by doubts now that there was finally hope. "He must refuse to come, of his own free will. How can you make him?"

Lemman laughed in a silvery lilt. "He is a man, and a child. If I care to, I can make him believe he's a locust or a grandfather or a statue of stone! He will see what I tell him is there, believe whatever world I choose to create for him. Have no fear for that, Meg Morgan. The fairy glamour has never yet failed with any living man. Do you think the Seelie queen the only one to hold such power?" She closed her eyes briefly. "He is in his chambers, thinking great thoughts, with his sword and shield spread before him. I will go to him now, and tell him pretty things, and sing him secret songs, until his mind is not his own. I will tell him that the Midsummer War is over and won, that he has acquitted himself like a champion and now reaps a hero's rewards. I cannot change his mind, but I can make him believe his duty is done. Thus, willingly, he will not go to his appointed place, and you will be there in his stead."

As she preceded Meg to the Rookery, Lemman offered one final piece of advice: "The minions of the Black Prince have been watching you all for quite some time. It will not take them long to divine the change of champions, nor would it be past them to attempt some treachery. The battle will be dangerous, but your journey to the battlefield may be just as hazardous. Go with care." And she went to find Rowan, to lull him with pretty lies and cozen him with unearned praise. Ere long, he found himself in a pleasant, proud stupor, and he lay content under her glamour without a thought of his obligations.

Meg ran to her own room to collect the Hunter's Bow, and as she strapped the full quiver to her back, she found that the dull target tips had changed of their own volition to wicked wedge-shaped points. The Seelie relics knew that war was upon them, and though they'd thought to have no part in this fray, they now made themselves ready. She touched the tip of one lightly, and it pierced the pad of her finger. First blood, she thought as she sucked her fingertip. If they can do that to me with a touch, what will they do to Bran?

She almost put the bow down, but gritted her teeth until her jaw hurt and clung to it. She remembered what Gul had told her about the one who made the bow, the Hunter. When an arrow hits home, his is the hand that launches it, but when the arrow misses, his is the hand that knocks it aside. Maybe there's a way around this, she thought. Maybe there doesn't have to be any blood on these arrows except mine. But she didn't know how.

The bowstring sang with an urgent pitch when she plucked it, and the leopard wood was warm to her touch. She shouldered the Hunter's Bow and scampered downstairs, pausing only to listen to the low sounds of Lemman's singing that came through Rowan's door.

The Rookery was dark and almost deserted, with most of the servants already in Gladysmere; those few who remained were busy in the kitchen putting the finishing touches on the lemon and ginger cakes that would be eaten after the Midsummer fires. Meg ran through the long, bare entrance hall to the front door. She flung it open, then slammed it shut again with a terrible scream. The servants, chatting over their work, didn't hear her. Nor did Finn, upstairs. But Dickie, on brief hiatus from his studies, was in the garden kitchen in search of sustenance, and he came running. (He'd changed for the better since coming to the Rookery—a few weeks earlier, that scream would have sent him running in the opposite direction.)

He found Meg still standing before the closed and bolted door, pale and panting. She jumped when he took her shoulder. "What is it?"

"There's something out there!" she said, looking as if she needed to sit down.

"What kind of something?" Dickie asked.

"I . . . I don't know. It was . . . it was . . ." That was just the trouble—she couldn't say what it was. It was horrible, she knew that much. Beyond that, she had no way to define it. When she opened the door, it had lurched toward her, making a sound like a slab of meat hitting the ground. But it didn't seem to have a proper shape, or perhaps its shape changed too fluidly to be identified. At first it seemed like a jellyfish, then a cloud, then a wet sheep without legs. It was like a cold, damp blanket about to envelop her, and then like a tentacled octopus, slimy, and as heavy as the ocean's depths. Even behind the closed door, it hovered in her memory, an amorphous form that threatened to overwhelm her by its frightful ambiguity. She was unaccountably terrified, with a tremulous, instinctive fear that went beyond the creature's appearance.

Dickie looked out the window, and to Meg's surprise didn't seem at all put out by what he saw.

"Couldn't you see it?" Meg asked. "Is it gone?"

"No, it's still there. Oh, look, now it's like a drowned dog! I never thought I'd see one!" Meg stared at him incredulously. Was this Dickie, or some apparition? "It's one of the Frittenings. They call it Boneless in some places, in others merely It. I've read all about them, but I never dreamed I'd be lucky enough to see one. Don't be afraid. That's what it wants. It can't do anything to you. It doesn't have a real body, or any powers other than changing form. But sometimes people die of fright when they look at it. It's kind of silly, really. Nothing scary in a soggy ball of yarn. Oh, that's better! Now it's more like a bloody side of beef. Oops, back to jellyfish again."

Timidly, Meg peeked out the window beside him. The thing was still there, changing shape furiously as she looked at it. She was a little less frightened, but, "I can't go out there, Dickie!"

"Why should you have to? It'll get bored and go away, eventually. Come up to the library, and I'll read you what they say about it in Shetland—"

"You don't understand. I have to go out. I have to get to the Green Hill and—" She stopped short, and he looked at her quizzically. Oh well, she thought. What harm can it do to tell him now? She explained the matter in three sentences, and was stunned to find that Dickie seemed to know all about the Midsummer War.

"And Rowan was chosen? That's odd. How'd you get him out of it? Oh, I see. That's the Hunter's Bow, then? My! I thought that was only a legend. What are you going to do about the eggs?"

Meg cut him off. "I need to go now. I have to get there—"

"Just after the sun sets, I know. Well, you don't have much time. Go on, then."

"I can't go out there . . . not with that thing looking at me."

"Don't be afraid of it. I told you, it can't hurt you, only scare you. I'll go out, too. Will that make it easier?" Who was this strange new Dickie, so casually brave?

"Will you come with me all the way?" she pleaded. "I think there might be other . . . things . . . that want to stop me."

"Oh . . . all right," he said, with a scholar's characteristic antipathy for the real world.

Dickie was right. Boneless hovered around them as they left the Rookery, and did its best to look disturbing, but when they showed no signs of being afraid, it grew disheartened and evaporated into a mist. By her side, Dickie babbled excitedly. "I really get to see the Green Hill? Wow, and the Midsummer War. You know, some say that it goes back to fertility rituals, but I think it really . . ." He found he had to save his breath for running. Meg set a fast pace, and he was hard-pressed to keep up with her.

The Black Prince's spies were in a tizzy that Meg Morgan seemed to be going in Rowan's place. While some little monsters darted off to try to warn their master before the war began, others set about interfering with her progress. Malicious stray sods tried to turn her around, but fortunately Dickie knew a charm against their trickery. All you have to do is turn a piece of your clothing inside out and they can't misdirect you.

On they went, past leering fairies who didn't quite dare attack, and into the woods. The moon was just full and, having risen a few hours ago, was waiting in the east to take the sun's place. In the west, the molten orb was sitting on the horizon—the Seelie Court would be gathering now, Meg thought as she pushed onward. In a few minutes, the Host would follow.

The evening was bright with the strange and shifting light that comes when two opposing heavenly bodies compete in the same sky, and Meg had no trouble seeing where to go. In fact, she rather wished she couldn't see quite so clearly, for the things that dogged their steps were getting worse, and she feared that at any moment they might spring on her. At least they kept her mind somewhat off what lay ahead of her in the next few hours. If she'd had a calm and uneventful stroll to the Green Hill, all the way there she'd have pictured Bran's death . . . and have tried with limited success not to picture her own.

Her hand stayed tight on the Hunter's Bow, though she did not draw it. Not only did she want to save her arrows for more dire need, but she guessed (rightly) that physical weapons would have little effect on fairies. Dickie seemed strangely unconcerned, and only exclaimed occasionally that one was a Jack-in-Irons (wearing a fashionable ensemble of chains and shrunken heads) and another a Redcap, who liked occasionally to redye his chapeau with fresh blood. To the one Dickie stuck out his tongue, to the other made an odd gesture, and both seemed utterly cowed. Dickie was as pleased as anything that his studies were serving him so well—so pleased, in fact, that he did not warn Meg in time to keep them both from stumbling into an oak coppice.

Oaks are the quintessential magic tree, long associated with old gods and the fairies. They live such a prodigiously long time that they are bound to be wiser than most other beings, and their roots are so firmly anchored in the earth that they have enormous strength, both physical and spiritual. Even the simplest peasant knows that "Fairy folks is in old oaks." Most oaks are benevolent enough, taking little interest in the affairs of others . . . until they are crossed. An angry oak makes a dangerous foe.

In the heart of Gladysmere Woods, there once lived a great oak, a mighty behemoth who had stood his ground since before the first Guardian had taken the land. He considered the forest his kingdom, and under the span of his canopy had cleared a vast shady spot where he held court to squirrels and birds while the other, lesser trees bowed around him. Then, one day, two drunken friends challenged each other to a contest—ten pounds lay on the outcome—as to who could first chop through half of the mighty oak of Gladysmere Woods.

Everyone in the county knew the great tree's reputation, and no others would dare harm it. But these fellows, for some reason, decided that the great old oak was the only fit challenge for them, so they set out to the solitary tree, drove a stake in the place they thought was the middle, and began to hack at the trunk with their axes.

It was a fool's mission, in more ways than one. They kept on all through the day, and made little headway through the dense wood. But a bet is a very important thing, and after going home to sleep their weariness off, they returned the next morning to hew and hack at the old oak. It took them three days to fell it, and in the end there was no winner, for the tree had its revenge. When only a narrow wedge of wood in the center was left holding the giant upright, the men crowded close, each trying to strike the winning blow. But felling trees is no sport for intimacy. In his fervor, one of the woodsmen miscalculated, and the stroke that went through the last of the trunk also went through a great deal of his friend's leg. As he fell to his knees to aid his dying friend, the tree toppled and crushed them both.

Even then the oak did not wholly perish. The tree that had withstood the centuries had fallen, to be prey to creeping slime molds and pill bugs, true, but the roots entrenched so firmly in the earth had a life of their own. From all around the stump of the fallen oak came up tender new shoots, deceptively slender and supple, but with the wisdom of the ages in their fresh young sap. And as it grew, the coppice seethed with a hatred of men, the creatures who had brought down but could not fully quell the majesty of the forest monarch.

Meg and Dickie found themselves caught in the midst of the

oaks before they knew it. Now the young trees were thick as a man's leg, with a tangle of grasping branches. Meg and Dickie struggled to free themselves, but the tree limbs held them tight, catching in their hair and fouling their clothes. Meg heard a rattling voice, like the wind through dry leaves, say, *Cold iron. Cold iron on my bones. Iron teeth tear my flesh. Vile little legged grubs bring iron once again. Strangle them before they bite. Break them before they cut with their cold, cruel iron.* Meg felt branches like rough hands close around her throat, and she tried to pull away, snapping brittle twig fingers all around her. But the branches held her fast, pressing ever tighter where the blood flowed on either side of her throat, and she felt her vision dim.

Then, from somewhere in the darkness that was closing in on her, she heard Dickie's voice, clear and confident, say, "Take off anything metal, Meg!" She tore off her belt with its steel buckle, and felt the wooden grip loosen somewhat. She managed to reach up to her hair and unfasten the silver clip that held her dark hair back. She could breathe now, and the blood was flowing freely to her brain once again, but she still couldn't pull out of the oak coppice. Dickie was free, and shouted to her from beyond the vengeful oaks to cast off whatever metal remained. With much regret, she slipped a little gold ring, a gift from her mother, off her pinkie, and let it fall to the leaf-littered ground. The oak arms released her, and in fact almost shoved her from the coppice. *Go, little grubs, and cut no wood.*

On they ran through the forest. The sun was gone now, tucked into bed behind the world, but still sending its last benediction of rays into Gladysmere Woods. Meg had only a few minutes to reach the Green Hill. She thought she was close, but it was hard to tell in the confusing light of silver moonshadow and golden-pink sunset. They passed the winding deer trail, and the bluebell meadow—the Green Hill should be near. She stopped a moment, catching her breath and getting her bearings. "This way . . . I think," she said to Dickie. Then her blood ran cold, chillier even than it had at the first sight of Boneless.

From behind her came a cry like someone being tortured. No, not someone—hundreds of someones, like a field full of fallen soldiers dying in the mud. She turned, and beheld that most dreaded of all the Host, the Nuckelavee.

To say that the Nuckelavee is like a centaur would give you the wrong impression. Centaurs have the body of a horse and the torso and head of a man—and so does the Nuckelavee. But centaurs are warlike and wise like kings of old, their man half sturdy and regal, their horse haunches strong, their coats glossy and rich in chestnuts and dapple grays. A great many of them are as handsome as any man you're likely to meet, and even the rougher sort are still pleasant enough to look at. Not so the Nuckelavee.

The Nuckelavee makes his home near the coasts, and rises out of the sea foam to bring blight and destruction. He is hideous to gaze upon, for he has no skin either on the horse half or the man. The Nuckelavee paused before Meg and Dickie, stamping its great mildewed hooves, and then began to approach the paralyzed pair like a walking anatomy lesson. Black blood coursed through its veins, and its exposed muscles were raw and red. White sinews and thick tendons twisted over its naked flesh as it moved. Behind it, vines withered and flowers bowed their heads and died, for the Nuckelavee spreads poison in its wake. A vile stench permeated the wood, and all living things with legs or wings fled.

Had she been the proper Seelie champion, bound and declared like Rowan, the Nuckelavee couldn't have touched her. It was against the rules (and how rulebound the fairies are!) to molest or hinder the designated champion. But she was as yet unofficial, and until the moment when Rowan failed to appear and she stood in his place, she was as fair game as any mortal who walked the earth. The dread Nuckelavee had traveled many miles from his salty home on the southern strand to serve his court, and he was hungry to rend and tear. He paced nearer and nearer, and Meg, with nerveless fingers, finally managed to draw her bow.

"No," Dickie whispered, and now at last, at this ultimate horror, he was trembling. "You can't hurt it. And don't run. It will hunt down whatever flies from it." He gulped, and took a deep, steadying breath. "You have to get to the Green Hill, Meg," he said, resignation plain in his tone. "If Rowan doesn't go, and no one shows up to take his place, the Host wins by default, and Rowan will still die at dawn without ever having raised his sword. Wait until I'm gone, Meg. Wait until I lead it away."

"Dickie, no!" It was too late. His short legs took off as fast as they were able, and his wheezing breath came hard. He wouldn't have had a chance, except that the Nuckelavee hesitated, looking at Meg. *There* was the one he was meant to stop. But she did not move, and the lure of fleeing prey was too much for him. With a scream he reared, his bare, bloody muscles bunching and dripping, and galloped after Dickie. When both were out of sight,

Meg ran in the opposite direction. Within a scant few paces, she burst through a curtain of brambles and stood disheveled, arms scratched and bleeding, her dark hair wild, before the silk-garbed, bejeweled, and shining nobles of the two fairy courts. Pale in the moonlight loomed the Green Hill. The sun's last rays had faded, and night held the land.

"The Time Is Come but Not the Man"

PHYLLIDA STOOD DIRECTLY BEFORE MEG, but she did not see her. Her gaze rested on the Green Hill crest, where a lone figure rose, dark, even in the strong light of the full fat-cheeked moon. Behind Phyllida, arrayed in order of age, were her family and Meg's. Lysander, seeming sturdy for all that he leaned heavily on his knobbly staff, looked as though he would like to move closer to his wife, to comfort her, as he was permitted to do in every other circumstance. But she was the Lady of the Rookery, the Guardian, and he only her consort. This task of bearing witness to the most dreaded scene she must endure alone. Near Lysander, Silly Morgan held her little brother against her hip, with his soft, round cheek pressed against hers. Could it be that Silly had finally come to realize the grave purpose behind all this pomp?

Indeed, the gathering was as magnificent as any festival. To the right of the Morgans, the Seelie Court waited, mounted or on foot. There at their fore was the queen—magically, impossibly fair, though even within this fairness, to Meg's clear-seeing eyes, there was a sickle sharpness, and a tension like that of a harrier as it hovers before a strike. Gul Ghillie—the Seelie prince—rode a stallion of steel gray, and both man and beast were armored in shining overlaid plates like a carp's pale scales. They tinkled when the horse stamped his foot anxiously. He, too, knew that there was a delay, an absence. The other members of the Seelie Court, from the proud lords and ladies with swords or long, cruel knives at their hips, to the assorted hobs and sprites and grotesques behind them (some with weapons just as fell, some with rolling pins or skillets or thorny sticks to strike the foe), were in an unmoving phalanx, waiting for their prince and general to sound the call to the fray.

But it was the Host, as challengers, that had the first word, and the Black Prince rode at the fore of his snarling and fair company—for you must not forget that some of the most malignant fairies are also the most enticing.

"So," he began, his voice rich and languid, his hand resting lightly on the hilt of his sword, "another seven years have passed, another teind to be offered. I come to do battle, Seelie swine!" He drew his weapon magnificently and held it aloft. "I come to claim what is mine—my kingdom . . . and my queen." He bowed insolently from horseback. "My champion stands ready on the Green Hill. Bran is his name. I think you are acquainted with him." The prince sneered. "He fights for me now!" He pulled hard on the reins and dug his heels into his steed's flanks to make him rear.

The Seelie prince's horse took a step forward without apparent urging, and his rider spoke. "Life, once begun, has no end. Conflict, when it is joined, will never cease. All things change, but all things endure. We have diminished, as the world has diminished. Once, gold fire burned hotter than it does now, and silver ice was colder. Still, since fairies and humans marched together into this land, we have maintained the rites of the dying year. And every seventh year, when the rule of these courts is decided, two humans meet in battle. One will stand at dawn to greet the shortening days. One will give his blood to the earth, to the Green Hill at the center of the world. Which is honored more, and which can, in truth, claim the longest life?"

He abandoned the ritualistic words and scrutinized the Black Prince. "I do not ken with what base trickery you convinced the noble Bran to fight for you. But know this. The outcome will be the same. Blood is yet blood, life is still life." He looked—sadly, it seemed—to the lone, dark monolith on the hill. The outline of an ax was clearly visible, silhouetted against the star-speckled sky.

The Black Prince laughed. "It takes no trickery to let a man do what he wishes! My champion came willingly, as they all must." His face turned sly. "But what of yours? The little manchild. Has your mighty champion changed his mind? Does your hero quake in his cradle? Come! The sun is set, the Midsummer War must begin! Where is your warrior?" And he laughed again, looking over the human gathering and seeing no more than an old woman and man, two girls, and a small child. He did not notice the Hunter's Bow in the elder girl's hand, nor did he discern the grim resolution in her countenance.

There was a flurry through the crowd, a hushed murmur from the Seelie and low rough sounds from the Host. The Seelie prince stood in his stirrups and raised his hand for peace. "The time is come!" he cried into the night. "The time is come, but not the man! Who stands as champion for the Seelie Court? Who will kill, or die, on the Green Hill?"

"I will," said a small voice that was almost lost in the strengthening wind. And then, "I will!" cried with something like a warrior's strength. From the cluster of mortals walked a girl as slim as the crescent moon, with the full moon's own glow upon her face. She stood upright, graceful, and sure. In her left hand she held the finest bow ever crafted. Already she had an arrow nocked to the string, and the deadly tip, crimsoned with her own blood, pointed at the earth. Into utter silence she called out again, "I will stand for the Seelie Court!"

Lysander had to grab Phyllida to keep her from falling backward in a faint. Silly screamed, but the fairies, taking it for some banshee war-cry, lifted their own voices in wild yells and ululation. From all around Meg came the glorious sound of a thousand swords being drawn, that slick hiss of metal on metal, and the harsher sound as the fairies beat their weapons against shields or their own armor in a martial tattoo, and advanced upon their foe. The Midsummer War had begun.

Now that she was committed, Meg was at a loss. Was that all the preliminary? Was she to go now and slay Bran if she could? He still stood there on the unravished summit as, all around the base and into the shadowed woods, Seelie fell upon Host and Host hacked at Seelie in a jumbled, disorganized melee. It was like the fairy dances, frenzied and, she would have said, joyous, were it not for the horrible things she saw going on all around her. She flinched as, to her left, a one-legged, one-armed, one-eyed member of the Black Prince's court smashed a mace into a creature that looked a great deal like the Rookery brownie. Beyond them, several grimacing Redcaps had banded together to drag a knight of the Seelie Court off his rearing and foaming horse. They piled on top of him when he hit the ground, and she never saw what became of him.

The Seelie Court was more than holding its own. Knights and ladies skilled in warfare charged through the ranks of the Host, lopping off heads and dealing deadly blows. But not a single weapon touched Meg, nor did the fairies seem at all aware of her. They had their battle to fight, the two humans theirs. Only once did a fairy pay her any mind. The Seelie prince, his sword blooded, reined in his horse at her side just as she'd decided the only thing for her to do was climb the hill and face Bran. He bent in his saddle, and for a moment his face shifted and he was the impish Gul Ghillie she knew so well. The sight reassured her somewhat.

"Have no fear, Meg Morgan. This was meant to be, though I could not see it. There are others, perhaps, greater than you or I, who knew this would come to pass. Trust them. But trust more in yourself. I've seen you split a hempen thread at a hundred paces."

He galloped off with a savage cry before she could tell him that merely hitting her target wasn't the problem. The problem was that the target was Bran. As fairies fell all around her, their strange blood like quicksilver on the wild thyme, Meg mounted the hill to her fate.

For the first few steps she could still hear the fierce fighting just behind her, the clash of swords and cries of the wounded, and, scarcely heard but even more terrible, the low sounds of bones being crushed under bludgeons. She spared a thought for Dickie, somewhere out there, pursued (though perhaps not pursued anymore) by the Nuckelavee. *There* was bravery. In the moment of crisis, insignificant, ignored Dickie had shown his mettle and very likely given his own life for her sake. She didn't know what made him do it, and was sure that she, in such circumstances, could never be capable of such heroism. She did not consider standing in Rowan's place to be particularly heroic; it was simply something that had to be done. She did not realize that necessity lies at the heart of most bravery. In any case, she did not feel very courageous now. Her legs trembled so she could hardly negotiate the slope.

As she walked, the sounds of battle grew dim behind her, until, halfway up the Green Hill, they were muffled to no more than the dull, constant roar of waves beating the strand. When she looked back, she found that a mist had settled over the lowlands, obscuring the fighters. None of them ventured up the hill. She and Bran were alone.

The woods might be shrouded in fog, but the hill stood in unnatural clarity, vivid in an uncanny light. Bran recognized it as the twilight of the fairy kingdom beneath the Green Hill— never in sunshine, never dark, but existing always in an eerily bright half-light. Colors were too sharp, but outlines were

muted, so everything seemed somehow less real, more beautiful than nature had made it. The thyme and pennyroyal Meg
bruised beneath her feet were brighter than spring's first leaves,
and the leopard spots of the Hunter's Bow glowed like radiant
amber. The air itself seemed bright and sharp—they might have
been submerged in an unrippled spring, or in a block of clearest
quartz. Bran was the only dark thing on the hilltop, and he stood
immobile, ax at his side, a pillar carved of wood.

I could shoot him now, Meg thought. He's standing plain in
the open—it would be an easy shot. All the more so because at
this distance she could not see his face through the shadows that
seemed to cling to him. It would be just like hitting a target. Forget that he's a man, forget that he's even alive. Just place the arrow
where you want it, as you have so many times before. Forget that
he has suffered. Forget that he's Phyllida's father. Forget that
he's your own great-great-grandfather. Forget that he is tall and
handsome and alive, so very alive, as you are now, as you hope
to remain. And remember what Phyllida herself has said to you,
that he will not hesitate to kill you, and what the Seelie prince
said, that one of you must die this night.

All of this she told herself as she stood midway up the Green
Hill, looking at Bran, her opponent, her enemy. But she did not
draw her bow.

"There must be some other way," she said aloud, and the air
around her seemed to shiver, like a still pond when a minnow
leaps for joy. Just because the same thing had happened every
seven years didn't mean it had to happen this time. This strange
world might be in Meg's blood, but a lifetime spent away from it,

nurtured in Arcadia's intellectual hills, deep pondering gorges, and lively skeptical streams, had taught her that tradition is only good to the extent that it makes people happy or serves a purpose. And history is not a course to be repeated but, rather, a litany of mistakes to help shape a better future. The gravity of ritual and the overwhelming force of the expectations of others had for a time stifled her powers of reasoning. She went along with all this—the Midsummer War, the kill-or-be-killed—because everyone around her seemed to assume that there was no other way. She forgot for a time that she was Meg Morgan, not a slave to tradition, not a pawn in this game between fairies and humans. With new strength, the strength not of a warrior but of a diplomat who is yet ready to fight should negotiations fail, she marched up to join Bran at the summit.

They stood perhaps twenty feet apart, just enough so that Meg would have time to draw the Hunter's Bow to meet even the swiftest charge. Her bow was down, but there was still an arrow to the string and three fingers curled around it. She could fire a killing shot in an instant.

Bran wore plated armor of some strange, darkly luminous metal, like silver when it tarnishes. A close-fitting helm capped his head, and his shaggy locks, escaping, curled back over it. The ax in his hand was wrapped in red-dyed cord, and the blade was flecked with a crusted, dark substance, for by tradition the Host weapon was never cleaned after it had done its job. Bran's full mouth was set in a grim line, and as she neared he shifted his grip on the ax. Meg, sure that he was set to attack her, half drew her bow. Before she could fully raise it, she looked into the eyes of the man she would have to kill, expecting to find bloodlust there, something hard and stern and unfathomable to her. But there was only sorrow in Bran's golden eyes, and something like the despair she felt herself. She lowered the Hunter's Bow.

"Why do you prolong it?" Bran said, his voice low and tight, lips scarcely moving. There was pain in that voice, but also a sort of savagery, like the pitiable beast caught in a snare. "Why didn't you finish me from down there?" He gestured to the base of the hill with his ax, swinging it in a wide arc. Meg flinched and again raised her bow, but held her ground. "It would have been easier for both of us. We shouldn't have to look into each other's faces . . . at the end. Shoot! Now!"

Meg looked at him without comprehension. Bran spread his arms wide and advanced on her. "This armor is nothing to a bow like yours. End it—now. Quickly, as you love me!"

And then it dawned on her, as she watched Bran come nearer, his face a mask of anguish and bitter expectation. He had never betrayed them. He had not forsaken his family to regain the paradise he had lost. No, Bran served the Host only as willing sacrifice. To keep Rowan from being slain, he made sure the Host champion was the one man who would let himself be killed in the Midsummer War. Bran had fooled the Black Prince, who thought to purchase his services with a promise of rewards. *Midsummer comes, and my time draws near. . . . Soon my pain will be ended. On Midsummer Night, I will know if such a price can buy me peace at last!* His longing to return to the fairy world under the Green Hill was like a sharp-toothed beast gnawing at his vitals. He would indeed pay a great price to escape the daily suffering he endured. But the price was not slaying his kin. It was his own life. In death, he hoped to win the peace that he could not find in the dry, colorless world.

"Bran . . . oh, Bran!" She could say no more.

"Don't hesitate, girl! Don't think about it. Draw and shoot. There is no other way!" His armored chest was laid bare, and the Hunter's Bow quivered in her hand.

She steeled herself. "I won't kill you. And if you won't kill me, then there's nothing they can do." She glanced down to the battlefield at the foot of the hill, but she could see no signs of life. "We'll just go down there and tell them. No one will die this year." It seemed perfectly reasonable to her. After all, the fairies could not force them to do battle—despite what she had once believed.

But Bran, to her amazement, only laughed grimly. "You think to change the order of things? You think the sacrifice will not be made merely because you say so? Even if we lay down our weapons now, one of us will die at dawn. My life is theirs, as is yours. At dawn, one of the eggs that hold our lives will be crushed." (But my life isn't in an egg, Meg thought. Only yours and Rowan's. What will that mean in the end?) "It will be mine, for your will to live is strong. And then I will die a death more horrible than any your arrow can inflict. Kill me, Meg. Better to be slain cleanly by a friend than to have my life ripped away from me, my body torn apart by the rabble. I am not meant to see the dawn. Do me the kindness of letting me die as I wish, cut down by the Hunter's Bow. It will be an easy death."

꒰ 263 ꒱

Meg, stunned by his words, backed up a pace. "I won't ... I can't! I'll tell Gul ... I mean the Seelie prince. He'll understand."

"Do you think they care for you, Meg Morgan? Or for me? We are nothing to them. We live for an instant in a brilliant flash, then fade away. What is that to one who will live as long as the earth itself? The war to them is only another bacchanal; they have no understanding of what it means to end a life, to fall at the hands of another. They ape our lives and our deaths down there, but it is no more than mummery. Come tomorrow, they'll all be the same as ever."

"But ... I saw them fighting. I saw fairies being killed."

"You saw what they wanted you to see—as we all do. In the fairy glamour, you saw a war, you saw Seelie and Host kill each other. But it's no more real than a dream, Meg. No more real than ... than the years I spent under the Green Hill. You and I are the only real things here. And soon it will only be you. There is no other way, child." His eyes were suddenly kind and pitying. "It should have been your brother. You should have been spared this. But it does not matter now. Do what you must, Meg Morgan, and do it quickly."

"I won't!"

"One of us must die this night! Do it!"

"No!"

"Then I will give you no choice," he whispered, and with a wild war-cry swung his weapon once around his head and then charged at Meg, ax poised to lop off her head.

Her eyes were closed when she loosed the arrow, but her aim was true. She opened her lashes to a brilliant dawn, not knowing if she'd stood on the Green Hill a minute or a year. Before her lay Bran, pierced through the chest by a white-fletched arrow, his arms splayed wide, the fell ax on the grass near his lifeless hand. A black cloud rose from the direction of the Rookery, grim against the golden sky. The rooks were coming to the battleground.

The Ash Is Hewn

SIX LORDS OF THE SEELIE COURT bore Bran's body home. The Seelie prince himself carried the unconscious Meg in his arms and laid her in her bed. She'd collapsed as the first crows settled on the fairy remains strewn at the foot of the hill.

Had she been awake, though, she would have seen a strange sight. Just a few minutes after dawn, as the survivors of the Midsummer War were regrouping, the corpses began to stir. Decapitated bodies groped the ground blindly in search of their missing heads. Fairies got into heated arguments about whose severed limbs were whose, and accused others of trying to get better arms and legs than they'd started out with. When body parts and owners were reunited, they snapped seamlessly back into place and worked as though they had never been sundered. Soon not even a bruise or a bent leaf on the ground indicated that there had been a fierce battle the night before. Bran was right. However terrible the war had seemed, it was in truth no more than a pantomime, a mockery of human life and death. The dead fairies were revivified, the injured healed, and all was exactly as it was before. Except for Bran.

According to the custom of the countryside, they laid Bran on the dinner table, for in most farmer and shepherd households that (or the marriage bed) is the only furnishing stately enough to display a body. The fairies left them, and Phyllida and Lysander stripped Bran of his armor. With gentle hands, as though any roughness could hurt him, any pain reach him, his daughter worked the arrow free and bathed the wound. When the blood was wiped away, there was scarcely a mark, only a narrow slit on his left breast. It did not seem possible to Phyllida that so small a wound could cause the demise of a man as great as Bran. Even on the endless banqueting table, he seemed imposing. Even in death, there was grandeur to his body, power in limbs now pale. Her father, her mountain! He had been gone from her life those many years, and she'd not lost hope. But what hope was left to her now? She bent her head to his chest, and wept for a father twice lost to her.

Upstairs, Meg was just coming around. At any other time, fainting would have been a matter for harshest ridicule. Now Silly was sympathetic and uncharacteristically tender with her sister. She petted her head and held her hand until Meg sat up and looked around. Silly expected her to burst into tears—and wouldn't have blamed her. But though Meg's face was ghastly, she did not weep. She felt drained and empty, too weary for words. If any emotion remained in her now it was anger—with possibly just a little relief when she remembered that Rowan's life had been preserved.

"Where is Rowan?" she asked.

"In his room," Silly said. "Asleep, or something like it. I shook him, but he wouldn't wake up."

"Dreaming of his victory . . . ," Meg murmured, then, "Dickie! Oh . . . he . . ."

"Dickie's downstairs. His clothes are a mess, and he looks a little smug, but he's fine other than that. What happened to him?"

Meg told her the story as far as she knew it, from finding Lemman's otter pelt to Dickie's heroism. Silly was fascinated by the horrible Nuckelavee and utterly overcome by the thought of Dickie's rash bravery. "And to think I've been making fun of him all this time, laughing at his sneezing and wheezing." And she made a noble vow never to think badly of anyone again . . . a resolution she managed to keep exactly one day.

"Did they bring Bran back here?" Meg asked.

"Yes. He's downstairs."

She swung her legs out of bed. "I'm going down to see him."

Silly caught her arm as she was leaving. "Don't be too hard on yourself, Meggie. You did what you had to do."

"Did I? That doesn't make it any better."

Meg crept quietly into the room where Phyllida was still bent over Bran's body. I did that, a little voice chastised her. That terrible thing . . . I did that. But he would have killed me. No, he wouldn't have. But I killed him. The guilt of a child obeying its elders or a soldier following orders is particularly poignant.

Meg made a little sound, and Phyllida turned, flinching like a frightened animal. How can I look at her and not hate her?

Phyllida thought. And yet how can I look at her and not thank the powers that she's alive? Meg stood at her side, mourner and victor, and looked down at the lifeless man, wondering, as all do when a vital thing grows still, whether it was not some illusion. Oh, if only it were another fairy glamour, Meg thought.

"I wonder . . . ," Phyllida began softly, but trailed off.

"What do you wonder?" Meg asked.

Phyllida said, as if talking to herself, "I wonder if it would have been best to leave him where he was. He was happy under the Green Hill. His return brought happiness only to me. He found none himself."

She fell silent, and after a time, unbidden, Meg told her the day's tale. Phyllida was momentarily roused from her sorrow when she heard of Lemman's restoration to fairyhood. "Bewitched the boy, did she?" Phyllida said with the barest glimmer of a smile. "And now he dreams that his deed is done. Has she gone? I'd like to see her, to wish her well. But no doubt she's eager to quit this place." She dabbed at her eyes with a handkerchief embroidered with thistle heads, and pulled herself away from Bran's body with some effort. By force of will, she became at once practical and businesslike. She was the Lady of the Rookery, the Guardian, and she had duties to do.

"Get Silly and James, and Rowan if you can rouse him, and come to the ash grove. We must cut down Bran's ash tree."

Rowan slept on, a faint smile on his face, and though Meg was somewhat alarmed that she couldn't wake him, he seemed otherwise healthy. Part of Lemman's glamour, Meg thought, and assumed it would wear off eventually. She gathered Silly and James, and on the way found Dickie. Since he'd played such a vital part in the previous night, she asked him to come along.

"How did you get away from the Nuckelavee?" Silly asked him. "It sounds terrible."

But Dickie shrugged it off as if it were no great matter. "Nothing's so bad if you know what its weaknesses are. A Nuckelavee can't cross freshwater, 'specially if it flows south. They come from the ocean, you know. This one must have taken quite a circuitous route to get here without crossing any. Anyway, I just ran until I came to the stream—which happens to flow south at that point—and then thumbed my nose at him from the other side. My friend Tim Tom was there. He's a Urisk. He doesn't look like much, but the Nuckelavee seemed to be afraid of him. Tim Tom sprang across the stream, and the Nuckelavee galloped away. Nothing to worry about, really." Still, he basked under Silly's admiring gaze.

They met Phyllida on the lawn by the ash grove, and stood with her until Lysander strode from the shed with an ax that reminded Meg unpleasantly of the past night. But this one was heftier—a woodsman's ax, with a thicker, duller head and a wooden haft worn smooth in the shape of Lysander's hands, which were nearly as strong at eighty-six as they had been at twenty. He presented himself before Bran's ash tree as though it were a person, taking off his hat and bowing.

"Bran is felled!" he called. Did the mighty tree tremble, or was it only the morning breeze that made its limbs quake? "Bran is hewn! Bran is dead!" And he raised his ax to smite the tree that was Bran's partner, that held a piece of his life.

But the ax never fell. Even in the bright morning sunshine, a new radiance was seen, pale gold and glowing as it came from the forest. Lemman walked like a wood goddess, a serene divinity come to ease their woe. For there was no doubt in the minds of those who saw her that any pain would be lessened, any trouble made lighter, just by her presence. Lysander froze at the sight of her.

"Stay your hand," she said. There was a gentle smile on her lips, as though she had an amusing secret she thought she might share. "Would you deny Bran his last chance at life?"

Phyllida stepped forward. "Bran was killed at the Midsummer War, slain by the Hunter's Bow. His body lies within the Rookery."

Lemman looked at Phyllida with mingled kindness and pity. "Ah, Phyllida! In all your years as the Guardian, haven't you learned that things are not always quite as they seem?"

"But he's dead, Lemman! He's been dead for hours. I tell you, he lies in the Rookery, and now his ash must be cut down." She felt as though Lemman was mocking her.

"But how can he be dead, good Guardian, if the egg that holds his life is yet unbroken?"

"That cannot be," Phyllida insisted. "It was broken at dawn, pushed from the nest by the bird that hatched from the other egg."

Lemman laughed, and the sound filled Meg with unlooked-for hope. "The two courts are in a tizzy, running mad through the woods!" Lemman said. "Never has such a thing happened. This child has stirred things up to no end, and now the cauldron bubbles over." She blessed Meg with a smile. "The white-feathered life-egg keeper has fled the country in disgrace."

"What do you mean?" Phyllida asked, knowing, but unwilling to let false hope tear at her heart.

"The two life-eggs can't be found!" Lemman cried, joyous at the joke. "The keeper's friend Micawber swears they were fine the day before the Midsummer War. The White-Handed Birch Lady says nothing, though I think she must have been asleep. Someone made off with the eggs, and the ritual cannot be completed. Though his body lies dead, Bran's life is held... somewhere. Who can say where? If his body and his life can be united, then it must be that Bran will live again. Even the laws of the fairies must bend to the laws of nature. He is not really dead as long as his life is preserved in the egg."

"Rowan's life is in an egg, too," Meg said. "When I took his place, it happened so fast—weren't they supposed to put *my* life in an egg? What's to become of Rowan now?"

At this, the faintest line appeared on Lemman's brow. "A life-egg only hatches when one wins the Midsummer War—then the bird flies back to the body, and the person is whole again. Now both eggs are in limbo. If Rowan's is broken before it is returned to him, he will die."

Meg stifled a cry in her hand. Would it come to this, that, despite the sacrifices, she would lose them both? "Where could they be? Who would take them?"

"Even the fairies do not know, though they search the woods now. The only thing certain is that Rowan's egg is yet whole, for he lives, though he sleeps between life and death. The charm I laid on him is passed, and now a greater spell holds him. His egg at least must be found, lest two are sacrificed in the Midsummer War."

"We'll find both of them," Phyllida said resolutely. All traces of tears were gone. She was a woman of action again. Bran was not dead, any more than when he'd lived under the Green Hill. For the moment he was out of her reach, but now that she knew there was a chance to win him back, no force on earth could stop her.

Let the eggs be discovered! Meg thought desperately. Let my terrible deed be undone!

"How can we find them?" Luck had brought her Lemman's otter pelt, but who could find two tiny eggs in all the world?

"The fairies search the forest," Phyllida said. "If they get the egg first, won't they . . . ?" She looked to Lemman.

"Yes. According to the rites of the centuries, they will break Bran's egg, and he will pass forever into unknown places. But Rowan's egg they will return, for his life is no longer forfeit."

"Will you help us, Lemman?" Phyllida asked, beseeching.

"What I can do, will be done," Lemman said. "In return for the kindness you have shown me in my captivity. But should my people find the eggs first, it will be as I have said. So it has always been."

"I'm sick of things being the way they've always been!" Meg shouted suddenly, and glared fiercely at Lemman, as representative of all her folk. Meg stormed off to the house. What could she do? How could she find them where all the fairies had thus far failed?

As she went through the Rookery, she slammed as many doors as she could. This made her feel a lot better for a little while. She had to do something to feel as though she was helping, but she really had no idea where to begin. She was on the verge of frustrated tears again when Finn, roused by the commotion, poked his head around the corner.

"'Sup, Meg? Skin yer knee? Didn't get invited to the fairy ball?" But she shot him a look of such ferocity that he sobered and asked her, with more sincerity than he generally displayed, what ailed her. Another time, she might have been softened by any genuine interest from Finn, but on that day she snapped at him.

"Get out of my way! I'm looking for something!" She tried to shove past him—though there was really no more reason to look in that room than any other—but he blocked her path.

"What are you looking for?" Anything she was that upset about was bound to be good.

"None of your business! Shove off!" Still he stood in her way, and asked her again.

She had enough self-control not to hit him. When she had tried twice more to sidestep him and failed, she finally said, just to get rid of him, "Two eggs. I'm looking for two eggs, okay? Now, get out of my way!" Here she did give in to some violence and pushed him, then ran past him into the downstairs library, where she hastily scanned every shelf without hope. She was about to run to the next room—she'd likely have searched every room in the Rookery until she collapsed from nervous exhaustion—but, once again, Finn barred her path.

"Two eggs?" he asked, and there was something in his voice, a certain slyness to his face, that brought her up short.

"What do you know?" she demanded, her body taut and her little face tense.

"Oh . . . well . . . there's eggs in the kitchen, and eggs in the henhouse. . . ."

"Finn!"

"Making an omelet? Soufflé?"

"Finn, please! Do you know where the eggs are? One's speckled brown, and the other's . . . Oh, I don't know what the other one looks like, but they were out in Gladysmere Woods, in . . . in a birch tree, I think. Oh, Finn, if you know, you have to tell me. Rowan's life depends on it. And Bran . . . he . . . he's . . ."

Rowan's life depends on it, eh? Of course Finn took this metaphorically. And Bran? How did he fit in? Well, anything he could do to hurt Bran was all to the good. He hadn't been in the dining hall that morning.

"I don't think I know anything about *those* eggs," he said.

"I'll do anything!" Meg said desperately. "I'll give you anything—anything at all! I need to find those eggs!"

Finn was exactly where he liked to be—in a position of power. Now, what could he get in exchange for some rotten old eggs? The Morgans didn't have any possessions he coveted, nor could he at the moment think of any suitably humiliating task for Meg to perform. Then something marvelous occurred to him. He'd found a hundred times more fairies than all the Morgans put together, for, as far as he knew, they'd never seen any after that first night. But they'd bested him in one way—they'd viewed the Green Hill. That was what he longed for—no man can get the barest glimpse of the Seelie queen and not burn for another sight of her. The weeks of searching, though they might have brought him geographically near the Green Hill, had afforded Finn no view of it. But the Morgans must know where it is.

"Take me to the Green Hill," Finn said.

Meg was momentarily shocked out of her worry about the eggs. "What do you know about the Green Hill?" she asked him.

He chuckled. "Oh, plenty. I know plenty about all the fairies. I've seen hundreds of 'em!" Gloatingly, he told her about the seeing ointment and all it had revealed. "And you thought you could keep it all from me. Ha! No one keeps a secret from Finn Fachan—not for long. And maybe, just maybe, I'll let you use some of the ointment. But I won't tell you how to make it. That's my secret."

If he was expecting her amazement to last, Finn was doomed to disappointment. Once she was over the initial surprise that he knew anything about the fairies, she was not particularly impressed. After all, she had, in the past night, seen far more fairies than she cared to, and would be just as happy never to see another as long as she lived. Finn felt momentarily crushed. Though he'd never admit it, the primary goal of his existence had become impressing the Morgans.

"If you ever want to see those eggs again, you better take me to the Green Hill."

Meg, though she was desperate, equivocated. "I don't think that's a good idea, Finn. The fairies don't like spies. They might do something nasty to you if you see the hill without their permission."

"None of the other fairies cared. They didn't even know I could see them. Come on, do you want the eggs or not? If you don't take me I'll break 'em."

Meg looked panic-stricken, and Finn knew he'd won. "I'll take you," she said slowly. "But don't blame me if something happens." The maternal instinct that arises in some girls years before they ever become mothers told her not to take him to the Green Hill. But those instincts were more strongly telling her to protect Rowan and save Bran, and she decided that if Finn wanted to play the fool he must chance the consequences.

"All right, then, where are the eggs?" Meg said. Finn laughed at her.

"Oh no, Meggie—not as easy as that. D'you think I'm stupid?" She didn't deny it. "You take me to the Green Hill first, and when we get there, I'll tell you where the eggs are."

"You really will? You promise?"

He shrugged. "You'll find out when we get to the Green Hill." Somehow, this reassured her. She would have been uneasy if he'd tried to swear his honesty. When people insist too vigorously that they'll be honorable, it generally means they're plotting treachery.

"Just tell me—are the eggs safe?"

"Safe and sound. Why are they so important to you?"

She couldn't tell him the truth, and stammered a story that sounded plausible. "Rowan stole them, and there'll be trouble if he doesn't give them back." If not for the sore temptation of the Green Hill, Finn would have left Rowan to his troubles. But alas, he thought, some sacrifices have to be made for the greater reward.

They slipped out of the Rookery, and Meg led him through Gladysmere Woods to the Green Hill. It stood bare before his eyes, and didn't look very impressive. A wren darting low above the slope was the only sign of life. But in his pocket was a little jar of seeing ointment, and soon, he thought, the fairy court in all its finery would appear to him. He imagined himself being welcomed by fairy ladies, praised for his courage and ingenuity in finding their lair, rewarded with secrets and treasures. . . .

"Where are the eggs?"

"In a mousehole in a little room on the fourth floor."

"Which one?"

"Which mousehole?"

"Which room!"

"I don't know. It's a nasty, dusty little place. Oh, I remember— the pear tree is right below it. You know, the one that climbs against the wall—"

That was all Meg needed. She took off back to the Rookery at a run.

Twenty minutes later, Meg held the two eggs in her cupped palms—Rowan's speckled and Bran's blue. There in her hands lay the lives of two men.

As she rose from the dusty floor before the garret mousehole, she was seized by an unreasoning fear: *What if I drop them? What if some stupid accident crushes their life-eggs?* The stairs she'd run up so heedlessly were suddenly a deathtrap, a hundred edges and corners to trip her and send the eggs flying. Now that the eggs were in her hands, she was paralyzed with the fear of her own failings. She looked down at her feet, knowing they could stumble; she looked at her hands, rough and scratched, with broken nails, and thought they were not delicate enough, not sure enough, to carry such a precious cargo. What if some tragedy should befall them on the short journey to Phyllida? Was the world really so arbitrary? She feared it was.

"Get ahold of yourself, Meg!" she said aloud. She'd done the impossible—found the eggs. Now all that remained was to walk down the stairs and tell Phyllida. Her knees were shaking with the first steps, but her body had a bit more confidence than her mind and had no trouble walking slowly down three flights.

"We'll do Rowan first," Phyllida said when Meg, sticking her tongue out for balance, found her beside Bran's body. "Life is more important to the living." Silly, springing around the corner and seeing her sister's success, rushed to hug her, but Meg cringed away with a look of horror and a little scream. "The eggs!" she cried, just as Dickie pulled Silly back.

"Here, give them to me," Phyllida said, and it was a relief for Meg to turn over the responsibility to those strong, certain hands. They climbed back up to Rowan's room.

Rowan lay as the old knights lay in their crypts, decked in the armor that had shielded them in life, each with his sword, his constant companion, folded in his arms in place of a lily. Rowan's face was very pale and his breathing shallow, but even in that limbo between life and death, he dreamed of his imagined victory, and a faint smile touched his lips. As they entered his room, Lemman appeared at his bedside and bent over him, touching his brow.

"He is strong," she said. "There is no question he will live. But word has spread among my people that the eggs have been found, and they send a delegation to see that the custom is followed, that the old ways are heeded."

"You mean—"

"I mean that they come to take Bran's life-egg from you, by force if necessary, and dash it to the ground, as should have been done at the first light of dawn. The Midsummer War calls for a death." She frowned, fierce and lovely. "I cannot say what will come to pass in this world if there is no sacrifice. Blood has been spilled on the Green Hill, and that may be enough. As long as one has killed, and one has died, who can say if it matters that he is restored to life the next day? Perhaps that will cast a spell even greater than death would bring. If I knew my duty, I'd take that egg from you myself."

Phyllida, holding both eggs, took a step back, and Meg placed herself between Phyllida and Lemman.

"Maybe I've lived as a human too long," Lemman said. "I should not like to see Bran pass forever from this world. Take Bran's egg, Meg Morgan, before my people come to stop you. Restore his life before they can make the sacrifice complete. We will see to your brother."

Trembling again, Meg took the little blue egg. "What do I do?"

"Simply break the egg above him. His life will know him, and seek him out."

"But I thought breaking the egg would kill him."

"Only if his life flies free apart from his body. It cannot live long out of its shell. It will search for him, but if he's not near, it will disintegrate. Now, go!" Lemman's eyes were unfocused, as though she was watching some distant scene. "They come closer. They will be here shortly. If you would save Bran, go. Let nothing they say stop you!"

Meg rushed away, pausing only for one last lingering look at her brother. What if it didn't work—what if the egg didn't restore Rowan to life? What if her interference in the Midsummer War, intended to save a life, only meant two were taken in the place of one?

Bran lay alone, with none standing vigil over his corpse. The dining hall's many curtains had been drawn tight, for a house of death closes its eyes, but a candelabrum was lit at his head, and one at his feet, casting a shifting, uncertain illumination over his body. The light gave some flush to his pallid flesh, and it almost seemed to Meg as if his chest rose and fell. When she touched him, however, his skin was deathly cold, with none of life's yielding quickness. His eyes were closed, and his lips parted slightly. His forehead, which had been clenched in a perpetual scowl, with indrawn brows, whatever other expression might have played on the rest of his face, was now smooth and unlined. He looked more content than he had ever seemed while alive, and as she held the precious egg above him, she had a moment of misgiving. Once before, he'd entered a state of happiness, one that seemed to the outside world like a prison, and had been ripped violently from it, unwilling. The loss had been so painful it seemed to him death would be better. Now he was peaceful, beyond earthly woe, and she proposed to fetch him back to a world that held little but suffering. He'd made his choice. Did she dare countermand him?

But it was only the hesitation of a moment, for Meg could not philosophize that deeply. The matter was simple. Two people had been, to all appearances, irrevocably changed—Bran in leaving this life, she in having taken that life (and, despite what you might think, the change to Meg was more severe). And here was the chance to remedy it. She had the power to resurrect Bran. There really wasn't any choice.

Before she could act, she heard a commotion outside. It was the sound of horns such as the Seelie Court blows, and the tramping of many feet. She heard cries of "Inside!" and "Get the egg!" and then the massive front doors groaned as they were forced open. "Quick, before it's too late!" a fairy voice called, which was Meg's thought exactly. She tapped the egg against Bran's belt buckle and broke it near his head.

There is the color of a raw egg yolk, and there is the color of a cooked egg yolk, and then, somewhere in between the two (when you have simmered the egg precisely four minutes), is the glorious orange-gold of the yolk that is gelled but not fully set. It is the most magnificent color known to man, grander than a sunset, richer than any precious metal, the color of light and life and happiness. From Bran's cracked blue egg came a little bird, sharp-winged and darting like a swallow, but as ephemeral as morning mist. Its entire body was that vivid yellow-orange, and it seemed to burn with an internal smolder. It sang one clear, sweet note, tucked its wings, and flew between Bran's parted lips. For a terrible moment, there was nothing; then Bran took a shuddering breath, and his lashes parted.

"Oh, Bran!" Meg cried, and threw herself over his chest, utterly unmindful of the deadly wound that pierced him. As she pressed herself against him in an ecstasy of relief, he gave a little groan and fell unconscious. He had been dealt a mortal wound the night before, and though his returned life force strengthened him, he was still in grave danger.

"Help me! Oh, help me, someone!" They couldn't hear her upstairs, but Lysander came running. Behind him came the Seelie prince.

"By the powers! He lives!" Lysander breathed as he drew nearer and saw the shallow rise and fall of Bran's broad chest.

"He is as the last flower before the frost," the Seelie prince said solemnly. "However the gardener may shield the blossom, he cannot stop the coming winter."

"Stay away from him!" Meg hissed across Bran's body, baring her teeth like a little wildcat. "I won't let you kill him!"

"It is not for me to give him life or death, little one," he said, not unkindly. "Nor is it for you. Do not try to cheat him of his fate. His path lies in the unknown lands. Let him go there."

"He will live!" she insisted. But Bran's breath was already growing weaker, and the beat of his heart beneath her hands was faint. Despairingly, she looked to Lysander.

"There is only one chance," Lysander said. "His ash must be split. If it lives, maybe Bran will live, too." He felt Bran's pulse and held his knuckles to those cold lips to feel his breath. "He doesn't have much time. Perhaps it would be better just to let him . . ." But when he met Meg's liquid, imploring eyes, he said, "I'll get the ax. You bring the others down to the grove again."

Meg cast a suspicious look at the Seelie prince. "I won't leave him alone with Bran. He wants him dead. I don't trust him."

"We don't have time, child—go!" Lysander said.

Meg didn't move, and glared at the prince. "Swear that you won't hurt him," she said.

"I swear by the Green Hill, and all that lies beneath it, that I will do Bran no harm."

"And the other fairies?"

"The oath of one is the oath of all. He will die easily enough of his own accord, without my help."

A moment later, she burst into Rowan's room to find him awake and very cross-looking. "You mean I didn't even . . ." he was saying, then spied Meg. "You! Of all the nerve—"

"Later!" she said. "Bran's alive again, but he's dying. Lysander's going to split the ash tree. We need your help!" Phyllida and Silly hurried out, with Rowan following, looking confused and angry. There hadn't been time to answer all his questions, and he was still trying to sort out what was real and what was only a dream given to him by Lemman. In his mind, he'd fought heroically on the Green Hill. But Phyllida told him he'd shamefully (to his way of thinking) slept the night away while Meg took all the glory. He had never thought he needed saving, and now that Midsummer was past and the fairies no longer held his life in an egg, the noble warrior's heart he'd borrowed was replaced by the somewhat petty, childish, though fundamentally good one he'd started out with. He was annoyed with Meg, as if she'd kept him from playing some game, or broken a favorite toy.

Some of his testiness was knocked out of him when he saw Bran, stretched almost lifeless on the banquet table. Now that his heart was beating, blood once more seeped from the gash in his chest. "He's alive?"

"Barely," Meg said.

"But . . . but I thought one of you had to die."

"He did die. But he's alive again." In April, such a conversation would have seemed absurd. "Come on—we have to get him to the ash grove."

Bran was well over six feet tall and powerfully built—not the sort of burden young people or old can easily carry. It took Rowan, Meg, Silly, Dickie, and Phyllida to get him outside, and even then they half dragged him. By some miracle, he was still breathing when they laid him at the foot of his ash, a thick, sturdy tree with a somewhat sloping trunk. The ash bent its spearpoint leaves low, but could not quite touch Bran's body where it lay among the thrusting roots.

Lysander propped a ladder against the trunk and climbed to the place where the ash naturally split into two main branches. It would take skillful ax-work to cleave the tree properly, for it must be hewn deeply enough for Bran to pass through the gash, yet cleanly enough so the tree had a chance of mending itself. Fifteen feet off the ground, Lysander examined the tree. The trunk was stout, true, but the branches were so well grown and heavy that their weight might be enough to split the tree to the ground, killing it. This is why splitting the ash hardly ever saves the very young or the very old. Saplings are too tender to recover from harsh treatment, and old trees are too ponderous, too set in their ways to take injuries without falling. Only trees—and humans—of middling age will spring back easily from grievous hurts. He checked the tree for any sign of weakness or rot that might thwart their efforts, chose a likely spot, and, balancing carefully on the ladder, raised his arms to deal the first blow.

Meg knelt at Bran's side, laying her hands upon him as if there was some healing virtue to her touch. She felt powerless, but at least her cool hands could soothe his brow, her fingers could tell him, through his insensibility, that someone was near, caring for him. He had seemed to her somehow more alive when he lay on the banquet table, for then he had been serene, and though he was cold he seemed strong, like a marble pillar. Now, alive, he looked nearer death than he'd been before. His body was no longer firm but flaccid, his head lolling to one side and his muscles without any will. He was flushed with fever, and burned under her cool touch. Above them, the ax fell.

A violent convulsion passed through Bran's body as the ax blade bit into his ash tree. Again the ax struck, and his body arched in response. His eyes opened, wide and staring, but he seemed to see nothing, not even Meg's anxious face a bare few inches above his own. With each chop at his tree, his body shuddered, but between strokes he lay immobile and ever weaker. He was hardly breathing—air seeped in and out of his parted lips, but this seemed to be more a special favor of the air than the result of any effort on Bran's part. The elements were conspiring to keep him alive a bit longer; would it be enough?

A terrible creaking came from above, and with it that dreaded sound of wood splintering on its own. All eyes turned upward and watched the great ash, now cloven several feet at its crook, hover on the edge of splitting. Lysander held his breath. He could risk no more chops—another might kill Bran's last chance. The tree, overweighed by heavy branches, groaned, and the split widened before their eyes . . . one inch . . . two . . . three. . . . The jagged crack snaked lower. . . . Then the tree seemed to find new strength. The fissure stopped, and the split tree held its ground, firm in its trunk and in its roots. The first stage was successful.

Lysander threw the ax away from him as though its mere presence might move the tree to break its equilibrium, and climbed down the ladder. Now came the tricky task of getting the limp and unresponsive deadweight that was Bran up the ladder, to pass his body through the split. Lysander took off his belt and looped it under Bran's armpits, hauling him up awkwardly, while Rowan and Meg grabbed whatever parts of Bran they could and followed him up the ladder, clinging to the side like monkeys, pushing and pulling as best they could. One careless moment and Bran (or all of them) would plummet to the ground, and that would surely be the end.

Once, Meg's foot slipped, and all was almost lost, but Lysander had one arm hooked securely through a rung, and his prodigious strength saved them. Each step on the ladder was an impossible obstacle, each inch gained a hard-won victory. Bran's head hung, with his chin tucked against his chest, unconscious and absolutely incapable of offering any help.

On they struggled, until, at last, as they neared their goal, their burden grew suddenly lighter. They looked up and saw leafy hands reaching down, strong forked branches catching at Bran's arms, snagging in his clothes, pulling him toward the cleft. They had done their part—Bran's ash tree was taking over.

"He'll pass through the split," Lysander said. "Then we'll take him down and put him to bed while I bind up the ash with rope. We won't know for many days if Bran will live. Trees never do anything quickly."

The three clung to the ladder and helped the tree guide Bran into the deep cleft. But as he lay propped against the gentle incline of the split trunk, high above the ground, the tree began to move of its own volition. The raw inner wood, bleeding pale sap, began to close around Bran's body. Before his kin could think to pull him free, the split bark seemed to seal itself, pulling the edges of its wound together, with Bran trapped in the center. Wood fibers were reconnecting, sap and pulp joining together to close the cleft. And in the middle, still insensible, was Bran, entombed in the healing flesh of his ash tree. In a matter of seconds, his body was hidden, encased in the ash, and only his head was visible, cradled at the top of the split, held gently in a woody embrace. Man and tree were locked together. There he was sealed, to live or die as the strength of his tree decreed.

Huddled together at the base of the tree, the Morgans, the Ashes, and Dickie looked wonderingly up at the encapsulated Bran.

"What do we do now?" Meg asked.

"The hardest thing of all," Phyllida said. "We wait."

Sometimes People Get What They Deserve

THERE IS NO PAIN, there is no sorrow, that can match the torture of waiting in uncertainty. Waiting is timeless, it has no beginning and no end. The mind becomes uncannily fertile, imagining every variation, every conceivable outcome. Hope burns painfully bright in the breast of the one who waits, but so does the certainty of tragedy.

For those who kept vigil at the base of Bran's ash tree, there was no hope of tranquillity. Every moment that he yet lived filled them with joy even as it destroyed them with the fear that each breath could be his last. While they sat among the roots or paced slowly, winding their way through the other ashes in the grove, they were not merely biding their time for an outcome. No, they were constantly conjuring in their heads all the wonderful and terrible ways the world could turn out. One moment, Bran was fully recovered; the next, irrevocably doomed. There was no peaceful middle ground in their thoughts, only that seesawing between extremes. They waited. And waited. And waited.

Eight days passed with Bran trapped in the cleft of his ash tree, and never was the pair left untended. His heart kept up a steady, slow beat, but he did not seem to improve. Likewise, though the tree had in part mended itself, it still wept sap from its jagged split, and seemed to heal itself no further than it had in those first few minutes when it encased Bran. The high branches of its canopy drooped, and the narrow leaves were beginning to brown and curl at the tips.

On the morning of the ninth day, Rowan and Meg were sitting together in a patch of clover at the edge of the ash grove. Meg was absently making a chain, and fat, dusty bees buzzed around their heads, sometimes resting on the children's knees when weary of gathering nectar.

"I still don't understand why you did it," Rowan said. Time had done much to cool his irritation, and now he was reluctantly grateful to her. He still felt he hadn't needed any saving and had been thwarted in his calling, but overwhelming this was relief that he hadn't been the one to injure Bran. He thought he could handle the hardships of warfare, but it had never occurred to him that the real trial comes after the fighting is over. He didn't think he'd much like to be in Meg's shoes, watching a man hover between death and life, knowing that she had been the one to put him there. Then again, if he lived, she'd be the one who saved him, for without his life-egg he'd have had no chance. Come to think of it, she'd as good as saved *his* life, too, Rowan mused. Imagine, their two lives rolled up in Finn's sock and shoved into a mousehole! However did Finn get hold of those eggs? Meg wouldn't tell her brother how she'd gotten the eggs away from him, but he knew from a certain uneasiness in her eyes when he asked her about it that she wasn't exactly happy about her methods.

Finn had come home late on the night after the Midsummer War, and expressed some faint sympathy for Bran's plight. He'd wished the man ill, but that's a far cry from wishing him dead. Though no one much cared to talk to him, he got the gist of the story from Dickie. Once, it might have impressed him, or scorched him with jealousy. But he had seen the Green Hill, he had seen the Seelie queen, and no other sight, no other thought had the power to charm him now.

As soon as Meg had led him to the Green Hill and run along home to the Rookery, Finn, concealed in the brambles surrounding the hill, had placed a daub of the seeing ointment in his right eye. At once the character of the hill changed. What had been merely a pleasant knoll was now charged with a vitality that seemed to hum through the air. Some people will feel this in all wild places—in fields that are alive with insects, in clumps of earth thrilling with crawling worms and bacteria. Such people experience an almost ecstatic awareness of the glory of life in even the smallest patch of nature. But for Finn, it took a magic ointment to open his eyes, and the rest of his senses, to what was already there.

The hill was a living thing. Even as a house takes on something of the personality of the people who live in it, the Green Hill was unmistakably a fairy home. Each herb that grew on the slope sang a faint paean to the people who lived beneath its roots, each insect droned its homage to the fairies. Above the Green Hill, the sky seemed more blue than any sky has a right to be, and the very trees that ringed it bowed to the sacred fairy mound.

Only Finn Fachan was out of place, the interloper. He was not invited, nor did he fortuitously stumble on the hill, but had won his prize by treachery, to which even the fairies are vulnerable. Through the centuries, there have always been men, too clever for their own good, who have sought to gain the secrets of the fairy world. And it is true that fairies, though masters at deception, can themselves be befuddled. But fairies are like the sea—time and again, you might sail through storms and laugh at the fierce salt spray, and think that you have beaten her, but the sea does not like arrogance, and will wait until your back is turned to drag you under or toss your ship on the rocks. Never turn your back on the sea, they say, and never cross a fairy.

Fearlessly—because he did not know enough to be afraid—Finn climbed the Green Hill and settled himself at the summit. For several hours he didn't see any fairies, and it occurred to him he might have been duped. The sun climbed higher, and the day grew uncomfortably hot and bright. Sweat started to bead on his forehead and drip down the back of his neck, and little sweat bees (which don't sting) hovered to sip the salts his body was shedding. Then, when the sun was directly overhead and he could hardly see for the glare, shapes finally emerged from the place where the brilliant, sunny green of the hill met the forest's deep shade.

Finn saw the Seelie Court that day, marching in their fairy rade. It is a rite that reconnects them with the real world, the world of humans and sunshine, to which they are bound. For the fairies, like captured humans, are sometimes wont to retreat to the twilight lands beneath the Green Hill, and if they stay too long, they may sink irrevocably back into the earth from which they were born. And so they emerge to salute the day, greet the trees, touch the flowers, and sometimes give a lucky mortal a glimpse of their grandeur.

Perhaps two dozen fairies rode past Finn that day, but in his eyes there was only one. There below him on her dappled palfrey rode the Seelie queen, bewitching, enticing, untouchable. It was all he could do to keep from jumping to his feet and running after her. But he knew that would give away his secret, and he didn't want to take any chances. The queen passed out of sight, and Finn was left in solitude.

No more fairies came that day, nor did the trooping court return by any path visible to him. As the sun set, he crept down the hill. Though dejected, he was not without hope . . . and not without a plan. He was wise enough to know he might have trouble finding the Green Hill again on his own, and so he'd brought with him a skein of red wool swiped from Phyllida's knitting basket. Every few paces as he made his way home, he tied a snip of wool to a bush or a low-hanging tree branch, leaving a foolproof trail to follow the next day. And, sure enough, the following morning, while the others were anxiously watching the tree-entombed Bran for any signs of recovery, Finn traipsed off into the woods and followed his well-marked trail straight to the Green Hill.

Every morning, he spied on the queen and made grand resolutions to greet her. But his dread of being banished from the Green Hill overwhelmed his desire to be near her. Better to do no more than see her each day, than to bask for a moment under her eyes only to be forever after exiled. He would not sacrifice the chance of future gain on an impulsive, premature act, for his sights were set high—he hoped to discover the entrance to the Green Hill itself, and introduce himself in the queen's own realm.

One day, he saw a courtier pause a moment to nudge a little stone with the toe of his boot. It piqued his interest, and when the troop melted into the forest, Finn investigated and found an innocuous piece of worn red shale lying in the grass. Tentatively, he shifted it to the left, and at once, grandly and silently, the earth heaved as it has not since glaciers shouldered up mountains and left gorges in their wakes. The hill lifted, and the vacuum it created as it rose sucked the air from Finn's lungs. He took a step back, and beheld the inside of the Green Hill.

The hill perched on alabaster columns, a many-legged turtle. A soft glow came from within, and, hesitantly, Finn advanced until he just peeked his head between two columns. He saw no fairies, or life of any kind, but the air was thick in a swirling silver mist, and he could not see well beyond a few yards. He took another step, and he was under the Green Hill. It seemed as if the hill was hollow, for above him arched a dome of dark slate blue, speckled with what might be stars—if stars could come to earth and then move of their own volition, for the lights shifted slowly against their false sky.

The movement of the mist around him made him dizzy, and for all that he stared hungrily about him, he could never, as long as he lived, remember quite what he saw that day. Sometimes it seemed that he stood in a vast hall illuminated with cold fire and pale jewels, and there was a rock-ringed well in the center. Other times he thought he was in a garden tended by fireflies, where the bloodless leaves knew no sun and the fruits never ripened. Once, when he looked at the floor, he saw no more than rough dirt strewn with hay, as in a stable; yet another time it seemed that an endless black chasm lay at his feet, with a narrow staircase spiraling down to the heart of the earth. Did the air beneath the Green Hill smell like sweet grass and new lambs? Or did it reek of brimstone and the dank, rich rot of decaying things? He could not tell, then or after, but only knew that something strange and old and unknowable was washing over him. Did he dare to take another step? Would the garden await his footfall, or would he plummet into the abyss?

His trial did not come that day. From behind him came the wild, joyous baying of hounds on a trail. The fairy dogs, with milky coats, and ears and eyes that burned red fire, had picked up the scent of Finn's trickery, and now the pack surrounded him, snarling and wagging their tails at the same time, as dogs will do when work and sport are one. The noon light shone through their carnelian ears, and a dozen pairs of ruby eyes stared him down. Before he knew what was happening, he was on the turf outside the Green Hill, and the pillars were gone, the ambiguous inside was sealed—the hill was closed and solid once again. He was found out, and the way was now barred to him.

The fairy hounds drove him away from the hill, but they showed him mercy, and did not hunt him till he dropped. They chased him only as far as the road, baying and nipping at his heels but never harming him. It was not the ending he'd anticipated—an inglorious retreat, without acknowledgment or reward. But what did it matter? He had been inside the Green Hill! He had seen the fairy home, looked into its heart. Could the Morgans say that? Finn had been chased away that day, but tomorrow was still before him. He could return to the Green Hill whenever he cared to. He believed he had discovered the key, that the fairy world now lay open to him. He did not know that no man may enter the Green Hill twice by the same path.

On the next day, the ninth day of Bran's entombment, Finn rose full of enthusiasm and confidence and set out as usual to the Green Hill. Just out of sight of the Rookery, he came to the first piece of yarn that marked the red trail he'd set.

He looked ahead for the next piece, and his mouth gaped in horror. There before him, on every tree, every bush, every creeping bramble and lowly herb, was tied a piece of red yarn. The entire forest was decked as though for a holiday in brilliant scarlet bows. Each was exactly like the ones he'd tied. His carefully marked trail was obliterated.

"No!" he cried to the heavens. He stumbled this way and that, trying to find a path in all the sameness, looking for any clue that might set him on the right trail. But the bedizened trees mocked him, and even the tiny flowers, prideful in their new finery, tittered at the fool who crashed and staggered through the woods, screaming protestations and pounding his fists against the rough bark. At length, deep in the woods and completely surrounded by red yarn bows, he sank to his knees.

It's over, he thought grimly. Dickie was right, Meg was right. The fairies don't want me there. I'll never find the Green Hill again.

But Finn did not have the constitution for lingering despair. He was young, his mind was lively, and he was supremely egotistic—it was not possible for him to fail. The Morgans weren't barred from the Green Hill. They could lead him back. He fell to plotting. Scowling at each and every one of the red bows around him, he headed back to the Rookery, working out the lies and half-truths he'd use to convince the Morgans to help him. Meg, he thought, would be his best bet.

"I've just seen the most remarkable thing," Finn began as he approached Rowan and Meg in the ash grove, intending to spin a convoluted tale, the exact details of which he'd not yet worked out. But, to his irritation, neither so much as looked at him. They were both gazing up into the tree, rapt and intensely still, like bird dogs at their quarry. Finn glanced up, but Bran was still in the same place. Finn grimaced. Country fools! He had to be dead by now. Why didn't someone take him down and bury him before he began to smell?

"You'll never guess what I've seen," he tried again, but Rowan hissed at him to be quiet. In the silence, while Finn tried to think of something particularly cutting to say, a faint sound rose above the bee buzzing and leaf rustle. It was like the low groan of ice breaking at the thaw. It was quiet, barely a sound at all, but, like the ice, it was the sound of a beginning. High in the tree, Bran made the first noise of consciousness.

The Morgans exchanged a glance. Hopelessness and hope had stood hand in hand for so long—did they dare give preference to one yet? Bran's head shifted on his wooden pillow, and then—oh, wonders!—he opened his eyes!

"Go get the others," Rowan said.

"No . . . you go." Already Meg was climbing up the ladder. As Rowan dashed off for the Ashes, and Finn looked up with cynical interest, she reached Bran's side and pushed the matted hair from his face.

He looked around in confusion—and wouldn't you, if for some reason you woke up in a tree?—and finally his bleary, befuddled eyes rested on Meg. She said nothing, only stroked his poor ravaged face. He had taken neither food nor drink in all that time, and what little she could see of him was angular and wasted. But the ash tree had nourished him somehow, keeping him in close symbiosis all those days, sharing its life with him. His body was still hidden within the trunk, but it seemed that there was now a little extra room around him, that perhaps, with a little judicious wriggling, he could be pulled free. He shifted his torso in his wooden tomb (which had turned into a cradle), and viscous waves of sap lapped at his neck.

"You . . . you . . . ," he began, his voice as hoarse as a raven's and as weak as a newborn kitten's mew.

"Don't try to speak, Bran dear."

But he paid her no heed. "You shouldn't have done this. You should have let me die."

Now, this isn't exactly the sort of thing a girl wants to hear when she has gone to all the trouble of killing you and bringing you back to life, not to mention suffering through the agony of waiting to see if you'd survive after all. It makes her feel unappreciated.

"You did die," she said, in rather too sharp a tone for a

sickbed. "And that seems to have satisfied all the Midsummer War requirements—since the world hasn't ended yet. Now you're going to live." Whether you like it or not, she added to herself. She smiled a bit ruefully. She'd expected thanks, but neither healers nor soldiers ever get the thanks they deserve.

Though Bran tried to focus his eyes on her face, they had been closed for days, and the morning sun was intense. All he could see of Meg was a pale moon surrounded by dark clouds against a piercing blue sky. "I wanted to die," he said weakly. "I can't go back under the Green Hill. I should have died."

Meg was angry now. After all she'd done . . . after all everyone had done! "Hang the Green Hill!" she said, and he winced as if at blasphemy. "Why do you think your life began and ended there, Bran? You said yourself it's all illusion and lies. Pretty lies, seductive illusion, and it holds you—I know how it holds you. But you're here now, alive, whole. Can't you see what's in the rest of the world, our world? Look at it all!" She swung her arm wide and teetered perilously on the ladder.

Around her, the land was green and fresh and fertile. Nut trees blossomed, fruit trees set out tiny, hard green nubbins that would one day be peaches and apples. The world was in flower, and in the fields around Gladysmere the wheat and barley were growing tall. Glossy black rooks danced in the sky, flying with overlapping wings and turning cartwheels against the azure infinity. "Look at it!" she cried again. And he looked. But all he could see was a firmament so bright the blue was almost white, and against it all, Meg's radiant face.

She did not know if she had convinced him. But she

determined that she would never stop trying until she made him see what a beautiful place the world is, how much better sunshine and birdsong are than all the allures of the Green Hill.

Phyllida and Lysander came, with Silly skipping after them. Dickie came, too, trailing a bit behind, always remembering that he wasn't a part of the family. But Silly, so happy to hear that Bran was awake, caught Dickie's hands and danced him around in a circle. Dickie Rhys he might be, but as far as she was concerned, he was an honorary Morgan. (James was in the kitchen, helping the cook make pastries—and by "helping" I mean "eating.")

Meg slid down the ladder and Phyllida took her place, climbing on bones that had grown oh so weary in the last weeks. Disturbing thoughts came more often to her now: What will be when I am gone? But when she saw Bran awake, the new weight of her years fell away. She felt his pulse and propped open his lids to peer into his eyes, and determined that he was strong enough to be moved—if the tree allowed him.

A few minutes later, Bran was on the grass, with all the family crowded around him. Naked and frail he lay, covered in red and amber sap. The raw lips of the gash made by the Hunter's Bow had sealed themselves, though a cicatrix would always mark the spot where his heart had been pierced. He was changed—how can a man not be who is killed, and then reborn from an ash tree? His family could not yet see it, and in their hearts was the fear that it had all been for nothing, that he would never know peace in this world.

But trees—rooted, stolid, steadfast trees—know the art of contentment. They rely on the chance of wind or squirrels to spread their seeds, and from the earliest days of sprouthood are at the world's mercy. Should rain fall in its appointed measure, should the winds not blow too hard or the hungry young rabbits not nibble away his greenery, the tree will live, and he will love his life. Men rarely see the moment they live in, for the past haunts them, the future lures them on with promises, so that now does not exist. Trees have no such blindness. All that comes is welcome, and they stand, well rooted, as the world goes on around them.

Bran had been nine days in the womb of his ash tree, and, like the tree, he had begun in his convalescence to have neither regrets nor anticipation. Now that he was torn from the tree, alone as the air dried his sap to hardness, he felt the old sadness creeping upon him. But the tree-ness was there, too, and though the loss never quite left him, it never again filled him with despair. The grass under him was soft and cool—could he mourn the loss of a bed of silken sheets with a fairy lady beside him when such a bed of grass lay under the sun's benevolent warmth?

His family only saw that he was recovered—not wholly, for it would be days before he could walk again, weeks before some strength conquered his newborn feebleness—though enough so that the real danger was past. Meg looked up to the ash tree and saw that branches that had drooped, leaves that had withered were once more fresh and green, reaching heavenward. Fresh sap bled down the bark, but the roots reached deep, the trunk stood firm.

From the woods came a tinkle of bells, and Gul Ghillie skipped into their presence. Though Meg was disposed to resent all fairies just then, Gul in his childish guise looked as innocuous as a village lad, and his irrepressible merriment made her forget—almost— that he was prince of the Seelie Court, and one of those who had brought this trouble upon them. As a rather decent playwright said, and many have said since, all's well that ends well, and she had already learned the valuable lesson that it seldom pays to hold a grudge.

Since Midsummer Day, she'd been convinced that fairies were vile, villainous, heartless, unnatural creatures, and that whatever charms they might possess were vastly outweighed by their vices. Now time had cooled her passion, and Bran's recovery erased fully half of the unpleasant memories. With him alive, what had happened had left the realm of tragedy and was now an adventure—and who can resist an adventure, particularly when it is already successfully completed?

She had begun, though, to see why there needed to be a Guardian, and people who understood the nature of fairies. They were dangerous, and their allure was such that many will walk headlong into that danger. Once, she had hoped for nothing more than to leave all this behind, never to see so much as a fairy whisker again. Now that things were seeming to work out well, she was glad to see Gul Ghillie, her first fairy friend.

Gul was singing a song about magpies as he skipped toward them. In his hand was what looked like an old-fashioned toy—a little hoop that he twirled around a short, sharp stick. He tossed the hoop in the air and then caught it, still whirling, on the stick.

"So," he said, drawing near to Bran, "the big brute lives, despite our best efforts!" But Meg could see relief in his eye, and she knew that, whatever the stories might say, whatever she herself had once thought, there are times when the fairies care for humans. Bran had ridden with the Seelie Court for years (though a heartbeat in fairies' endless time) and had been well loved. Whatever rules might have bound them to seek Bran's death, these were not enough to kill all feeling for him. The fairies had grieved when Bran was taken from them, and would have grieved more deeply at his death. Still, they would not have sought to prevent it, and that is one of the things that is hardest for us to understand about the difference between humans and fairies.

"You've done a great deed, Meg Morgan," Gul said, turning to her. "You've laid a spell on this land far greater than death can bring, and it will not be forgotten. In the years to come . . ." But he spied Finn smirking at him. Finn, you will remember, did not know that Gul Ghillie was anything other than a mortal boy, and found it amusing that a mere village lad should take such a grandiose tone.

Gul laughed, but beneath that merry sound was something that made Meg shiver even in the late morning sun. "And you, Finn Fachan. You've been up to a thing or two yourself, haven't you? Gadding about the forest while the rest of the household is occupied. Seen a few things, haven't you?"

"Oh, well, nothing much," Finn stammered. The boy's unblinking eyes made him uncomfortable. Did Gul know his secrets? Finn preferred to reveal things in his own good time. What was this boy about?

"You've watched the Asrai bathing in the willow's shadows," Gul said, his voice low and intense, not at all a little boy's voice. "You've seen the Glastig in her wild dance, heard the hammers of the Knockers as they mine for ore in the valleys. Things that are meant to be hidden are known to you, Finn Fachan." He leaned close, conspiratorially. "You've been to the Green Hill—I know you have!" Finn couldn't quite suppress a grin. He was proud of his accomplishments. "And you've seen the Seelie queen and all her court. Tell me . . ." He bent to whisper in Finn's ear. "Tell me, in which eye did you put the ointment? With which eye did you witness the forbidden things?"

Finn did not see the danger. "My right eye," he said, and was about to pull Gul to the side to talk about it further. Here was a confidant at last. Gul might know the way to the Green Hill. Maybe he would lead him back.

Gul laughed, a wild sound that made Finn tremble. Though he was still a boy in appearance, it suddenly seemed as if there was something unnatural about Gul Ghillie. He tossed the ring he played with high in the air, and all eyes followed it. Then, shifting the sharpened hazel twig in his hand, he lunged forward. Swifter than an adder's strike, keener than an adder's tooth, the hazel point struck home in Finn's right eye. He fell back, clutching his face and screaming as if he were dying.

"That eye shall never see again," Gul Ghillie said. "Count yourself fortunate I didn't take both." With that he disappeared.

Everyone's thoughts were still with Bran, and I'm afraid Finn didn't get all the sympathy he deserved (however much that was). But, obedient to triage, they turned from the stable Bran to the screaming Finn and comforted him as best they could. Phyllida brewed him a draught from a dark-leafed shrub that grew in one shadowy corner of the herb garden, and though he choked at its bitterness, it seemed to quiet him and dull the pain of his blinding. They put him to bed, then refocused their attention on Bran, bringing him into the Rookery and helping him take a few swallows of rich beef broth.

Meg was the only one who stayed at Finn's bedside. Part of her felt he had gotten what was coming to him—for which she was immediately ashamed of herself. No spying, no trickery should bring such a punishment. What harm had he done to the fairies? She herself had brought him to the Green Hill. Why wasn't she punished? Her sense of fairness rebelled, and her humanity recoiled from the fairy way of justice.

But whereas her ancestress Chlorinda had run in fear from all this, it filled Meg with a sense of purpose. Here was poor Finn (for whom, as you know, she'd always harbored a soft spot) lying injured only because he was seduced by the fairy glamour and didn't know enough to keep himself safe. For all his cleverness, he didn't really understand the fairies. Well, Meg thought she understood them by now. She could have kept Finn from harm. She had come to appreciate Phyllida's role, the good she must do in mediating between the foolishness and ambition of humans and the mercurial nature of the fairies. It seemed a worthy profession, a noble calling.

Then such thoughts vanished in the general ickiness of eye injuries, and she sank to a back corner as the doctor, fetched at last from the next village beyond Gladysmere, tended Finn's eye. Very lucky, the doctor said, that the stick hadn't pierced through to his brain. Gul Ghillie's vengeance had been precise—Finn's right eye was blind, but no more damage was done.

The next morning when he awoke, full of the strange dreams Phyllida's potion had brought him along with oblivion, Finn examined himself in the mirror. He couldn't quite bear to look at the actual injury, but he rather fancied himself in the dashing black silk eyepatch Phyllida had sewn for him overnight.

It is odd, though, how ineffective most punishments are. They are meant, I suppose, to instill a sense of remorse in the heart of the wrongdoer . . . but do they ever? Does the incarcerated felon ever truly regret his actions, or does he only regret being caught? The loss of his eye taught Finn nothing, save perhaps to be more cautious, more crafty. He was not sorry that he had seen the Green Hill, only that he'd been found out. As his left eye stared at his new face, his sightless right eye still beheld the Seelie queen and her court, and the ambiguous wonders that lay hidden in the fairy home under the Green Hill.

A Letter

DEAR MOMMY,

That part was easy. Meg, alone in her bedroom, chewed on her pen and gazed out the window, looking for words. There were Rowan and Silly, hacking gleefully at each other with sticks, now that their Seelie weapons were gone.

Mommy, I fought in a war. She crossed the line out.

Bran watched the warlike antics from a lawn chair. Phyllida tempted him with tea and biscuits, but he was itching to be up and at work again, and sometimes had to be physically restrained.

Mommy, I killed a man. But it's okay, he's alive again. With a rueful little laugh, she drew a heavy mark through that sentence, too.

Finn sat by himself, scowling at everyone.

Finn had his eye put out by a fairy. Yes, Mommy, a fairy. She'll think I'm mad, Meg mused, and crossed that out as well. There had never been anything she couldn't tell her mother, and she ached to relieve her own burden by sharing it. Somehow, the words would not come.

Her eyes traveled away from her family, out to the deep forest, where she could just see the emerald crest of the Green Hill. Suddenly she bent and scribbled on a fresh page.

Oh, Mommy, I wish you were here. No, I don't. If you were here you would have stopped me . . . but it doesn't matter. It's done now. If you could only see for yourself how wonderful it all is. Wonderful and terrible. I never knew. . . . I wish I was home, but I wish I never had to leave the Rookery. Oh, Mommy, I miss you!

She knew it was vague and troubling, but she could write nothing better. She sealed it quickly and ran downstairs to drop it on the silver tray of outgoing letters.

"Come on, Meg," Dickie called. "Lysander's gonna teach us cricket."

She played, and for a time forgot her worries, while from the shrubbery fairy eyes watched her and spoke in hushed tones of the changes one little girl had wrought.

"The world," Gul Ghillie said, "will never be the same."

"Never *was* the same," the brownie said cryptically, and spat on the ground.

Three weeks later, Meg's letter made it across the Atlantic, and Glynnis Morgan, reading it, murmured, "Oh dear . . . I wonder if I should bring them home."

But by then, it was already too late.

Acknowledgments

I would like to thank my agent, Shawna McCarthy, who won me over by comparing my writing to that of E. Nesbit and C. S. Lewis and (after my head returned to normal size) helped my career take off with her amazing talent. You are reading this book thanks to my wonderful editor, Reka Simonsen, to whom I owe the deepest gratitude.

My sister, Marla Jane Sullivan, gave me my first book about fairies—real fairies—and so this book is probably her fault. She's far more brilliant than I am, and will probably become a great novelist now, just to remind me of that fact. My father, John B. Sullivan, saw to it that I had the best education, bits and pieces of which have been remarkably useful. Thanks, Dad. Incidentally, this book had its first germ in Alison Lurie's folklore class at Cornell. Thanks also to my husband, Andy DeLay, a NASCAR radio talk-show host who, for my sake, tries very hard to believe in fairies.

My beloved mother, to whom this book is dedicated, deserves all my love and gratitude, because she supported ne'er-do-well me when I quit one of my many jobs and devoted myself to writing this book.

And most of all I must thank my best little friend, Buster, Bubeleh, Robbie.